ANNE
DEATH IN THE

C000212014

ANNE Morice, *née* Felicity Shaw, was born in Kent in 1916.

Her mother Muriel Rose was the natural daughter of Rebecca Gould and Charles Morice. Muriel Rose married a Kentish doctor, and they had a daughter, Elizabeth. Muriel Rose's three later daughters—Angela, Felicity and Yvonne—were fathered by playwright Frederick Lonsdale.

Felicity's older sister Angela became an actress, married actor and theatrical agent Robin Fox, and produced England's Fox acting dynasty, including her sons Edward and James and grandchildren Laurence, Jack, Emilia and Freddie.

Felicity went to work in the office of the GPO Film Unit. There Felicity met and married documentarian Alexander Shaw. They had three children and lived in various countries.

Felicity wrote two well-received novels in the 1950's, but did not publish again until successfully launching her Tessa Crichton mystery series in 1970, buying a house in Hambleden, near Henley-on-Thames, on the proceeds. Her last novel was published a year after her death at the age of seventy-three on May 18th, 1989.

BY ANNE MORICE
and available from Dean Street Press

ANNE MORICE

DEATH IN THE GRAND MANOR

With an introduction and afterword by
Curtis Evans

DEAN STREET PRESS

Published by Dean Street Press 2021

Copyright © 1970 Anne Morice

Introduction & Afterword © 2021 Curtis Evans

All Rights Reserved

First published in 1970 by Macmillan

Cover by DSP

ISBN 978 1 913527 91 4

www.deanstreetpress.co.uk

INTRODUCTION

By 1970 the Golden Age of detective fiction, which had dawned in splendor a half-century earlier in 1920, seemingly had sunk into shadow like the sun at eventide. There were still a few old bodies from those early, glittering days who practiced the fine art of finely clued murder, to be sure, but in most cases the hands of those murderously talented individuals were growing increasingly infirm. Queen of Crime Agatha Christie, now eighty years old, retained her bestselling status around the world, but surely no one could have deluded herself into thinking that the novel *Passenger to Frankfurt*, the author's 1970 "Christie for Christmas" (which publishers for want of a better word dubbed "an Extravaganza") was prime Christie— or, indeed, anything remotely close to it. Similarly, two other old crime masters, Americans John Dickson Carr and Ellery Queen (comparative striplings in their sixties), both published detective novels that year, but both books were notably weak efforts on their parts. Agatha Christie's American counterpart in terms of work productivity and worldwide sales, Erle Stanley Gardner, creator of Perry Mason, published nothing at all that year, having passed away in March at the age of eighty. Admittedly such old-timers as Rex Stout, Ngaio Marsh, Michael Innes and Gladys Mitchell were still playing the game with some of their old élan, but in truth their glory days had fallen behind them as well. Others, like Margery Allingham and John Street, had died within the last few years or, like Anthony Gilbert, Nicholas Blake, Leo Bruce and Christopher Bush, soon would expire or become debilitated. Decidedly in 1970—a year which saw the trials of the Manson family and the Chicago Seven, assorted bombings, kidnappings and plane hijackings by such terroristic entities as the Weathermen, the Red Army, the PLO and the FLQ, the American invasion of Cambodia and the Kent State shootings and the drug overdose deaths of Jimi Hendrix and Janis Joplin—leisure readers now more than ever stood in need of the intelligent escapism which classic crime fiction provided. Yet the old order in crime fiction, like that in world politics and society, seemed irrevocably to be washing away in a bloody tide of violent anarchy and all round uncouthness.

Or was it? Old values have a way of persisting. Even as the generation which produced the glorious detective fiction of the Golden Age finally began exiting the crime scene, a new generation of younger puzzle adepts had arisen, not to take the esteemed places of their elders, but to contribute their own worthy efforts to the rarefied field of fair play murder. Among these writers were P.D. James, Ruth Rendell, Emma Lathen, Patricia Moyes, H.R.F. Keating, Catherine Aird, Joyce Porter, Margaret Yorke, Elizabeth Lemarchand, Reginald Hill, Peter Lovesey and the author whom you are perusing now, Anne Morice (1916-1989). Morice, who like Yorke, Lovesey and Hill debuted as a mystery writer in 1970, was lavishly welcomed by critics in the United Kingdom (she was not published in the United States until 1974) upon the publication of her first mystery, *Death in the Grand Manor*, which suggestively and anachronistically was subtitled not an "extravaganza," but a novel of detection. Fittingly the book was lauded by no less than seemingly permanently retired Golden Age stalwarts Edmund Crispin and Francis Iles (aka Anthony Berkeley Cox). Crispin deemed Morice's debut puzzler "a charming whodunit . . . full of unforced buoyance" and prescribed it as a "remedy for existentialist gloom," while Iles, who would pass away at the age of seventy-seven less than six months after penning his review, found the novel a "most attractive lightweight," adding enthusiastically: "[E]ntertainingly written, it provides a modern version of the classical type of detective story. I was much taken with the cheerful young narrator . . . and I think most readers will feel the same way. Warmly recommended." Similarly, Maurice Richardson, who, although not a crime writer, had reviewed crime fiction for decades at the *London Observer*, lavished praise upon Morice's maiden mystery: "Entrancingly fresh and lively whodunit. . . . Excellent dialogue. . . . Much superior to the average effort to lighten the detective story."

With such a critical sendoff, it is no surprise that Anne Morice's crime fiction took flight on the wings of its bracing mirth. Over the next two decades twenty-five Anne Morice mysteries were published (the last of them posthumously), at the rate of one or two year. Twenty-three of these concerned the investigations of Tessa Crichton, a charming young actress who always manages to cross paths with murder, while two, written at the end of her career, detail cases of Detective Superintendent "Tubby" Wiseman. In 1976 Morice along with Margaret Yorke was chosen to become a member of Britain's prestigious Detection Club, preceding Ruth Rendell by a year, while in the 1980s her books were included in Bantam's superlative paperback "Murder Most British" series, which included luminaries from both present and past like Rendell, Yorke, Margery Allingham, Patricia Wentworth, Christianna Brand, Elizabeth Ferrars, Catherine Aird, Margaret Erskine, Marian Babson, Dorothy Simpson, June Thomson and last, but most certainly not least, the Queen of Crime herself, Agatha Christie. In 1974, when Morice's fifth Tessa Crichton detective novel, *Death of a Dutiful Daughter*, was picked up in the United States, the author's work again was received with acclaim, with reviewers emphasizing the author's cozy traditionalism (though the term "cozy" had not then come into common use in reference to traditional English and American mysteries). In his notice of Morice's *Death of a Wedding Guest* (1976), "Newgate Callendar" (aka classical music critic Harold C. Schoenberg), Seventies crime fiction reviewer for the *New York Times Book Review*, observed that "Morice is a traditionalist, and she has no surprises [in terms of subject matter] in her latest book. What she does have, as always, is a bright and amusing style . . . [and] a general air of sophisticated writing." Perhaps a couple of reviews from Middle America—where intense Anglophilia, the dogmatic pronouncements of Raymond Chandler and Edmund Wilson notwithstanding, still ran rampant among mystery readers—best indicate the cozy criminal appeal of Anne Morice:

> Anne Morice . . . acquired me as a fan when I read her "Death and the Dutiful Daughter." In this new novel, she did not disappoint me. The same appealing female detective, Tessa Crichton, solves the mysteries on her own, which is surprising in view of the fact that Tessa is actually not a detective, but a film actress. Tessa just seems to be at places where a murder occurs, and at the most unlikely places at that . . . this time at a garden fete on the estate of a millionaire tycoon. . . . The plot is well constructed; I must confess that I, like the police, had my suspect all picked out too. I was "dead" wrong (if you will excuse the expression) because my suspect was also murdered before not too many pages turned. . . . This is not a blood-curdling, chilling mystery; it is amusing and light, but Miss Morice writes in a polished and intelligent manner, providing pleasure and entertainment. (Rose Levine Isaacson, review of *Death of a Heavenly Twin, Jackson Mississippi Clarion-Ledger*, 18 August 1974)

> I like English mysteries because the victims are always rotten people who deserve to die. Anne Morice, like Ngaio Marsh et al., writes tongue in cheek but with great care. It is always a joy to read English at its glorious best. (Sally Edwards, "Ever-So British, This Tale," review of *Killing with Kindness, Charlotte North Carolina Observer*, 10 April 1975)

While it is true that Anne Morice's mysteries most frequently take place at country villages and estates, surely the quintessence of modern cozy mystery settings, there is a pleasing tartness to Tessa's narration and the brittle, epigrammatic dialogue which reminds me of the Golden Age Crime Queens (particularly Ngaio Marsh) and, to part from mystery for a moment, English playwright Noel Coward. Morice's books may be cozy but they most certainly are not cloying, nor are the sentiments which the characters express invariably "traditional." The author avoids any traces of soppiness or sentimentality and has a knack for clever turns of phrase which is characteristic of the bright young things of the Twenties and Thirties, the decades of her own youth. "Sackcloth and ashes would have been overdressing for the mood I had sunk into by then," Tessa reflects at one point in the novel *Death in the Grand Manor*. Never fear, however: nothing, not even the odd murder or two, keeps Tessa down in the dumps for long; and invariably she finds herself back on the trail of murder most foul, to the consternation of her handsome, debonair husband, Inspector Robin Price of Scotland Yard (whom she meets in the first novel in the series and has married by the second), and the exasperation of her amusingly eccentric and indolent playwright cousin, Toby Crichton, both of whom feature in all of the Tessa Crichton novels. Murder may not lastingly mar Tessa's equanimity, but she certainly takes her detection seriously.

Three decades now having passed since Anne Morice's crime novels were in print, fans of British mystery in both its classic and cozy forms should derive much pleasure in discovering (or rediscovering) her work in these new Dean Street Press editions and thereby passing time once again in that pleasant fictional English world where death affords us not emotional disturbance and distress but enjoyable and intelligent diversion.

Curtis Evans

ONE

ONE damp and cheerless day last July, my cousin, Toby Crichton, telephoned to invite me to spend a few weeks at his house at Roakes Common and, in doing so, put his finger on what I can only describe as the fatal switch. Possibly, the reason why I can only so describe it is that I am writing this saga in the intervals of rehearsing for a Victorian melodrama and the florid prose is rather infectious. Doubtless, the style will cool down, as the narrative proceeds, particularly if I am fortunate enough to secure a contemporary part, in the course of it.

However, fatal switch or not, Toby's doom-laden words sounded innocuous enough at the time, although rather puzzling and I asked him: 'Why so long?'

I occasionally spent a weekend with him and his wife, who was an actress named Matilda Spragge, and they sometimes reciprocated by gracing, not to say overcrowding, my London flat for a night or two during the week. A stay of two or three weeks boded something more than normal cousinly give and take and, knowing Toby as I did, a degree of caution seemed advisable.

'I'll explain, when you get here,' he said, which was not reassuring, and I told him he would have to do better than that.

I half expected him to ring off in a huff at this point, for he was not one to suffer opposition with a light laugh. Perhaps I should have been sorry if he had, for the fact is that, despite his tiresome prejudices and quarrelsome disposition, Toby had a unique place in my affections. He had been immensely kind to me when I had been a stout, despairing schoolgirl of fifteen and he an established playwright, nearly twice my age. Experience has taught me that his championship sprang merely from the chronic perversity which governed all his actions and that he would barely have noticed my existence if everyone else had not thought me so awful, but at the time

I loved him for it with mute and passionate gratitude. Some of the early hero-worship lingered on and I should not be surprised if traces of it were to remain for the rest of my days.

Instead of hanging up, he said in his crafty way: 'It is for Ellen's sake, chiefly. Matilda is going out on tour and I have a deadline to meet. I shall be practically incommunicadikins and I thought you might come and keep her company.'

Knowing that Matilda had been out on tour a dozen times since their marriage and that Toby's career had consisted of a series of lurches from one deadline to the next, I said warily:

'What sort of tour? Lapland?'

'Somewhere like that,' he agreed. 'I've forgotten the details. All I know is that she won't be able to get home, except for the week when they play Dedley.'

Dedley, which is within twenty miles of Roakes, is a city on the normal five- or six-week circuit for pre-London tryouts, which also includes such accessible towns as Brighton and Oxford, and it occurred to me that there might be some domestic fraças behind all this and that Toby's second marriage was cracking up as disastrously as his first. If so, I concluded that Ellen might be in for something a good deal more fraught than a spell of loneliness. Having been abandoned by her own mother at the age of five, she had become accustomed, if not attached, to Matilda in the four years since she and Toby had embarked on the frail craft of matrimony. I lifted that last phrase from my Victorian play and I do think it has a certain whimsical charm, though using it here, of course, in the ironical sense.

Ellen was then eleven years old and, although that is not usually regarded as a specially tricky time of life, compared to some which come later in the female span, I nevertheless suspected that it would give her a considerable jolt, besides opening up some nasty old wounds, if the frail craft were heading for a rough passage through the divorce courts. Rotten actress though she was, I had to admit that Matilda had turned in a creditable performance in the real-life stepmother rôle and I believed her to be fond of Ellen, too, in her own bossy and undemonstrative way.

A vague idea of conferring with Matilda and playing on these finer feelings of hers partly accounted for my eventual acceptance of Toby's invitation, although I should not pretend that this decision, which was later to involve me in so many tribulations, sprang only from the purest of motives. The truth is that I had just completed six episodes of a television crime serial and could afford, for once, to relax from the slog of job hunting. I was in a particularly self-indulgent mood because mine had only been a tiny part in the original script, but it had turned out so well in performance that they had written me into the later episodes as well. Believing, though wrongly as it turned out, that I now had both dainty feet on the ladder to stardom, I was in the mood to treat myself to two or three weeks' holiday.

I acquainted my agent with this development and she covered the telephone with her hand, saying: 'Good idea, my darling; bring the roses back to your cheeks; and give loveliest love to darling Toby, won't you, my darling?'

She promised to call me on the instant if anything turned up for me, adding that if matters turned out as she hoped this might happen a lot sooner than her darling expected.

With these false but none the less comforting words to cheer me on my way, I hurled myself into a taxi and, when I had fought off all the merry, twinkling porters who sprang forward to assist me, sank back into my dirty corner of the two-fifty from Paddington, opened a bag of apples and a new biography of Mrs P. Campbell and prepared to while away the long and tedious journey to Roakes Common.

(ii)

There are two methods of travelling by rail to Roakes, though neither has apparently been designed with any idea of the passenger's reaching it in less time than it would take to get to Siberia. Toby maintained that it was just this inaccessibility which gave the village its unspoilt charm and that we should all be prepared to suffer the inconvenience in a cheerful spirit. He and Matilda both suffered it with exemplary cheerfulness, as each had a car and would not have dreamt of travelling by any other means. Toby's car was an old green Mercedes, which he drove with great speed and nonchalance, as though he were on the Dodgems and the object of the exercise was to bang into every other vehicle on the road.

Roakes Common is a hamlet to the north-west of London and some eight hundred feet above sea-level, so they tell me. It consists of twenty or thirty houses, two pubs and a combined post office and store, set in a hundred acres of commonland. The Common is divided down the middle by the road which joins Storhampton, in the Thames Valley, with Dedley, twenty miles to the north.

Toby's section of the Common was on the eastern side of this road and was shaped like a horseshoe. The road made a line across the top of the horseshoe and a rough, stony track formed the curve. Half a mile separated the two points at the top, where this track joined the road, and a pub, like a cosy sentinel, stood at each corner, the Bricklayers' Arms on the Dedley side and the Bull Inn on the other. I doubt if there were any contours to justify it, but at Roakes we always spoke of going up to the Bricklayers' and down to the Bull.

Five private houses were dotted at intervals round the inner curve) all facing out over the Common and screened from the road by a row of beech trees. At all times when not actually making the journey I was ready to concede that it was worth some sacrifice to preserve such a haven, only fifty miles from London.

Dedley is a hideous industrial city on the main railway line, but is farther from London and farther from Roakes than Storhampton, which is the terminal point of a meandering branch line. Going via Dedley meant travelling twenty miles beyond the ultimate destination and then backtracking by road. Storhampton station is a mere eight miles from the goal, but necessitates a change at Threwing Junction, which is the place where they lock up the waiting-rooms and slam down the shutters of the buffet as soon as the London train is signalled.

So far as I was concerned, the decision usually depended on the state of my finances and this time, with three economical weeks ahead, I had settled for the Dedley route, and Toby, who unlike Matilda is not at all cheese-paring, had not grumbled about driving all the way to meet me. The big surprise was that he actually arrived at the station on time and was waiting on the platform when my train limped in. I spotted him from afar, owing to what his neighbour, Mrs Grimbold, gushingly referred to as his theatrical appearance. This is not quite the phrase I would have used, but there was a certain flamboyance about him which may have reminded her of the dear old days, when she was a girl and madly in love with Ivor Novello. He even wore a hat, and a squashy green one at that, but I suspected that the reason for this was that it toned with the Mercedes.

He did not come so far out of character as to pick up my suitcase, but kissed me on the forehead, saying: 'How nasty your hair smells. Ellen's waiting in the car. We're parked on the double yellow, so she has to stand guard, lest the coppers pounce. By the way, Tessa, *on ne parle pas du petit chien*,' he added mysteriously.

'Which *petit chien* would that be?' I asked. 'And *pourquoi pas*?'

'Ellen's *chien. Il est mort.* It's a long *histoire* which I'll tell you in *privé.*'

Since there was not a soul within earshot who could conceivably have had the faintest interest in the matter, I was at a loss to understand why these warnings had to be couched in such a strange tongue, but I assumed that it was to impress me with their gravity. So I assured him that his *mot* was *ma commande* and we proceeded onwards, to the nearest double yellow.

Ellen was waiting, very composedly, with not a policeman in sight. She had grown even more stunning than when I had last seen her, which is saying a lot. She had inherited her mother's thick flaxen hair and her father's small, straight nose and enormous dark green eyes. It had been shrewd of her to get the permutation right, because the other way round could have spelt disaster. Toby's head consisted mainly of eyes and forehead, and what little hair he did possess was of the most undistinguished variety, whereas his first wife, if memory serves, had shifty blue eyes and pink eyelashes. However, one would naturally have expected Ellen to organise things properly. She was about the most capable and poised young female of my acquaintance, with an innate serenity which had a most heartening effect on everyone around her.

She greeted me with her usual benevolence, and in return I gave her an affectionate hug. I thought she was looking more serious than usual, which could have been accounted for either by Matilda's departure or by the mysterious *mort du chien*. Either way, I reckoned that discretion lay in silence.

Toby kept up a ceaseless babble throughout the half-hour drive, and once we had stopped swerving in and out of the suburban traffic and were in open country, with all the cursing bus drivers, tooting motorists and fainting pedestrians safely behind us, I felt able to give about half of my mind to what he was talking about. This proved to be Matilda's play. He and Ellen had been up to Manchester a day or two before for the opening night, an experience which, according to him, was among the more unspeakable in a life which had known its share of ups and downs.

He continued to abuse the play for several miles, as well as the iniquity of managements who expected people to pay to see such rubbish, all of which led me to conclude that it was probably quite good in its way and likely to run for at least two years.

Most of the plays that Matilda had appeared in had been quite good in their way, and several of them had run for two years. They were all farces, and in each of them Matilda had been cast as a stately aristocrat who remained implacably aloof and only faintly surprised, while everyone else tore round the stage, hiding under beds and getting locked in wardrobes, usually dressed in each other's clothes, or only in underpants, if they happened to be clergymen. Matilda, being statuesque and junoesque, to mention only two, did provide rather a chucklesome contrast to all this mayhem and certainly her air of unwavering indifference and disdain did not overstrain her dramatic powers, slight as these were. Apart from the salary she was excessively bored by the whole proceedings, and spent most of the action totting up the housekeeping expenses and deciding where the axe should fall next.

I think the main reason why Matilda looked so imposing, on and off stage, was that she had originally intended to become a ballet dancer and the early training was responsible for her regal bearing. It always came as a slight shock to see her standing next to Toby, who was quite a small man, and to realise that they were exactly the same height.

After listening for a while to his invective, most of which I had often heard before, I twisted my head round and asked Ellen what she had thought of the play.

'It was all right,' she said. 'Jolly amusing, in some bits.'

'She has a funny sense of humour,' Toby explained.

'That is better than having a sad sense of humour,' Ellen said calmly.

It was the kind of remark which sometimes prompted me to ask myself if whether there were not some deep waters beneath the clear, sunlit surface which Ellen presented to the world and which gave rise to some disturbing conjectures in the weeks ahead.

Two

No DOUBT every Eden has its snake lurking somewhere in the grass, and Roakes was no exception. There, the snake took the form of a whole family, Cornford by name, and its habitat was no less than the Manor House. This was by far the largest of the houses surrounding the horseshoe, holding a commanding position, at its base. Until recently and for generations before, the Big House and adjoining farmland had belonged to the Davenport family, who were also Lords of the Manor. Little by little, strips of the land had been sold off and the neighbouring houses built. On the death of the last owner, which occurred soon after Toby's arrival on the scene, the remnants of the estate had finally been disposed of, and the house itself acquired by Douglas Cornford, the son of an industrial tycoon from the Midlands, as a home for himself, his wife Bronwen and their two children. It proved to be an unlucky venture, for the family evinced no joy in their new surroundings, while growing daily more inimical to all their neighbours. Their flat Midland accents, surly manners and urban attitudes grated on everyone, and the mention of their name could be relied upon to set the ball of conversation spinning, in any of the nearby houses.

This time it was Ellen who introduced the Cornford theme, soon after she had carried my suitcase up to my bedroom.

'You're in the blue room,' she announced, pushing open the door, and she was dead right. Every inch of the room, including carpet, wallpaper, bedcovers, towels and ashtrays, were either blue, or patterned in blue and white. There was even a cake of blue soap on the wash basin. Only the waxy oak panelling had been left untouched and I did not doubt that Matilda would get around to this, given time.

'Heavenly,' I said, examining the bedside lamp to see if it had a blue bulb.

When I turned round Ellen was sitting on the bed, looking alert and expectant, as though ready for a bit of a chinwag, and she said: 'You're going out to dinner tonight. Did Daddy tell you?'

'He did not. Who with? And why me?'

'Both of you. With Sylvia and Gerry.'

'Really? And who might they be?'

'They might be anybody,' Ellen said, switching on her prim manner, 'but they're the Grimbolds. You know, the people who moved into the White House when the Mortimers left. Only they call it White Gables now. She's called Sylvia, and she's quite old and awfully kind and gushing.'

'And Gerry's the cigar-store Indian, who never utters? Yes, it all comes back to me,' I said, without enthusiasm.

'Sometimes he utters to himself, though.'

'Go on! How do you know?'

'I've seen him doing it, on the Common. Sylvia doesn't care for walks, so he goes by himself and strides up and down in the wild part, talking to himself like mad. I suppose he doesn't get much chance when he's with Sylvia, so he has to do this to keep in practice.'

'Thanks for the warning. I suspected there was something odd about him. Anyway, I can't go to dinner with them. I'm here for the express purpose of Ellen-sitting, didn't you know? You and I will have a cosy evening on our own.'

She shook her head: 'Not tonight. Mrs Parkes is coming to spend the evening with me. That's the gardener's wife,' she explained, probably to forestall inquiries as to who Mrs Parkes might be. 'They've got the flat over the garage now, so it's no trouble for her.'

'It's going to be a trouble for me, though,' I said. 'What's come over your father? He never mentioned anything to me about hobnobbing with the neighbours. Honestly, you can't even rely on misogynists these days.'

'You'll have a smashing dinner, though, Tess. I went to tea there once and it was gorgeous. Everything homemade.'

'Is that why Toby accepted? Is he getting greedy in his old age?'

'No,' Ellen said. 'He kept trying to get out of it, but Sylvia is very persevering and he ran out of excuses. She wants him to join her anti-Cornford League. So in the end he said he would go, if he could take you as well.'

'Now I know you're joking,' I said, falling back on the bed. 'Toby in the anti-Cornford League? Not possible. He's always been so holy about the Cornfords, standing up for them like a brave little Lord Fauntleroy whenever they were attacked.'

'Yes, but that was only because everyone else was so down on them, you know. Anyway, something has happened to make him change now. You heard about Oscar?'

Oscar was the name of Ellen's dog, a rakish, one-eyed old Pekinese that she doted on like a mother. In view of Toby's warning, the question put me in a quandary and I hedged:

'Well, I had noticed he wasn't around, now you mention it.'

'He's dead.'

'Oh, Ellen, I am sorry,' I said, trying to sound surprised as well as sad. 'What happened?'

'He had to be killed.'

'What a shame! You mean, put down?'

'That's what they called it. I call it being killed.'

'Poor old Oscar! How ghastly for you. But still, if he was ill and in pain, it must have been the kindest thing.'

'He wasn't a bit ill,' Ellen said.

'You mean, he was run over, or something? What did happen?'

She drew a deep breath and said: 'It was the day after we came back from Manchester. We took Oscar with us. He always came everywhere with us. Well, you see, it was dark when we got home, so we didn't notice.'

'Didn't notice what?' I asked.

'I'm telling you. You remember how Oscar used to dash out of the house every morning when I took him downstairs?'

I nodded.

'He always did exactly the same, every day. As soon as I opened the front door he bolted across the lawn and through that little gap he'd made for himself, on to the Common, barking like mad. Then, after a few minutes, he'd come trotting back, very happy and pleased with himself. Remember?'

'Yes, I do. It was about the only time we ever heard him bark.'

'I know; and the day after we got back it was just the same as usual. I watched him go tearing off and then I went to the kitchen to get his breakfast ready, only . . .'

'What?'

'Well, before I got there, even, the barking stopped and it changed into a sort of screaming. He was screaming and screaming.'

'Oh, my goodness, Ellen!'

'I was scared,' she said. 'I wanted to run away and get the screaming out of my head, but Daddy was asleep and there was no one else here, so I went out on the Common. He'd stopped screaming by the time I got to him. It was just a sort of whimpering noise and there was blood all over him.'

'Was it a trap?' I asked.

Ellen paused for a moment to collect herself. Then she said:

'It was a sort of trap. Barbed wire. It was very low down, you see, and he'd caught his good eye on it.'

'Oh no!' I said, horrified. 'Barbed wire on the Common? Who would do such a thing, and what for?'

'Mr Cornford put it there.'

'Oh, Ellen, surely not? It's forbidden to put any sort of fencing on the Common and, anyway, why should he want to?'

'He wanted to kill Oscar, of course. He'd fixed it up, just opposite our gate, while we were in Manchester, so that we wouldn't know it was there.'

Ellen's set expression warned me not to argue this point, so I changed my tactics and said:

'You must try to understand that something of this kind was bound to happen, sooner or later. He probably couldn't see all that well, with only one eye, and he was getting old.'

'He wasn't old,' she replied. 'He was the same age as me, which isn't terribly old, even for a dog. And he enjoyed life, he really did, Tess. He loved sleeping on my bed and pretending to chase rabbits on the Common and all that. The vet said he was good for quite a few years, only it wasn't fair to keep him alive.'

'Well, at least you can be sure that he didn't suffer. It would have been just a tiny pin-prick, and then he'd have gone to sleep without knowing anything at all.'

'I expect he knew he was blind,' Ellen said. She had stood up by this time and had her back to me. She appeared to be counting up the blue coat hangers in my wardrobe and I could not see her face, but she went on in a voice too cold and level for my comfort:

'You needn't bother to smooth it over for me, Tess. I've stopped crying about it now, but, whatever you say, the Cornfords did kill Oscar. They did it on purpose and that makes them murderers.'

THREE

(i)

TOBY's conversion to neighbourhood togetherness was less wholehearted than Ellen had led me to believe, and he went through all the familiar stratagems to get out of dining with the Grimbolds.

The first ploy was to stare at me incredulously when I referred to our engagement, as though I had shown rather bad taste and would instantly be shamed into dropping the matter. When that failed he mumbled something about there having been a vague arrangement, but the details escaped him and most likely Mrs Parkes wouldn't bother to turn up, as she was most unreliable, and we should just have to wait and see.

Mrs Parkes reported for duty on the stroke of seven, looking about as unreliable as the Duke of Wellington, and Toby fell back on a tangled web of lies and excuses, including a script which had to be finished, a nasty touch of migraine coming on and a strong disposition to believe that he had seen both the Grimbolds driving away from their house only ten minutes before.

However, when each of these frail pillars of resistance had crumbled into dust, he gave in and, with many a moan and a whimper, set forth at my side to walk the two hundred yards up the track to White Gables.

The Manor House loomed up between our house and the Grimbolds', a bleak, castellated Victorian pile, in no way enhanced by the addition of modern, wrought-iron gates. The evening sun, reflecting sightlessly from the highest row of stark, uncurtained windows, added an extra inimical touch and I staggered about on my high heels, clutching Toby's arm and squealing:

'Ooh, ooh, isn't it scary? Like a home for retired homicidal maniacs.'

'Not nearly so cosy,' he said crossly. 'All those places have chintz with everything, nowadays,' and stamped on, too dispirited even to laugh at his own joke.

He was still in a sad humour when we arrived at the Grimbolds, and Sylvia got off on the wrong foot by inquiring about dear little Elaine even before we had our coats off.

Toby stared at her, affecting total non-comprehension, and when I had sorted out the slight confusion she fluttered about in ecstasies of self reproach, saying:

'Oh, Ellen, of course, of course. Silly me! Such a sweet little old-fashioned name, how could I forget it? Sit down, both of you and tell Gerry what you'd like to drink.'

'She was named after Ellen Terry,' Toby said. 'I do not recall that there was anything particularly old-fashioned about her.'

'Oh, goodness me, how frightfully romantic! Are you related?'

'Closely,' he said. 'She is my daughter.'

'No, no, silly boy, I know that. I meant, are you related to the Terrys?'

'Yes,' he replied.

This was untrue, but in the somewhat trying circumstances I decided to let it pass and weighed in with a couple of anecdotes from my book about Mrs Patrick Campbell. During the second one Toby picked up a handsome, illustrated tome on Chinese art from the coffee table, then realising from Sylvia's surreptitious glances that it had been put there on purpose to ensnare him, instantly replaced it.

Gerry had taken no part in the opening skirmish, but had stalked about the room like a robot, handing out great goblets of foaming alcohol, without saying a word. I concluded that he was storing up a fund of material for an interesting chat with himself on the Common the following day.

Things brightened up considerably, when we sat down to dinner, for in the food and wine department Sylvia was certainly no mean hostess, and I wished that Matilda had been there to observe the mellowing effect of such lavishness on even the most unpromising of social occasions. I had seen her go into a deep trance when out shopping, and all because she was wondering whether half a pound of sausages would go round or whether to lash out on a whole pound.

Toby and I gobbled up second helpings of everything, and by the time dinner was over Sylvia and Gerry were practically our dearest friends.

For my money, the evening could have tailed off at that point, like the last act of a period comedy with lots of world-weary epigrams, as various threads of the plot became disentangled to everyone's satisfaction. Unfortunately, Sylvia had provided herself with a different script and was only now working up to the climax.

'So now, dear people,' she began, when with the help of sign language from Gerry we had decided which of about sixteen different liqueurs we would sample. 'Now, tell me what is to be done about those dreadful Cornfords. Let us get down to brass tacks.'

'Rather indigestible, after all that soccolate shoufflé,' I suggested wittily and made a note to tell Toby of an interesting development about himself, which was that he had acquired two extra heads. A possible explanation for this then occurred to me and, with immense care, I deposited my glass on the coffee table, sat back in my chair, did some breathing exercises and blinked my eyes rapidly before attempting to refocus them.

'Better now?' Toby asked coldly.

'Yes, thank you. I was momentarily overcome by the brandy fumes, but it has passed.'

He leant forward and moved my glass farther out of reach, saying to Sylvia:

'The poor girl is pickled, but it would be kinder to ignore it. In any case, she could hardly have anything constructive to contribute.'

I felt a strong desire to crush him, with a stinging retort, but although the words sounded all right in my head I distrusted my ability to bring them out in the right order and contented myself with some stinging looks, instead. This was fine for Toby and Sylvia as, with me now as *hors* as Gerry from the *combat*, they had a clear field. Bringing out her first brass tack, Sylvia said:

'Poor old Miss Davenport is the one Gerry and I feel worst about. She has the Cornfords right on her doorstep and it is no secret that they make her life intolerable. Apart from that, I do think it is time for all of us interested parties to put our heads together and decide what is to be done to safeguard our own interests.'

I regretted this speedy brushing aside of poor old Miss Davenport, as I had hoped to hear some of the details of her intolerable life. It began to look as though the meeting had really been called to promote the protection and greater glory of Sylvia, but, if so, she had reckoned without Toby.

'I detest these dreary, rural vendettas,' he said, 'and I do not see that anything is to be gained by talking about the Cornfords. My attitude boils down to this: either they go, or I do.'

'Would you not admit that it was rather a selfish attitude?' Sylvia asked, with a saintly smile.

'Yes, I would,' he agreed warmly. 'I thought I had made that clear.'

'And perhaps also rather a defeatist one?'

'Oh, I'm not proud,' Toby assured her, in a tone which belied the claim. 'I came to live here, because it offered peace and quiet. If they cease to be available, I shall go away again.'

'That is so easy to say,' Sylvia protested, 'and it may be easy for some people to do, but we are not all such happy-go-lucky bohemians as you. Some of us have chosen to put our roots down here and we do not see why we should be hounded and terrorised out of our own property.'

I could see that Toby did not relish being described as a happy-go-lucky bohemian and that, if she persisted in using such insulting terms, there was a danger of his swinging round again and coming out in defence of the hounds and terrorists. Sylvia saw it too and back-pedalled rapidly:

'Take Miss Davenport, for one. I am sure the poor old dear could not afford to live anywhere else, however much she might want to.'

'What makes you think she does want to?' Toby asked. 'I've not heard of her organising any movement for the suppression of the Cornfords.'

'My dear man, you are surely not deceived by that? Let me tell you that Miss Davenport belongs to that fine, old-fashioned breed who simply do not blurt out their troubles to all and sundry. She would be too proud.'

'Unlike some!' I thought.

'She is one of the old school and they have their code, you know. I'd describe her as a real lady if I didn't know you'd laugh at me, you old cynic.'

'I am glad you have decided not to risk it,' the old cynic replied, 'because, in fact, if this picture of yours were anything but the figment of an overheated imagination she would be quite indifferent to the Cornfords. If the kind of romanticised, upper-class person you so fondly describe had ever existed, which I doubt, she would certainly not have concerned herself, one way or the other, with such lesser breeds as the Cornfords.'

'She may not feel them to be on her own social level, I grant you that. Which of us does? But she cannot fail to be affected by their disgusting behaviour. Do you know, when I popped over to see her this morning with a basketful of our raspberries, do you know what I found?'

'No, Sylvia, I do not.'

'Both the Cornford children in her little front garden, if you please! As soon as they caught sight of me they bolted over the fence like ninepence, you may be sure, but I saw them as clearly as you're sitting there. And so, of course, I looked around a bit to see what they'd been up to, and what do you think?'

'Nothing. What should I think?'

'Why, there was Miss Davenport's dear little kitty, crouching under a bush and terrified out of its poor little wits. It arched its back and spat at me when I put my hand out, and you know very well that dumb animals don't do that unless they've been ill treated. Those two brats had been tormenting her, you may be sure, and if there's one thing Miss Davenport does care deeply about it's her pets, which makes it doubly cruel.'

'Yes, most unpleasant,' Toby agreed, 'but none of it alters my views. On the contrary, it bolsters them. Why should one have to live among such savages? I don't propose to and I don't intend that Ellen shall. Miss Davenport has all my sympathy, but she is a big old lady now and must decide for herself. Ellen is different.'

'It is all part and parcel, in my opinion,' Sylvia said. 'Don't think me hard. I could have wept when I heard about the poor darling doggie. It upset me for hours. Gerry will tell you. It was sheer sadistic cruelty, and they deserve to be punished for it. Did he ever give any reason for putting up the barbed wire?'

'There was some story about making an enclosure for his geese. He had intended to graze them on the Common.'

'Geese? What geese? It's the first I've heard of any geese.'

'And is likely to be the last. He seems to have counted the enclosure before the geese were hatched. There was some rigmarole about having ordered them and having to get something fixed up in advance. All rubbish, no doubt, and entirely irrelevant, too, because neither he nor any of us is entitled to fence the Common. You can graze your geese on it if you have a mind to, but you have to hire a goose girl to keep them in bounds, and there aren't so many of them about these days, I daresay.'

'The surprising thing is that he consented to take it down without a dreadful fuss.'

'There was a dreadful fuss. The rumour is that Mrs Cornford screamed without stopping for two days. And he didn't consent to take it down, he was forced to. We had to invoke the Domesday Book and Ye Ancient Laws of Commonie Righties and I don't know what all. The Clerk of the Parish came in person to threaten him with a week in the stocks; and Miss Davenport was most helpful. It turns out that she has medieval law at her finger-tips. That is presumably why cat-baiting is now on the increase.'

'Egged on by their mother, no doubt. She is the arch villain, you know.'

'So you always insist, but I don't agree with you,' Toby said, as at various times in my life I had heard him say before.

'Oh, Gerry and I are both convinced of it. We feel that Douglas Cornford would be quite a harmless little person, if he were left to himself. It is that shrew, Bronwen, who makes all the trouble.'

'You are entirely mistaken, Sylvia. This is the kind of thing all women say and it is merely a symptom of their own prodigious vanity. They have such an over-rated opinion of their own sex that praise or blame for a man's behaviour is invariably attributed to his wife. I don't suppose you would find a single man to agree with you about the Cornfords, except Gerry, of course.'

'Gerry's judgement is quite good enough for me, thank you. He has had great experience of the world and you would be surprised to hear some of his comments on Bronwen.'

'Indeed, I would,' Toby said, 'but they would not alter my decision to move, as soon as I have found somewhere else to live.'

'I think it is a very selfish and spineless attitude, but I quite see how it will be. Everyone worth speaking to will leave, and we shall be left here with none of our own sort,' Sylvia said bitterly, not explaining why she was so eager to hang on to a neighbour of whose character she held such a poor opinion.

'Cheer up! You will still have Miss Davenport.'

'Oh, Miss Davenport is a saint; reminds me so much of a maiden aunt of mine, quite the *grande dame*, I can tell you and don't I just wish there were more of her sort left in the world? But, when it comes to things of the mind, books, music, everything which makes the difference between living and mere existence, well, I confess that poor old Joan Davenport and I simply have nothing in common.'

'A terrible pun rears its head,' Toby said, 'which probably shows how late it is getting, even if we didn't have the sleeping Tessa to underline it for us.'

I was nowhere near asleep as it happened but had closed my eyes, the better to concentrate on the dialogue. However, as this seemed to be degenerating into acrimony on one side and self-aggrandisement on the other, I was not sorry to be hauled to my feet and dragged forth into the starry night.

'Somehow I don't see much future for the anti-Cornford League, if tonight was any example of its aims and achievements,' I remarked, as we plodded round the Common.

'Preposterous woman,' Toby replied. 'I was fooled into believing that she had something sensible to suggest, but it was only a roundabout device for pooling the latest gossip. Books and music, indeed! The *Daily Sketch* and Anniversary Waltz are about her criterion.'

'It was a good dinner, at any rate,' I reminded him. 'Ellen will be pleased to hear that.'

'Oh yes, excellent; and I am happy to say that I am one of those philistines for whom the difference between living and mere existence is a scrumptious old soccolate shoufflé.'

(ii)

The telephone rang, as we opened the front door and Mrs Parkes, hatted and coated, was in the hall and moving towards it.

Perhaps, if I had not still been somewhat fuddled by the brandy fumes it would not have occurred to me that my agent could be ringing me up at ten minutes before midnight, but I plunged forward and grabbed the receiver.

It was Matilda.

'Hang on,' I said, 'I'll just . . .'

I had been about to say that I would hand her over to Toby, but she cut me short, in her usual imperious fashion.

'Is that you, Tessa? It's you I want. Can anyone hear you?'

I looked behind me. The front door was open, but there was no one in sight. I concluded that Toby was escorting Mrs Parkes back to her quarters.

'Okay, just at the moment,' I said, 'but it may only be a moment.'

'Then, listen carefully. There's something you've got to do for me and it's vital. Do you understand?'

'Perfectly,' I said, thinking that it was typical of Matilda to beg a favour, in the terms of an ultimatum.

'The point is, I wrote two letters this afternoon in my dressing-room. I finished the second one about two minutes before my call and I only had time to stick them in the envelopes before I went down. Do you follow me?'

'Like a trusty spaniel,' I said, 'who knows exactly what Mistress is going to say next.'

'Precisely. The minute I was on I got this frantic idea that I'd put them in the wrong envelopes. I belted back immediately after the curtain and I found that that bloody officious dresser of mine had already posted them. She probably wanted a nip before they closed and made my letters an excuse for leaving the theatre.'

'Hard cheese!' I said. 'What do you expect me to do about it?'

'It's quite simple. One of the envelopes was addressed to Toby. It may have the right letter inside, but I dare not risk it You've got to get hold of it before anyone else does.'

'Oh, is that all?' I said, but the sarcasm was lost on her.

'Absolutely all. You can manage that, I suppose?'

'What time does the post arrive?'

'My letters caught the afternoon one from here, so it ought to be in your morning delivery. That's about nine as a rule, so there's no problem. Toby never comes downstairs before ten, and Ellen . . .'

'Hasn't so much incentive for early rising, these days.'

'Yes, I know, poor darling. I must write to her.'

'Just so long as you remember to put it in the right envelope,' I said.

'Oh yes, very funny. Now, you're sure you've got it all straight? If so, I'll ring off and leave the rest to you. This call must be costing the earth.'

'I'll do my best. That's as much as I can promise.'

It must have been enough, for she hung up, saving herself a few pennies, by dispensing with the farewells. I turned round and saw that Toby had returned and was standing by the front door.

'That was Matilda, was it?' he asked. He was still wearing his hat, but he was so morbidly attached to it that it gave no indication that he had not been indoors long enough to over-hear some revealing words and so I said:

'If you knew, why didn't you came and speak to her?'

'Did she want me to?'

'I don't know that she did. She was ringing up about Ellen. Wanted to know if she was getting over the shock of Oscar, etcetera.'

'And what did you tell her?'

This was not precisely the cue I had been expecting and I fluffed my next line disgracefully:

'Oh well, I said yes and no sort of thing.'

'And I am sure Matilda thought that was well worth the expense of a call from Manchester?'

'Well, it's cheaper at night, you know.'

Toby laughed: 'So it is; and you needn't look so guilty, Tess. I am well aware that Matilda is up to something, but I infinitely prefer not to know what it is. If she is trying to involve you, in some way, that's your look out, but you will be doing a favour to us both, if you keep her secrets to yourself.'

'I am not involved in anything,' I said. 'And I haven't the remotest idea what is going on. I wish I had.'

'As I've told you, I am thankful I haven't.'

'But you must know something, Toby? Is Matilda planning to leave you, or what?'

'Not so far as I know. I prefer not to talk about it.'

'You have talked about it, by accusing me of being involved, and it's not much fun keeping secrets when you don't know what they are.'

'The less you know, the better. Matilda is a hard nut and one that you are likely to crack your teeth on.'

'Don't you mean, burn my fingers pulling her chestnuts out of the fire?'

'Perhaps I do. Shall we leave it at that and go to bed?'

As a curtain line, this left something to be desired and I made one last attempt to get some sense out of him:

'Before you go, Toby, just tell me one thing. I'm not trying to pump you, just to satisfy my vulgar curiosity. I'd really hate you and Matilda to split up, mainly because of Ellen, but if that's the way things are I might as well be warned. The rumours are bound to be flying around before long. Ellen will ask questions and she won't be the only one. So what am I supposed to answer?'

He had continued his relentless ascent of the stairs during this speech and he turned at the top and looked down on me:

'You may say this,' he announced portentously, 'Matilda and I have no plans for a divorce. We are just bad friends.'

(iii)

There is no denying that it was thanks to Matilda that my honour and integrity were preserved unblemished. Of course, it is possible that she was a brilliant psychologist, but I doubt it. I believe the reason why I was not seriously tempted to read her letter before destroying it was simply that she did not forbid me to, presumably seeing no necessity. The paradox is that, had she required me to swear on my unborn children's heads, guide's honour, cross my heart and hope to die, or any of the normal feminine voodoo, there might have been a sharp tussle between my curiosity and my conscience, and who is to say how that would have ended? As it was, I was so eager to get the wretched job done and Satan behind me that I almost jumped the gun.

For reasons which are no doubt clearly set out in the Post Office rules, the postman always stopped his van midway between each pair of houses round the Common. His routine was then to walk a few yards back in one direction, followed by a few yards forward in the other, before returning to his van and crawling to the next stop.

I had been watching for his arrival, in the manner of a starving hawk on the look-out for prey, and as soon as the red van got into position I nipped through the gate and practically tore the bundle of letters from the postman's hand.

'Easy on, now; easy does it,' he said, in some alarm, as though I were making a personal assault on him. He held the letters aloft and out of my reach and then I noticed that he was not concerned with me any more, but was looking at something over my shoulder. I wheeled round and saw Mrs Cornford emerging from the Manor gates and bearing down on us with many a glowering look. She was clad in her favourite costume, consisting of black woollen trousers, fawn macintosh and green headscarf, which hid all but a few strands of her red hair and made her look like a character from some dreary communist play about to deliver a swingeing attack on the imperialist war-mongers. I had never seen her dressed in any other way, winter or summer, and the facial expression was more or less the perennial one, too.

'Just what do you think you're doing?' she snarled at me.

It always enrages me to be asked what I think I am doing, as though, in my case, intention and result were unlikely to coincide and I said, in a high-pitched voice:

'Tampering with Her Majesty's mail. Reading all your post-cards. Auntie Glad's having a smashing time in Penzance, you'll be glad to hear. No doubt, she wishes you were there.'

She stared at me in sullen stupefaction, then said in a flat voice:

'I think you're mad.'

The postman who had profited by this fiery interlude to sort the letters into two separate bundles, handed her one of them without a word, and she snatched it up and marched away, head down and arms tightly clasped across her chest.

Having watched her retreat, the postman turned to me and said kindly:

'They're awkward customers, up there. You want to go a bit careful. Here you are, then, Miss, here's your little lot and let's hope he's written.'

I was still shaken by Mrs Cornford's rudeness and so mortified at having allowed it to ruffle me that I was scarlet in the face, trembling like a leaf and only too thankful to allow his coy interpretation to pass. It enabled me to simulate a few more blushes and stammers and to make a plausible exit.

Even before I re-entered the house, I had picked out an envelope in Matilda's handwriting and, tossing the others on to the hall table, I bolted upstairs and locked myself in the bathroom. After one final glance at the letter I ripped it into shreds, dropped them down the lavatory and pulled the plug.

However, even during this spate of frenzied activity a little nagging query was popping about in the back of my mind, informing me that there had been something odd about the packet of letters which the postman had handed to Mrs Cornford. It fidgeted me not to be able to pin it down, and yet the harder I concentrated the more obstinately its significance eluded me. It was not until weeks later that the truth hit me and fell into place, as one more piece of the puzzle.

FOUR

(i)

IT PROVED to be uphill work, in every sense, to get Ellen out on health-giving, fresh-air excursions. She had her own sitting-room, still known as the nursery, which was equipped with all the books, games, records and television sets which the childish heart could desire and really preferred to spend every waking hour in these cosy quarters.

I could not blame her, because the weather had gradually deteriorated from mild, to cool, to downright chilly, since my arrival, and neither of us felt inclined to break the ice on the swimming pool, or even to wrap ourselves in overcoats for a game of croquet. Ellen possessed a bicycle which she used for occasional jaunts to the village shop and suchlike, but situated as we were, on the topmost ledge of a ridge of hills, anything farther afield inevitably ended with an uphill walk home and me pushing the bike.

I should have been too nervous to drive the Mercedes, even if Toby had offered it, and although Matilda's tamer vehicle was in the garage, she had prudently removed the keys. The only means left to us was our own legs, and unfortunately all the surrounding walks had painful associations for Ellen, because she had travelled them with Oscar.

I asked Toby whether it would not be a smart move to buy her a puppy, but he said gloomily that it was not in his hands. If I would care to obtain the Cornfords' approval, it might save trouble later on, but for his part he was convinced that what Ellen needed was not a new dog but a new home.

This defeatist attitude irritated me almost as much as it did Sylvia, but I did not fan the flames by arguing. As Ellen, having lost her beloved dog, now stood in imminent danger of losing her beloved home and her fairly beloved stepmother, it behoved me to concentrate on the immediate task of diverting her mind from these past and future sorrows.

In desperation I suggested one morning that we might call on Sylvia and sample her coffee and home-made buns.

'Not today,' Ellen said firmly. 'Sylvia's never at home on Saturdays.'

'You speak with much assurance,' I said. 'How come? Do you keep tabs on her movements?'

'No, but everyone knows that Saturday is her day for the adopted babies.'

'And a busy day it sounds. Has she many?'

'They aren't hers. It's when she interviews the people who want them. She belongs to a society that sends out orphan babies to people who haven't got any of their own. Sylvia goes spying on these people, to see if they'd make good parents.'

'I wouldn't call that spying,' I objected primly. 'It sounds a sensible idea. But why Saturdays? I should have thought even the most dedicated adopters might have other things on their minds, at weekends?'

'That's the whole point. If she goes on an ordinary day the place is all spick and span, with frilly curtains and everything. But on Saturdays she catches them when Mr is at home, too, and then sometimes it's different.'

'Really? You mean that at weekends Missus slops around, tending her bruises, while Mr sleeps off his hangover, that kind of thing?' I asked, rather fascinated by this new glimpse of British domestic life.

'I suppose so. Anyway, after one of her Saturday pounces she sometimes has to cross a family off the list.'

'And you mean that Sylvia does this chore every single weekend?'

'Never misses.'

'Good for her! And what an example she must feel it to be to the lower orders. So who else is there? I feel in a visiting mood.'

I could tell that this was not shared. 'Not Miss Davenport, if you're thinking of her,' Ellen said.

'Why? What does she do on Saturdays?'

'It's not just Saturdays, it's every time I meet her. She wants me to join her Brownie group and the Sunday school class and all that.'

'Quite right, too. Where would the British Empire have been, without its Brownies and Sunday schools, I should like to know.'

'I shouldn't think there'd have been one, if Miss Davenport was in charge. She'd never have got to the right country, on the right day. I expect she'd have gone to India, by mistake for Russia, or something.'

'Russia was never in the Empire, as I recall.'

'Well, I bet you anything Miss Davenport wouldn't have known that. Half the time when it's Brownie Meeting she forgets to turn up, or else she thinks we're the Mothers' Union and spends the whole time telling us what to do with the left-overs.'

'I can see that you are beginning to take after your father and are catching his anti-social attitudes. You would do well to guard against it.'

'We could go and see the Flyaways, if you like,' Ellen said, evidently taking the warning to heart.

'Oh, do let's. Who are they? Michael, John and Wendy?'

'No, Peter and Paul. They love being called on.'

'You mean that garrulous old couple next to the pub? Is that the best you can do? Don't you know anyone around here with children?'

'There's the Cornfords,' she said, regarding me gravely.

'So there is, but we might not get quite the welcome I had in mind. Tell me, though, Ellen, as a matter of interest, did you ever try to make friends with them, when they first came here, before all the rows started?'

The interest I spoke of lay in discovering what, if any, of the Cornfords' aggressiveness was retaliation for early snubs. Knowing how snobbish country communities could be, I half suspected this one of something less than effusiveness, in opening their hearts and homes to a strange family, from an alien background. Ellen knocked some of the stuffing out of this charitable theory:

'Miss Davenport was frightfully keen on the idea, at first. She kept telling me, before they came, how lovely it would be for me to have some little playmates and how she was going to arrange a tea party for us. Only she called it a bun fight.'

'Naturally. And what became of that idea?'

'She kept trying to do it, I think, but she said they always made some excuse why they couldn't go, so, in the end, she gave up. I expect it was true, because Matilda tried to be chummy, as well. She called on Mrs Cornford, and she invited her and Mr Cornford to a drinks party on Sunday morning.'

'And didn't they come to that, either?'

'Yes, they did, but it was an awful flop. At least, Mr Cornford wasn't so bad. Matilda had invited people from the company, as well as some locals, and Mr Cornford was jumping about and giggling like mad, but Mrs was awful. She just stood about and frowned at everyone when they tried to talk to her. I think she must have hated it, because they never came again and they never invited Matilda back, and that was more or less the end of it.'

Perhaps I should have paid closer attention, for Ellen was rarely imprecise in her wording, but I said:

'Right, then; Peter and Paul it is. Let's go.'

(ii)

Anti-social or not, Ellen was certainly well versed in local lore and, as we strolled along, was able to fill some of the gaps in my memory concerning the Flyaways. She even told me what their surnames were, but as I instantly forgot them again the information was wasted. More to the point was her reminder that Paul was the chubby, bucolic one and Peter the bearded member of the partnership, who looked like an abstract painter. Whereas, in reality, Chubby was the painter and Beardie the gardening expert, whose weekly contributions to a woman's magazine enabled them both to live in reasonable style in their modernised cottage, known as Oldacre. We agreed that, once you had grasped this paradox, it was no more trouble to sort them out than if they had been type-cast.

'I hope our sociable efforts won't be in vain,' I said. 'What a pity to have discovered so much about them, only to find they are not at home.'

'They will be. They do all their weekend shopping at Dedley market on Friday afternoon. They hate going to the shops on Saturday when they're so crowded.'

She was right, as usual. We found them both in the garden at the back of the cottage, although, contrary to the memorised facts, Chubby was sweating up and down the tiny lawn, in hot pursuit of a motor mower, while Beardie reclined on a wooden seat, which had *'A Garde . . . a . . . ovesom . . . hin . . .'*, inscribed in poker work, on the back.

'Someone Has Blundered,' I murmured.

Not so. Their opening words explained that bearded Peter, having tumbled out of a tree and broken his ankle, was directing operations from his chair, while tubby Paul had nobly relinquished the abstract brush and canvas for the more pressing demands of the *ovesom old garde*.

They greeted us enthusiastically and with audible sighs of relief; no doubt because we provided Paul with an excuse to cast aside his infernal machine and Peter with a new audience for the Saga of the Out-Patients Department, where he had waited for his leg to be encased in plaster.

'Four hours we were down there, in this dungeon,' he wailed, fixing us with his snapping brown eyes.

'Four and a half, it was,' Paul assured us, gazing from his melancholy blue ones. 'You remember, Pete, I looked at my watch as we went in, and it was four hours and twenty minutes till Nurse came for you. And you in this excruciating agony! As though I'd be likely to forget it . . .'

'. . . Four and a half hours in this dreadful dungeon,' Peter continued, as though there had been no interruption, 'and all those awful crocks hobbling in, hundreds of them; and each time a new one arrived we had to move up one place on this bench and they brought us cups of tea, on a trolley. It was like a concentration camp, really it was.'

'Have a drink, won't you?' Paul said, abruptly transferring his attention to Ellen and myself. 'Or some coffee? Coffee's on the hob and it wouldn't take a jiff. How about you, Pete?'

'Oh, I can't say that I feel like coffee. Haven't we got something in the fridge? Oh, it is lovely to see you both. I've been feeling ever so sorry for myself, cooped up here like this. Old Doc Macintosh says it'll be six weeks, at least, before I can put my foot to the ground. "That's fine, that is," I told him, "And what's to become of the garden in all that time, I should like to know? Rack and ruin, I suppose?" "You can thank your stars it wasn't worse," was all he said, so I told him, I said . . .'

'. . . could easily nip across to the pub and fetch some lager,' Paul said. 'They'd be open by now, and it wouldn't take a sec. Which would you honestly rather? Lager, or beer, or there's . . .'

I had been about to declare that we honestly did not want either, but could not get the words out before Peter was off again:

'This is only a temporary plaster, you know. The doctor who put it on, rather nice chap he was, said the ankle was much too inflamed for him to make a proper job of it and I'd have to go back for a check-up, on Tuesday.'

'Wednesday, you mean. It's Wednesday you have to go back. I remember, because of early closing.'

'Oh, Wednesday, is it? Head like a sieve. Well, I just dread having to go through all that again. Wouldn't you?'

'Which shall it be?' Paul asked. 'Just say the word. There's tea, you know, if you'd prefer . . .'

'. . . never had such a thing happen to me in my life, and never would have believed all the trouble it could cause; little thing like a broken ankle!'

'Get along with you, Pete. It's not a little thing, by a long chalk. Doc says the X-rays show fractures in three places. Call that a little thing?'

'Well, that's enough about me. Tell us what's going on in the big world. You're on the stage, aren't you? You are a lucky person. I had dreams of treading the boards myself once, but it was not to be. Just not talented enough . . .'

'Will you listen to the boy? It was your father wouldn't hear of your taking it up, and that's the plain truth. Terribly stuffy old party, Pete's father, by all accounts,' Paul assured us earnestly. 'Wicked waste, if you ask me. You should have seen our friend here, when the Storhampton Strollers did *French Without Tears* last year; brought the house down.'

Like many people who had lived together for years, passing their days in close proximity, Peter and Paul invariably spoke as a duet, but rarely in harmony. It was disconcerting, because at times they interrupted and contradicted each other in their bantering way, but suddenly and without warning would address themselves to a third party, demanding his full and exclusive attention. After about twenty minutes of switching my sympathetic ears and eyes from one to the other I found myself not only growing utterly bemused but beginning to understand so well what Sylvia saw in Gerry.

Since the idea of hot and cold drinks now seemed mercifully to have been abandoned, I decided to extricate myself and Ellen from the wear and tear of listening to them both simultaneously and suggested to Paul that he might show me the garden since all I had seen of it was the terrace where we sat and the patch of lawn beyond. I noticed Ellen giving me a reproachful look when I said this, but, believing that she had as much to gain as I by separating our hosts, I ignored it.

The manoeuvre, from my point of view, was entirely successful. Paul quietened down perceptibly as soon as his friend was out of earshot and further endeared himself by telling me how beautiful Ellen was and how much they both loved her. I decided that if Peter were saying equally charming things about me to Ellen, she could have little to complain of.

The cottage could more accurately have been named Old Halfacre, for this was approximately the size of the garden. It was L-shaped, but with the L standing on its head. There was a long, rectangular strip, stretching from the back of the house up to a meadow, and at right-angles to it another piece of identical length and breadth running alongside the meadow. It was separated from the square within the L, which contained the much smaller garden belonging to Miss Davenport, by a high yew hedge, and from the field, by a haha.

'It was all part and parcel, once upon a time,' Paul explained, when I had commented on this unusual layout. 'Before our time, of course. Our cottage was lived in by the gamekeeper, or bailiff, or one of those, in the old days. Then they built the cottage between us and the Manor and they lopped off a chunk of this garden, to go with it. Of course, the Davenports could do as they liked then. If the bailiff, or whoever he was, had dared to complain, he'd have got the push very likely.'

'What made them build a cottage there at all? So close to the house, I mean?'

'It was for Miss Davenport's governess. Our Miss Davenport, when she was a girl, that is. She was dotty about this old governess of hers, and when she retired couldn't bear the idea of being parted from her. I suppose the family weren't too keen on having her living in the house for ever, so they built the cottage for her. Then when she died she left it in her will to Miss Davenport which came in handy, because soon afterwards the old boy popped off, too, and, contrary to what everyone thought, he was flat broke. Everything had to be sold up to pay the debts. If he hadn't made an outright gift of the cottage I daresay that would have gone with all the rest of the estate, and Miss Davenport would be living in a home for indigent gentlewomen.'

He sounded rather regretful that the poor woman had escaped this fate, so I asked him what she was like as a neighbour, and he replied somewhat truculently:

'Could be worse, I suppose. A bit snooty, you know. Only to be expected, really. It takes more than two world wars and a social revolution for that breed to get it into their heads that they're no longer the top dogs. Anyway, she has her uses. She's a kind of buffer state between us and the Cornfords, and long may it last, is what Pete and I say. Come and admire the water garden. Pete is sure to ask what you think of it.'

The water garden, consisting of a lily pond about the size of a washing-up bowl, ringed with stunted Japanese conifers, was only one of numerous subdivisions which the ingenuity of Peter had contrived to delight the eye. Although so modest in dimension, the garden had been laid out patchwork style, according to a most grandiose design, rather like Hampton Court scaled down for a jigsaw puzzle.

Besides the water garden there was a rose garden, a heath garden, woodland garden, rock garden and even a miniature orchard, with half a dozen baby apple trees. Each section was separated from its neighbours by a low wall, or a box hedge, or a trellis of climbing roses. I guessed that it was useful, from a professional journalist's point of view, to have so many varieties of horticulture collected together under one roof, as it were, but the overall effect was fussy in the extreme. By far the most attractive section, to my taste, came right at the end of our tour. This was a square plot where nothing grew, except grass. It was bounded on one side by the high yew hedge, while facing us as we entered was a tall, honey-coloured brick wall which enclosed the Manor kitchen garden. The single embellishment here was a small bronze sculpture, roughly representative of a thin, curving blade, and I was gratified to find myself for once in the presence of a work of art, without any need to simulate my admiration. Praise on this occasion would have come easily, and I spun round, all agog, only to find that the unusual silence of my companion betokened not the diffidence of the artist but the fact that the artist was undergoing some disagreeable sensations of the first magnitude.

It was clear that congratulations would have been out of place and I soon saw why. Beside us in the paddock and only a yard or two beyond the haha, stood large heaps of grey slab-like bricks and propped up against one of these piles were some sheets of red, corrugated iron. Paul was gazing at this sorry collection with the expression which Dr Faustus might have worn when he perceived Lucifer prancing up to claim his dues. He was also making stifled, gurgling noises, which was worrying, but before I could hit him on the back or take other first-aid measures my attention was drawn to another quarter, by a new sound.

Two humpty-dumpty figures had manifested themselves on top of the wall. Only their heads were visible, but presumably they were standing on ladders, for as soon as they saw me look up at them two pairs of hands shot up and performed various obscene and cheeky gestures. At the same time, the two faces twisted into horrible grimaces and some ugly invective issue from the two little rosebud mouths.

'Oh my God!' Paul muttered. 'Oh God, how ghastly!'

I entirely concurred, but it was some consolation that the power of speech had been restored to him, and gambling on the chance that he was also capable of movement I grabbed his arm and started to drag him away from the hideous scene.

All the work and ingenuity which had gone into constructing the numerous little separate enclosures certainly paid dividends in this crisis, for it required only a few tottering steps to be out of range of our tormentors and we both collapsed on to a circular stone bench, beside the lily pond.

'Dear little pets,' I said. 'Do they often get up to these pranks?'

'Oh yes, quite often, if they know we can see them. One tries to ignore it as a rule, but today I could have killed them, I honestly could. It was the shock, you know. I just saw red.'

'Don't blame you. I saw red, myself. Do the parents know about it?'

'My God, the parents are worse than the blasted kids. No, it's not those wretched boys I mind about, they don't know any better the way they're dragged up, but it's that . . . that excrescence in the field. Didn't you see?'

'I saw some dirty old bricks and stuff. What does it portend?'

'Just that they obviously intend to build some hideous monstrosity and completely ruin our view, that's all.'

'They own that field, do they?'

'Yes, worse luck. We've always been on tenterhooks that something like this would happen and now it has. I don't know what it'll do to Pete when he finds out. I just dread to think of it. He's put his heart and soul into this place; it means everything to him.'

'Well, hold your horses,' I said, 'because I don't believe they can just shove up any old building, when the whim takes them. There are all sorts of things, like planning permission and so on, to stop people building, even if it is on their own property.'

Paul shook his head dismally. 'You don't understand. It's much more complicated than that. With those fifteen or twenty acres of his, Cornford rates as a farmer. He's more or less compelled to cultivate part of the land, to make it productive, and farmers can always get permission to put up barns and sheds, just by saying they need than.'

'He'd still have to prove that he does need this one.'

'So what? He only has to say he's going to breed pigs, or battery hens, or some hellish thing, and he can build the Albert Hall there for all the Council cares. The fact that it's going to ruin the amenities for a few non-farming neighbours wouldn't cut any ice at all.'

'Then couldn't you appeal to him, direct? I mean, ask him to put it in another spot, where it wouldn't bother you?'

'Ha ha!' Paul said, in a voice to chill the blood. 'Oh, very funny, I must say, and very naive, if you'll pardon the remark?'

'Of course I will, if it relieves your feelings,' I said kindly, 'but why shouldn't my idea work? He may not have thought of it from your point of view, and some people say he's not such a bad person, at heart.'

'I daresay and they may be right, for all I know, but I don't suppose you've heard anyone with a good word to say for his wife?'

I had heard one, as it happened, but considering the source did not think it worth mentioning, and agreed with Paul, looking around me nervously.

'And I can just picture her reaction if we were to go crawling on our knees and begging them not to spoil our view.'

'You consider that she would disregard your pleas?'

'You can say that again! She'd laugh in our faces, that's what. Oh yes, her ladyship would laugh her head off. She's at the back of it, you can take it from me. She'd just love to see us squirm.'

'Then, as far as I can see, the only solution is to build a high wall along that side of the garden. Shut them out and let them get on with it.'

'High walls cost money, in case you didn't know. Making the haha was ruinous enough. Besides, what's the use? Shut them out in one place, and they come creeping back in another. They mean to drive us out of here and they won't give up till they've done it.'

'Where's the advantage in that? Someone else would only come in your place.'

Paul shook his head. 'You don't understand. They want to buy up all the surrounding properties. They tried to do it in a straightforward way, at first. Came round to all of us, in turn, as sweet as honey, asking if we'd sell. Of course, they drew a blank everywhere, so then they started their campaign to force us out; sort of persecution, really.'

I could see that, if all he said were true, he was up against some formidable opposition and in any case he was in no mood to listen to words of comfort from me, deriving more of that commodity by wallowing in his own bitter thoughts. So I said no more and we sat in glum silence for a few minutes, while the iron gnawed away at his soul and the damp, cold stone seeped into my bones. At the moment when I could endure it no longer, I began to speak and so did he. The trick must have become second nature to him, after all the years with Peter. Not being so adept in the art of simultaneous dialogue, I courteously yielded the floor.

'You were going to say that it was time you went back to Ellen,' he said, supplying my lines for me, since I had declined to do so, 'but I was going to ask you a favour.'

'Anything you like.'

'It's just that I'd be ever so grateful if you didn't mention any of this to Pete.'

'Well, that's easy and quite understandable. I expect you prefer to break it to him yourself, and to choose the right moment?'

'I can't see that there would ever be a right moment.'

'All the same, I advise you not to put it off too long. You wouldn't want him to get the kind of shock you've just had.'

'No, but I've been thinking. You see, it could be days, weeks even, before that happened. He can't walk, remember. The doctor says it'll be six weeks before he's able to get around. We're going to fix him up with some crutches, but even then he'll only want to use them for essentials, like getting out to the patio and popping into the bathroom and that.'

'What about your upstairs windows? Don't any of them overlook that field?'

'Yes, most of them do, but that's the beauty of it. He can't manage the stairs, either. We've already fixed up a camp-bed for him in the living-room, and our bathroom is on the ground floor, too. There's nothing special has to be done in that end bit of the garden, and so long as I tell him I'm keeping the grass down he won't worry.'

'Well, it's your business,' I said, 'but I'm afraid he's bound to find out, in spite of all your safeguards. It's true what they say, you know, bad news does travel fast.'

I did not remind him of another saying concerning the minor misfortunes of one's friends, mainly because he clearly did not regard this as a minor misfortune but a major tragedy, well up in the King Lear bracket.

We began walking back to the cottage, and he said in a sort of frenzied mutter: 'I've got a few days' grace, anyway; maybe a week, with luck. It ought to be enough to work something out. Just a little time is all I need.'

Short of lobbing a bomb over the Cornfords' wall I did not see that there was anything effective he could do, given an eternity, but I hoped that a little time might at least reconcile him to the inevitable and induce a calmer state of mind.

I raised no more objections and we proceeded in silence until Peter and Ellen came into view. Whereupon, with many false smiles and nods, we broke into animated conversation on totally different subjects, a *tour de force* which, despite his longer training, I flatter myself I performed with quite as much artistry as he did.

(iii)

I dropped the mask as soon as Ellen and I were alone and gave her a résumé of the recent distressing scene. I had not been asked to keep my mouth shut, except where Peter was concerned, and, had I been asked to choose between Ellen and the tomb as guardian of my secrets, the decision would not have been lightly taken.

'Tell me something,' I said, when we had examined this latest Cornford outrage in all its aspects. 'Everyone around here, with the notable exception of your old man, seems to take the view that Mrs Cornford is the *éminence grise* of the outfit. Do you concur?'

'You what?' Ellen said in deliberately moronic and adenoidal tones.

'I mean, they believe it is Mrs Cornford who dreams up these horrid tricks and Mr Cornford is just the carrier out of same.'

'Then he must be a donkey,' Ellen said dismissively.

'Yes, we know he's a donkey. They're both donkeys to set out to make enemies where they might have nothing but friends. What I'm getting at is this: do you think she's the wicked donkey and he's the silly one, or the other way round?'

Ellen thought about it seriously for a while, then said:

'I can't see that it makes any difference.'

'Perhaps not, but if one were planning measures to outwit the adversary it might be an advantage to know exactly who the adversary was.'

'You mean like sticking pins in a wax figure until the person died and then finding you'd made the wrong wax figure?'

'That is rather a drastic example of what I had in mind, yes.'

Ellen's beautiful eyes grew particularly soulful at this point and I made a mental note to keep a close check on her handkerchief drawer and other childish hiding-places.

'I can't see what difference it would make,' she insisted. 'If the wicked one died, Silly would run out of ideas, and if Silly died, the wicked one wouldn't have anyone to carry out his evil purposes.'

I could not refute the logic of this, though dismayed to find that Ellen could apparently envisage no other solution than the death of at least one of the Cornfords.

'You don't feel that a more gentle approach might work? If, for instance, some disinterested party were to talk to them like a sister and find out which shoulder had the chip on it and why?'

'Is that what you mean to do, Tessa?'

'It had crossed my mind. I've nothing to lose and they can't kill me,' I said, inadvertently resurrecting the subject of sudden death.

Ellen was not so confident: 'They killed Oscar, didn't they? And they looked as though they'd like to kill Daddy and Miss Davenport when they were made to take the barbed wire down.'

'Yes, but it's not quite the same thing. I should pretend to be on their side.'

'Well, I expect you mean to be kind, Tess, but if I were you I should let Matilda deal with them.'

'You think she may be able to?'

I will not say that the advice had aroused my jealousy because that is not a thing I ever say about myself, being wholly free from the taint, but I did wonder what qualities that great big, untalented and stingy female was supposed to possess which made her more fitted for such a delicate task than me.

'Yes, I do, Matilda can always deal with things when she makes up her mind to. For one thing, I don't believe they'd have dared to kill Oscar if Matilda had been here. They're jolly scared of her. Most people are.'

'Not you, though?'

'Not so much, now. I used to be when I was small.'

'And now you've grown fond of her?'

'Oh, she's all right,' Ellen said with her sweetest smile, 'but I'd much rather have you, old Tess.'

'Reciprocated, old Ellen,' I said, and we bowed to each other in a stately fashion, like the Tweedles Dee and Dum.

FIVE

(i)

THE next day was Sunday, and out of a clear blue sky came the *diva ex machina*; in other words, Matilda in a borrowed Jaguar. She told us that it belonged to someone in the company called Dickie and that they had driven down together as far as his mother's house near Goring, where she was to collect him the following morning.

Sunday was the one day of the week when neither Mrs Parkes, who did the cooking, nor Mrs Grumble, who toiled round with a duster, was in attendance. I do not think that she can really have been called Mrs Grumble, but Toby seemed convinced that it was her name and she was never known by any other.

Since Matilda was well aware of the domestic routine I regarded it as typically inconsiderate of her not to have warned us of her arrival, and what made it all the harder to bear was that she looked so stunningly chic and elegant, not a false eyelash out of place, after three hours in an open car.

As it was a hot day for once, we had planned to lunch at a small riverside hotel and then to hire a punt for an hour or two. We had all been looking forward to this treat, specially Toby who loved to trail his languid, artist's fingers through the cool waters while two females battled away with the paddles, but, of course, Matilda soon changed all this.

Her first objection was that the hotel we had chosen was practically next door to Dickie's mother's house and we should all be bound to run into each other, probably at adjacent tables in the dining-room, which would be too boring for any words.

Toby politely agreed that there were few things more excessively tedious than meeting people one knew, particularly if they happened to be the sort of dear friends who had lent one their brand-new car, and suggested that we should repair to a different hotel on another stretch of the river.

Matilda countered this move by saying that she had already driven more than a hundred miles and the last thing she felt inclined for was dashing about the countryside sniffing up petrol fumes. Furthermore, she could not in the least understand why we should want to spend the best hours of the day in some nasty, crowded restaurant when we had this beautiful, peaceful garden all to ourselves, etcetera, etcetera, but I knew that what really stuck in her gizzard was the expense of the outing.

Inevitably, the rest of us hesitated and were lost. Matilda marched upstairs to her bedroom, but before we could profit by her absence to formulate an acceptable compromise she had marched down again, wearing only a bathing suit. She then stretched herself out on a mattress on the lawn, observing that we did not know how lucky we were to be able to do this every day.

Toby resignedly fetched his hat and installed himself in a deck-chair in the shade of a nearby apple tree. I could tell that he was inwardly raging, but he would have stood by and watched her knock the house down, brick by brick, rather than be embroiled in an argument. Ellen and I obediently trundled off to the kitchen, to make a salad and open some tins of paté and so forth.

Matilda received our little spread with rapturous enthusiasm, asking us repeatedly to tell her what could be nicer than a delicious picnic in the garden, and since none of us had any spirit left to do so the self-congratulatory idyll might have continued indefinitely had not the Cornfords chosen this moment to light their bonfire.

Only a very small slice of Manor House territory bordered our garden, just a few square yards at the edge of their orchard. None the less, this was the spot they had picked, as soon became clear, on which to burn their grandmother.

The smell was pungent and nauseating, and, more unpleasant still, fragments of the old lady's charred clothing, borne aloft over the hedge, floated lazily down again, to drop unerringly into our plates, our wine glasses and the salad bowl.

'How revolting!' Matilda said, flicking angrily at some black blobs which had landed on her thighs, and voicing for once the opinion of us all, 'Don't just sit there, Toby. Go and tell her to put it out, for God's sake.'

'I shall do no such thing,' he replied. 'It was your idea to have luncheon in the beautiful garden. If you are not enjoying it, you have only yourself to blame. Personally, I detest eating out of doors. Something like this always happens.'

'Oh, don't be absurd. Whoever heard of lighting a bonfire at this hour, and on Sunday of all days? She must be out of her mind.'

'Then tell her so yourself,' he replied, getting up, 'for I don't propose to. I am going indoors. You may bring my second course to my study.'

I did not tell him that there wasn't a second course, as it might have spoilt the dignity of his exit and put Matilda one up again.

'Well, I'm not afraid of her,' she said, 'only I can't go calling in this outfit.'

She looked down at the two strips of white lastex in which her beautiful form was clothed, and I was bound to agree that it was not the most suitable gear in which to do battle with the neighbours, although I would gladly have taken tickets just for the pleasure of seeing Bronwen's face had she done so.

'You'll have to go, Tessa. You look respectable enough. Go and tell her to put the bloody bonfire out, or else.'

'Oh, not me,' I said. 'Respectable I may be, pure in heart, certainly, but my strength is as the strength of none and I don't mind who knows it.'

I saw Matilda glance speculatively at Ellen, but either her own scruples, or Ellen's wide, innocent gaze deterred her and she said crossly:

'You're really too feeble for words, Tessa, but we'll just have to move all these things round to the nursery terrace. The bore of it is that we'll be out of the sun there, won't we? Oh, it really is the bloody limit!'

'You could telephone them,' I suggested. 'Ask them to hold up the *suttee* ceremonies, until you're in a position to raise hell in person?'

'So I could. Clever girl! It's working again, is it?'

'Is what?'

'The telephone. It's on again?'

'I was not aware that it had ever been off.'

'Oh, don't be stupid. You surely don't imagine that I'd come all this way without trying to let you know in advance?'

As this was precisely what I did imagine and what everyone who knew her would have imagined, I let the question go by.

'Naturally, I tried to ring you up.'

'When was that?'

'Twice. The first time on Friday evening, and again yesterday, about twelve.'

'Didn't you report it?'

'Of course. Both times. I spoke to the Supervisor and the Engineer and about fifty other people, but I don't know whether they'll bother to do anything about it until after the weekend. Besides . . .'

'Besides what?'

'They all said the number was temporarily unobtainable, which I could have told them myself, having wasted several hours trying to obtain it, but I have an idea that's the jargon they use when the line has been disconnected on purpose. I thought Toby might have forgotten to pay the bill. In fact, I meant to ask him about it.'

'Yes,' I said, gnawing my knuckles and gripped by direst forebodings, 'I believe you're right and I shall go and ask him myself.'

I paused in the hall as I flew to perform this mission and picked up the telephone. The line was deader than the tomb.

Toby was bent over his desk, deep in the Sunday papers. 'Have you brought my afters?' he inquired.

'No, I've come to ask you what you do with your bills.'

'What a fascinating question!'

'So give me a fascinating answer.'

'I will, because, you see, I have a system. It may be unique, for all I know.'

'I shouldn't be at all surprised.'

'Well, I have a special drawer for them, you know, and as soon as one arrives, which they seem to do rather frequently these days, I methodically pop it in. In that way they don't get mislaid.'

'In that way do they ever get paid?'

'No, not often,' he admitted, 'but there they all are. When I feel like paying one, I can lay my hands on it in a trice.'

'The only thing that surprises me,' I said, 'is that you don't spend more of your life in the Magistrate's Court.'

'Ah well, my system is elastic enough to take care of that. The really exigent creditors always open the offensive by sending a registered letter. Didn't you know that? What a sheltered life you've led! Naturally, those get priority.'

'They don't all do that, Toby. I can tell you one that doesn't and that's the Post Office. God knows why not. You'd think they'd be the one body of men in the land who could afford to. They send a little, flimsy, printed thing, with "Unless" on it.'

'Well, I know all about that. I'm not a child. But it's all printed in red, which is just as good.'

'Only on the inside,' I said with icy calm. 'On the outside it is printed in black.'

'I never did! Are you sure?'

'Positive.'

'How interesting! I don't ever remember noticing that. And yet we are not often cut off. I take it that this one has slipped through the net?'

'Right.'

'Most annoying! Still, as I've told you, I can put my finger on it in a flash. As soon as I've had my pudding I'll write a cheque.'

Not wishing to antagonise him at this delicate juncture I went downstairs and fetched him a banana and some cheese and biscuits. He had been as good as his word and I returned to find him rummaging about in such mountains of accounts rendered that I concluded that at least half of them must have been rendered for the first time during his teens. One or two had fallen to the floor, so I set the tray down on his desk and went on my hands and knees to scoop them up. One item caught my eye immediately because it was not a bill but a torn off sheet of ruled paper with a message printed on it in capital letters. It consisted of the six words: 'YOU WILL BE PUNNISHED BY DEATH.'

'What's this?' I asked, holding it up.

'What? Oh, God knows.'

'I should think He might. It reads as though He had written it Himself.'

He looked at me intently for a moment, then shifted his eyes, and taking the paper from my hand he crushed it up and dropped it in the ashtray:

'Nothing of importance, obviously. And what is that might I ask?' he added, scowling at my tray of dainties.

'And look! Another lovely glass of wine for you,' I said soothingly. 'Have you put your finger on it yet?'

'No, but yes. Yes, here we are! And just as you said, red inside and black out. I don't call that quite playing the game, do you? Well, our troubles are over. They shall have their cheque tomorrow.'

Even this was not soon enough so far as I was concerned, so I asked him what the time was.

'Oh, plenty of time. It's not two yet and the post doesn't go till four something.'

'What time does the pub close?'

'Now what are you on about? What's the date? So many questions! I suppose it doesn't really matter. I can date it for the first of last month. Two o'clock, I imagine. What do you want the pub for?'

'I thought I might nip down there and use their telephone. Do you think if I spoke to the Supervisor in honeyed tones and explained that your cheque had been posted on the first of last month and he would get it tomorrow, do you think he would trust me and reconnect us?'

'No, I shouldn't think so for a moment, and anyway, why bother? Personally, I'm in no hurry. The last few days have been so peaceful. Now I understand why?'

I did not stop to explain to him that my chances were slipping by, nor to speak of all the jobs I might be losing so long as my agent and I were out of touch, because the sands of time were running out.

'I think I'll try, just the same,' I said, heading for the door. 'There might just be time before they close.'

'Take that car Matilda brought,' he called after me.

'She'd have a coronary,' I shouted back.

'Serve her right,' he bellowed.

He could be very ruthless when he chose, and so could I. I happened to be passing Matilda's room at the time and the door was open. There was a set of keys on the dressing-table and I whipped them up and galloped on my way.

(ii)

Taking the Jaguar proved to be immeasurably slower than going on foot. It took me ages to find the reverse gear and I kept leaping forward, when I meant to go back. I became so obsessed with the terror that one more bound forward would send me crashing through the hedge that it almost overrode the earlier fear that Matilda would emerge round the side of the house and catch me red-handed.

Luckily she did not, and I finally managed to turn the monster in the right direction, churning up great chunks of the Common in the process, and streaked off along the track, whimpering to myself: 'Be careful, do be careful, go a bit slower, fool,' until normal reactions reasserted themselves. These prompted me to stamp on the brake, stall the engine, get into reverse unintentionally, wipe the sweat from my brow with a quivering hand and at length crawl up to the saloon bar entrance in such a state of jitters that it required half a dozen deep breaths to steady me sufficiently to totter inside.

It was then just on two o'clock and the bar was almost deserted, but there was none of the brisk activity usually associated with closing time. The two remaining customers both had full glasses and the landlord and lady were lolling about behind the bar with all the insouciance of two innkeepers who had just heard that the licensing laws had been repealed, that very morning. I was asked to name my poison and requested a large brandy, which was handed to me without a murmur.

I took a refreshing gulp and studied my surroundings. It was a profitable exercise, as they go, and provided some interesting facts. In the first place, one of the customers was Douglas Cornford. He was sitting away from everyone else at a table by the window. He was drinking beer from a pint-sized mug and staring vacantly at nothing, with a distinctly inane smile on his face.

I counted this as a mark for the Bronwen-for-Ringleader brigade. Judged on present form, Mr Cornford would barely have been capable of lighting a match in the recent past, far less a bonfire.

I was not certain that we had ever actually been introduced, or whether he was sober enough even to see me from that distance, but I gave him a half nod and he responded by smiling a shade more soppily than before.

The other customer was a stranger to me, but one finds all sorts in such places on a Sunday, so there was nothing remarkable in that. There were two things about him, however, which did strike me very forcibly. One was that the back of his head bore a strange resemblance to that of the actor who had played the part of the detective in the crime serial which I had just completed. He had been a very good actor, with a deep, attractive voice, and this man's voice was not unlike it. I was in a good position to make these comparisons because the other immediate thing I noticed was that he was leaning on the bar and speaking into the telephone.

I slowed my drinking down to spaced-out, lady-like sips because I did not want to finish the brandy and have to order a second before I could get my turn at the telephone, and I embarked on a round of small talk with the landlord, whose name was Leslie Brock. He had been an R.A.F. pilot, before turning to pub keeping, and his wife, Marge, had enjoyed an equally dashing and adventurous past. They were a middle-aged couple and it was *deuxième noces* for them both, but the union had been blessed with a baby son, known as Jumbo, who was the light of their lives. Leslie had previously been married to a lady greyhound trainer, and Marge to a draper in the north of England, so they'd had a rich and varied background and it was always a pleasure to talk to them.

On this occasion they had much to impart, for it transpired that Leslie was shortly leaving for a ten-day holiday in Toronto, where he had a brother, a twin brother, as Marge informed me proudly, whose son was to be married on the morrow.

'And a very slap-up do, it will be,' Marge assured me. 'The girl's people are rolling. Father owns half a million sheep. Or was it cows, dear? They're identical, you know,' she added confidentially, referring, I supposed, to Leslie and his twin and not to the animals.

'You're not going with him?' I asked her.

'Not something likely. You know how it is, love, in a place like this? On duty seven days a week.'

'Don't you ever get a holiday?'

'Yes, but we have to take it in the slack season: January, February. We went to Majorca this year. Smashing!'

'What happens then?'

'Oh, the Brewers provide a replacement couple, just for the fortnight, but you wouldn't catch them doing that at any other time.'

'Can't you and Leslie even go out together in the evening?'

'Once in a blue moon we do, when we can get a pal to take over. Peter and Paul are awfully good, like that; babysitting thrown in. They're gems, those two, but you couldn't expect anyone to take it on for ten days. No, I'll have to let the lord and master go gallivanting off on his own this time and trust him not to get up to mischief, won't I?'

She tilted her head and smiled provocatively at Leslie, who grinned back and winked at me in the style of a lord and master who wished it to be known that he proposed getting into all the mischief which Toronto could lay in his path.

'Want another of those?' Marge asked me, reverting to a more business-like tone. 'If so, better make it snappy, duck. We've got to close in a mo.'

'No, thanks. You're late, as it is, aren't you?'

'Not to worry; we don't get that number of coppers round on a Sunday.'

'In that case, could you hold things up for a tiny minute longer? Our telephone is out of order and I wanted to make a call on yours, as soon as this gentleman has finished with it.'

'This gentleman has already finished with it,' he said, moving away from the end of the bar where it stood. Then, addressing Leslie, he went on: 'How much do I owe you altogether? The call came to three and nine.'

Apparently it had been worth every penny, too, for he was looking highly amused and pleased with himself. I felt a crazy twinge of envy of whoever it was he had been speaking to. The resemblance to my actor friend, I now saw, was largely illusory. This man was a good deal younger and better looking and had eyes of a stunning aquamarine.

'Go ahead, dear, it's all yours,' Marge told me, waving at the telephone.

A part of my mind had been engaged in calculations as I talked to the Brocks and it had reached the conclusion that my telephoning should be confined to essentials. Obviously, neither the time nor the company were propitious for a protracted argy bargy about unpaid telephone bills, specially as the latter included Douglas Cornford, who, as I perceived from the corner of my eye, was still mooning in his chair by the window. So I dialled the number of my agent's flat in Chelsea.

Her daughter answered, and informed me in a sleepy voice that her mother was spending the day with a client in the country. It was bad news, because this daughter was a frightful dimwit and could scarcely be relied upon to grasp a message, far less pass it on. Nevertheless, I persevered, and when I was going through my piece for the second time she unexpectedly came to life and drawled that it was a fabulous coincidence because she did believe that Ma had been trying to contact me and was a bit stroppy about never getting an answer.

I managed to keep my head despite the sickness, racing pulses and tears of frustration which this information inflicted, and I told her very slowly, four times over, that I would telephone the office at five past nine the following morning. She promised faithfully to relay this to the right quarter and then presumably forgot all about it and went back to sleep.

When I had simmered down sufficiently to re-focus attention on my surroundings I found that the beautiful young man had departed and that Leslie and Marge were flitting about, making everything ship-shape on both sides of the bar.

'I'm afraid I don't know what I owe you,' I said, 'but it was a call to London and the pips went twice.'

'Fair enough,' Leslie said. 'We'll check up and let you know next time you're in.'

'It was awfully stupid of me, but I . . .'

'Not to worry,' Marge said, which turned out to be among the more rash statements ever uttered, because an instant later worry was what she got and plenty more besides. The door was flung open and Mrs Cornford swept through it like a tidal wave, swamping us all with the force of her fury.

It was comical in a way, but I could sense a breath of alarm blowing round the room, and this certainly was a Bronwen in a far uglier mood than at our previous encounter. She was dressed in her usual style, but her manners touched new depths, for she planted herself midway between the door and the bar and proceeded to let fly in both directions. Her husband got the first wave:

'So this is where you are!' she bawled at him. 'I might have known it, mightn't I? This is where you meet your fancy women, is it? Right on your own doorstep. How dare you? How dare you, I say?'

He did not tell her how, and in truth I had rarely seen a less daring creature than he looked at that moment. He had half risen from his seat on first sighting the apparition and, seeming now paralysed into this position, was staring at his wife with glazed eyes and gaping jaw.

'Oh, I say! Look here, now!' Leslie said from the safety of his stronghold behind the bar, and she whirled round and unloaded some venom on him:

'Oh yes, I know all about you, too. You're well and truly mixed up in it, aren't you? Covering up for him and conniving at his affairs. I know all about it and you needn't think I don't, you and your filthy immorality and living in sin. Mr and Mrs Brock, my foot! That's a laugh, that is. Yes, and I know how you break the law, too, keeping open till all hours, so's he can meet his tarts here. You won't get away with it; I'll see to that. The Brewers are going to hear about you two, and you'll soon get what's coming to you. And as for you,' she snarled, suddenly rounding on me, to my great terror and dismay, 'You and your smart cars and your theatrical ways, I suppose you think that excuses everything, but it doesn't, see? You get going and get out of here, back to that brothel where you belong.'

I would willingly have done so, at the double, had she not blocked my exit, but all I could do was to shrink back in my corner and make S.O.S. faces at Leslie, as the virago advanced towards me. I saw him square his shoulders and lift the bar flap and then a number of unexpected things happened simultaneously. Mrs Cornford, who had been peering malevolently at my face, faltered, stopped in her tracks and brought a hand slowly up to her eyes. At the same time she began to sway wildly to and fro on her feet. I was sure that she must fall over and, indeed, she did, although whether this would have happened without help from an outside agency there was no time to assess. Intervention had come, not from Leslie but from Mr Cornford, who restored to courage and movement when the brunt of the attack had passed to another target, leapt forward with great agility and landed his wife a powerful slap across the face, which put her out for the count.

A moment later Leslie had entered the fray and was tugging at Mr Cornford, now down on his knees and giving every sign of being about to batter his wife to a pulp. Marge followed, more slowly, brandishing an empty beer bottle, whereupon I, remembering in time that discretion was considered to be the better part of valour, flung myself on my hands and knees and crawled under the bar.

When I raised myself on the other side a fresh surprise was awaiting me. The blue-eyed boy had returned to our midst and had hurled himself into the centre of hostilities. It was a pleasure to see with what expedition he sorted out the shambles. Having thrown Mr Cornford aside in one graceful movement he scooped Mrs Cornford off the floor and laid her on a wooden settle, commanding Marge to bring cushions for her head and Leslie to fetch water and a tot of brandy. These orders being promptly obeyed, he slopped the first over her face and a dollop of the second down her throat.

Mrs Cornford choked, opened her eyes and struggled to sit up. She looked pale, but not interesting.

'Take it easy, now,' he said, pushing her down again. 'Lie still for a minute and you'll be all right.'

'All right now,' she burbled. 'Got to go. Lemme go. Wanna go home.'

'You can go home in a minute. One of us will take you.'

I wondered who that would be, but in fact it was Douglas Cornford who slouched forward and said sheepishly:

'I'll take over. Sorry about all this, but it'll be okay now. She gets these turns. Not really responsible, while they're on her, don't you know?'

The young man stared at him and then at all of us in blank astonishment, which Marge was quickest to interpret.

'He's the husband,' she explained. 'No fooling.'

'I see. Well, all the same, since you've just been forcibly restrained from beating her up, are you sure you're the right one to look after her?'

'Honestly, you don't understand. I know it looks bad, but a good thump is the only thing to bring her out of these fits. I've got to do it, for her own sake.'

'Maybe so,' my hero said, 'and it's none of my business, but I think she ought to see a doctor.'

'She's not hurt, I tell you.'

'Nevertheless, if she's subject to the kind of brainstorm or fit, which requires physical violence to control, I should say she's in need of medical treatment.'

'She is. We've got the pills and so on, and I know exactly what to do. That's why I want to get her back home as quick as I can.'

'Have you a car?'

Mr Cornford shook his head. 'It's not far.'

'Take mine,' I said. 'It's outside and the key's there. Go on! I can walk much more easily than you.'

His wife set up another whimper when she heard this, but the fight had gone out of her and she allowed herself to be hoisted up and dragged towards the door. As she staggered away we had the final, astonishing glimpse of her putting one arm round her husband's neck and gazing up at him with the adoration of a young bride being carried over the threshold.

The door closed behind them, and as though the curtain had come down the three of us drooped and flopped and draped ourselves into silent poses of total collapse. Marge was the first to recover.

'Come on!' she said. 'Strikes me what we all need is a stiff one and to hell with the law! It's not every day you get a punch-up in the saloon bar, thank the Lord. What'll it be, love? Another brandy? That's it. Crikey, I really thought he was going to do her in that time, didn't you? What's yours, Mr – er?'

'Price is my name, Robin Price. Thank you, I'll stick to pink gin, if I may. This round is on me, by the way.'

'It's not, you know,' Leslie said, locking the door, as he spoke. 'Serving drinks out of hours is not our normal practice, whatever some people say, but there's nothing to stop us entertaining our own friends and you've certainly earned one, old chap.'

'Hear, hear!' Marge said. 'It was darn lucky for us, you coming back like that. We could have had real trouble on our hands, with that lovely pair.'

'Why did you come back?' I asked, for it seemed to me that this development had provided the silver lining to our storm clouds. I hardly expected ever to see him again, but at least I had learnt his name and could henceforth identify him, in my dreams.

'It was pure fluke,' he answered. 'I was sitting out there in my car, working out my route on the map, when I noticed this woman coming towards me. She was weaving a bit and I thought she might be drunk. There was something fairly odd about her altogether. Then I saw her come in here and my curiosity got the better of me. I wanted to see what she was up to.'

'Just pure, straightforward curiosity?'

''Fraidso.'

'You're not a psychiatrist, or anything like that?'

'Not a psychiatrist, or anything remotely like that.'

'Well, it was lucky for us,' Marge said again. 'Les could have coped on his own, I expect, but with the two of them to his one it might have been dicey.'

'Do they often do this kind of thing?' he asked.

'Not often, and I've never known them so bad as today. She has come storming in here, once or twice, always with the same rigmarole about it being a den of iniquity and us harbouring her old man and I don't know what all.'

'And does she usually find him here on these occasions?'

'Funny, now you mention it,' Leslie said thoughtfully. 'This is the first time she has. Isn't that right, Marge? He comes on his own fairly regularly. We'd rather he didn't, on the whole. He's not violent, or anything, as a rule, but he sits there on his own, not speaking to anyone and getting a bit sozzled, and it's apt to be off-putting for the other customers.'

'Why do you let him in, then?'

'Well, it's tricky, in a small place like this. Can't afford to make enemies. But he's given us enough excuse this time, and I shall tell him so.'

'What do you think is wrong with her?'

Marge tapped her forehead. 'Batty, poor devil. Right round the bend, if you ask me.'

She and Leslie appeared to take all these questions in their stride, but it was beginning to impinge on me that there were an awful lot of them being fired around. I had the sensation that we were all taking part in an early Priestley, with Robin Price as a questing spirit, manifested to us by some Trick of Time and that the events we had just witnessed had actually taken place a hundred years before. It was becoming a bit static, too, so instead of just sitting there I did something. I climbed down from my stool, saying:

'I must go and see what's happened to the car. Thank you both for the drink.'

'No call to fret about the car, love. He's a good driver, even though he does go at the rate of knots and they live right next door to Mr Crichton, don't they? You'll find it there, all right, don't you worry.'

'Yes, but my cousin may wonder how it got there, all by itself. I'd better start walking.'

I pitched my voice up at the end of that speech, so that the last word came out round and clear, and Robin Price said:

'Oh, we can't have that. You must let me drive you.'

'I would with pleasure, but it really isn't far, like the man said, and I should think you've had enough delays already.'

'Not quite enough,' he said, putting his glass down on the counter. 'Come along; I won't hear of your walking, after all you've been through.'

''Bye, 'bye,' Marge called after us, game to the last, as Leslie unlatched the door. 'And don't do anything I wouldn't do.'

'I wonder what there is that Marge wouldn't do?' I said. 'Is that your car? How nice!'

It was a black Sunbeam convertible, quite new, and I was so pleased to find that he was a man of means, as well as parts.

'They are obviously a sterling pair,' he remarked as we drove along, 'and a great asset to the neighbourhood, no doubt. I am glad I was able to give them a hand.'

'You saved my life,' I said with quiet simplicity.

'I did nothing of the sort, I regret to say.'

'Oh, but yes. I am certain that maniacal woman meant to kill me.'

'Even so, she was flat on the floor with her eyes shut by the time I arrived on the scene, so whoever you have to thank, unfortunately, it's not I.'

'Never mind,' I said. 'Perhaps you'll get another chance.'

I cannot think what induced me to say this. The words came out at random. I had actually been thinking how glad I was that he had not been present to hear any of the spiteful abuse which Mrs Cornford had hurled at the Brocks. I neither knew nor cared whether they were legally married, or not, but if not, they could hardly wish to have the fact broadcast, even if only for Jumbo's sake.

He may not have heard me, for we had arrived at the house by this time and he was bringing his car into port, beside the Jaguar.

'So that worry is over,' he said. 'Will you be all right now?'

'It's not mine, you see,' I explained. 'That was the real worry. I had only borrowed it.'

It had occurred to me that, if he were to fall in love with me, which was now my life's object, it had better be on the clear understanding that it wasn't for my money.

'That proves you to be a person of upright character and high moral integrity,' he said, 'which just goes to show.'

'How lovely! What does it go to show?'

He looked amused. 'Why, that first impressions can sometimes be right, of course.'

Six

(i)

THE nearest public telephone box was half a mile away, beyond the Bricklayers' Arms, but although Matilda was still safely asleep at eight-forty-five the following morning I was not tempted to borrow the Jaguar. I was a person of upright character and high moral integrity, and looking every inch of it I strode off across the Common, my pockets jingling with such a collection of small change as to confound the most remorseless operator's efforts to cut me off in mid-stream.

I needed every penny, too, because, as I had foreseen, when the secretary finally did rouse herself to answer the telephone, she told me that my agent was speaking on the other line. If I were ever to ring that office and not be told that my agent was speaking on the other line it would probably so undermine my confidence that I should tear up my contract on the spot.

When at last communications were established there was further expenditure of time and coins while we ploughed through all the How Are You, My Darlings and How Were Darling Toby and Ellen and What's This I Hear About Matilda? Matilda belonged to a rival firm and did not rate a darling.

'All I know,' I said, 'is that at present she's down here and tucked up in her chaste little boudoir.'

I did not add that she had arrived in a Jaguar belonging to a Dickie because I knew precisely what my agent could do with an item of that sort, and after all Matilda, with all her faults, was one of the family. Furthermore, I have invariably found that it pays, in the cruel, ruthless, cut-throat, etcetera, world of the theatre, to play it innocent, even at the cost of some temporary popularity.

'Well, it must be nice for you, having her there. Has the play folded?'

'By no means. Doing rattling business, by all accounts. They were at Nottingham last week and they open in Oxford tonight, so this is just a temporary stop-over. She's leaving this morning.'

'Oh, Oxford, are they? I must try and get up to see it. When are they bringing it in?'

'Some time next month, I believe.'

I felt inclined to point out that I was not shovelling in all these florins and the like just in order to have a cosy chat about Matilda, but naturally I had to be subtle about it, so I said:

'And how are you? And how's Venetia?'

'Very, very well, indeed, thank you, my darling.'

'Good. She sounded rather well when I spoke to her yesterday, which reminds me that she said something about your trying to get in touch with me.'

'Did she? What a clever old pusscat! I have been.'

'Well, now you are,' I said, 'and I am all ears.'

'Yes, but don't get carried away, my dove. It is only a teeny, weeny part. You may not want to interrupt your holiday for it.'

I did not care for the sound of that 'interrupt'. 'Cutting short' was more the phrase I had been hoping for.

'What is it? A shampoo commercial?'

'No, not quite as bad as that. They want you for a live television. Half-hour job.'

'Oh God! Did you say live?'

'Yes, I was afraid you'd feel like that, my darling. It's not a bad part, though.'

'Who wrote it?'

'No one we've ever heard of. It's experimental, *avant garde* type.'

'Worse and worse,' I thought, saying: 'How much? And when?'

'Next week. Three days. Thirty guinea fee and three days usual rehearsal money. Shall I send you a script?'

'Might as well. Three days for rehearsal isn't very much.'

'As I pointed out, my darling. In fact, they'd have made it two, if I hadn't insisted. It's a tight budget and, anyway, the director is very keen about that element of spontaneity, if you know what I mean.'

'I do know just what you mean and I also think he is very likely to get it.'

'Shall I say you'll do it, then?'

'Why not?' I said. 'May as well have a go.'

'Oh, marvellous! You are such a dear, good, co-operative client. If only they were all like you! I'll fix it up right away.'

'Thanks a lot. Sixpences are running out. Don't forget to post the script.'

I rang off, feeling that I had conducted the business rather smoothly, and I enjoyed a pleasant homeward stroll across the Common, planning how to lay out thirty-one pounds, ten shillings, plus usual rehearsal money. There was a little red and white number in a little King's Road hovel which had taken my eye, and if I could find a red linen coat to match, who knows? Red or white shoes? That was the question; that and the slightly more formidable one of how to be sure of wearing the outfit on the very day when I was skimming down Bond Street, at twelve-thirty in the morning and chanced to come face to face with R. Price, Esquire.

The sun struggled out to greet me through the morning mist, and as I tripped along savouring the unusual combination of being rich, warm and in love all at the same time, I noticed, with mild surprise that, just ahead of me, there walked a medieval priest, with his medieval beast some paces behind. It was, in fact, Miss Davenport, taking an early morning bracer with her cairn terrier, but her emaciated figure, shrouded in a black cloak, with a black pancake on her cropped grey hair, had irresistibly brought to mind one of those small-part players who stand around for hours on end waiting to say: 'Tis heresy she speaks; let the Maid be burnt,' in a play about Joan of Arc.

I was also reminded of the differing verdicts which had been passed on Miss Davenport during the past few days. To Sylvia she personified the very parfit English gentlewoman; to Toby she was a harmless old lunatic, well versed in the intricacies of Common Law. Peter and Paul saw her as an arrogant snob, and even Ellen had shown less than her usual amiability in describing her.

Personally, I had no strong views, one way or the other, except that every time I saw her she gave me the uneasy feeling that her gaunt looks and dusty clothes might signify the direst poverty and that, for my own peace of mind and the proper enjoyment of red linen coats, etcetera, somebody, somewhere, ought to do something about it.

Evidently, though, there was no cheese paring where the dog was concerned, for it was as stout as a barrel and waddled along behind her, exuding resentment at every pore. As I watched, the distance between them gradually widened, until suddenly the dog stopped dead in its tracks just as though it had been shot and stuffed, all in the same instant.

I concluded that this must happen at that very spot on every walk, because, although there had been no sound, Miss Davenport wheeled round and retraced her steps, flapping the lead in a threatening manner. In doing so she became aware of the spectator and waved the lead at me instead.

'I know who you are,' she announced as we came face to face over the motionless dog. 'You're the cousin. Ellen told me you were coming. Fine morning, isn't it? Going to be a scorcher.'

She had bent down to fasten the lead to the dog's collar and I noticed that it was a great, heavy chain affair, more suited to a pet tiger than to the portly, grizzled object at her feet.

'There we are, Fido! Now, be a good little boy and come along.'

'Is his name really Fido?' I asked.

'Sometimes it is. He has several. Fido is one of than, but it depends on the mood.'

'His mood, or yours?'

'Mine, I daresay. His mood is never to answer to any of them. It is all one to him.'

'Perhaps if you found a name he liked and stuck to it, he'd get used to it and learn to respond?'

'I rather doubt that, you know. He's an independent spirit, aren't you, old boy? That's what I like about dumb animals, don't you?'

It wasn't, but I pride myself on my tact, so I said:

'I don't know all that many. Living in London, you know . . .'

'Yes, dreadful for you. Can't stand the place, myself. Perhaps you don't mind?'

'No, I'm in favour.'

'Extraordinary! Filthy place, I always think. Give me God's good, clean air any day of the week. Still, you're right to like it, at your age. I approve of that. Young people should live in the world, however nasty it may happen to be. Roakes and such places are for back numbers, like me. The young haven't earned them, is what I say. I think Ellen would be better off at school, don't you agree?'

'She is at school,' I pointed out. 'It's the holidays now.'

'I know that, my dear. I meant a boarding school, where they play games and rub shoulders, that kind of thing.'

'Did you go to one of those, Miss Davenport?'

'No, I didn't. I had a very happy childhood, as a matter of fact. And look where it's got me.'

We had been strolling along during this conversation, with Fido, or whatever his name happened to be at the time, making heavy weather of it, between us and had now reached Toby's gate.

'No team spirit, that's my trouble,' she added, by way of farewell and strode on, along the Common.

I went into the garden and found Toby and Ellen playing croquet. There was plenty of team spirit in evidence there, for their happy innocent faces revealed that they were both cheating like mad, a fact which, being well known to each of them, added considerably to the white-hot excitement of the game.

In the hall Matilda was surrounded by her usual impedimenta of gloves, white leather jewel case, chiffon scarves, and all set, it seemed, for imminent departure and Dickie collecting. One way and another, all at that moment seemed for the best, in the best of all possible worlds and to crown everything the telephone rang. It was some cheerful Charlie, testing the line.

'Everything should be okeydoke now,' he assured me.

'Everything's absolutely super whizzbang,' I agreed.

Little, as the saying goes, Did We Know.

(ii)

'Who won?' I asked.

'It was a draw,' Ellen replied.

'A draw?' Toby echoed haughtily, using his Lady Bracknell voice. 'A draw, did you say? May I remind you that when I came storming through to the winning post you were still three hoops behind?'

'Daddy hit the post first,' Ellen explained to me, in an aside, 'but he started off first, so he had one more turn than me. If I'd had my right number of turns, I might have caught him up. He can't prove that I wouldn't have, and in cricket that would count as a draw.'

'If it were cricket,' I said, 'you would both be given out, for bickering. I never knew such an unsporting pair in my life.'

'You won't say that when you see what I've got for you,' Ellen told me. 'You'll say I've been jolly, jolly sporting,' and she began to scrabble about in her reticule. She owned about a dozen of these, mostly cast-off evening bags of Matilda's and the current favourite was a very gaudy affair, made of emerald green satin. The hoard inside, so far as I could see, consisted of a much folded theatre programme, a diary, several photographs of Cliff Richard and an assortment of foreign coins. There was also a set of keys, which she dangled triumphantly before my nose.

'Very pretty. Where did you find them?'

'I didn't find them. Matilda gave them to me.'

'You're joking!'

'No, I'm not. I asked her if she'd let you drive her car sometimes, if you promised to be awfully, awfully careful, and she gave me the keys.'

'Just like that?'

Ellen's eyes became so huge that I knew we were approaching the nub.

'She did say that you might not be able to, because the battery was flat,' she admitted.

'Oh, I see. Well, that would account for it. Unless, of course, you're prepared to push us down to Storhampton?'

'I won't have to, because Mr Parkes has taken it to the garage to be charged, and he said that it might be ready by tomorrow.'

'I wondered why he wasn't working in the garden, this morning,' Toby said.

'He had to go, anyway, because the mucky old lawn mower has taken a fit into its head again and he's got to get that seen to. That's what he told me.'

'Things do just happen to turn out your way, don't they, Ellen?'

'Aren't you pleased?' she asked reproachfully. 'I thought it would be helping you.'

'Jolly pleased,' I said. 'You're a clever angel and I'm pleased as punch.'

'So am I,' Toby said. 'Now, perhaps, I shall be allowed to work in peace without you both plaguing me to drive you hither and thither through the countryside.'

An interesting phenomenon about Ellen's eyes was that it took her about five seconds to get through the motions of a single wink.

SEVEN

THE news of my forthcoming live broadcast got a scathing reception from Toby:

'You must be raving,' he announced in tones of pity and horror. 'Everyone knows it's the fatal error.'

'Everyone except me, apparently, and about forty other actors who do it every week.'

'They may prefer it to starvation. That's about all one can say.'

'I hope it is not all you can say. I'd really be glad to hear what your objections are.'

'Haven't you watched one? If so, you must have seen how catastrophic they are. Everyone is so intent on not fluffing or moving out of their marks that they say practically anything that comes into their heads. Nobody ever gives the right cue, and you just have to shove in what you can of your lines and hope for the best. The result is totally incomprehensible and hideously boring.'

'Oh, is that why they're incomprehensible and boring?' I asked with genuine curiosity. 'I had always assumed it was because they were loaded down with symbolism and allegory and so forth, which I never managed to catch on to properly.'

'There's probably a good deal of that, too,' Toby admitted. 'All the more reason not to touch it.'

'Have you ever tried writing one, yourself?' I asked.

He returned my look with the bland and innocent gaze, which Ellen had inherited, and said: 'I wouldn't demean myself, darling,' which made me wonder.

That was always the trouble with Toby. Much of what he said sprang from the observation of a highly individual mind, but at other times he was inspired solely by sour grapes, or the uncomplicated desire to take the opposite view from everyone else. To a straightforward person like myself it was apt to be bewildering, and I neither felt safe in following his advice, nor in ignoring it. However, as he had said, even live plays were preferable to starvation, which coincided with my own precept, of never turning down anything, unless it specifically involved being shot from the cannon's mouth.

'Of course, I wouldn't dream of doing it if you feel I should be letting you down,' I said.

'Me, Tessa? But I never watch the things and neither do my friends. It is kind of you to see it in that light, but quite unnecessarily scrupulous.'

'Oh, very funny indeed! You know perfectly well what I mean. I am supposed to be down here to look after Ellen and now I am proposing to go back to London for three or four days. Would you call it a shabby trick?'

'No, I wouldn't. It is not a phrase I customarily use. When will all this occur?'

'Next week. Second half of.'

'Oh, splendid. That is just the time we can most easily spare you. Matilda will be here.'

'She will?'

'Yes, she will. It is her Dedley week. She will be able to commute.'

'Has she said so?'

'She has no need to. Can you see Matilda paying to live in an hotel when there is free board and lodging only twenty miles away?'

In view of certain hints and rumours circulating about Matilda at this time, I was not at all sure that he had assessed the situation correctly. However, it was not in my best or even my second-best interests to apprise him of these matters, so I retired to a chair by the pool to apply myself to the script which had arrived with the morning post.

It was the third fine day in succession and Ellen had been persuaded to take the plunge. She surfaced a minute later, her long hair streaming behind her, and assured me through chattering teeth that it was lovely, once you were in. Apparently, it was, too, because she was still there about two hours later, although turning a funny shade of blue. So I interrupted my studies to haul her out and set her off on a brisk trot round the garden to get the circulation started up again.

By this time I had wrung every drop of sense that I could out of my part and was pretty well word perfect. This was not quite such a feat as it may sound, because unfortunately it was one of those plays about non-communication and the few passable lines that it did contain had all been given to computers.

It was set in the year two thousand and something and the author's comforting idea was that by then the computers would have taken charge of just about everything, from foreign policy down to bingo, with the result that Man had lost the power of self expression and was reduced to conversing in grunts and loosely connected monosyllables.

All this was directly opposed to my own experience, for I have found that the less Man has to do the more garrulous he becomes, and the same goes for Woman. However, mine was not to reason why, and at least my own part was that of the one remaining human being who retained some half-stifled yearnings towards loquacity. It transpired that, just before the action started, I had in some manner never quite accounted for unearthed a tattered old copy of Shelley's poems, which, after laborious study and to the bewilderment of my fellow-men, I went about quoting all over the shop and urging everyone else to do likewise.

I eventually got crushed to death for my pains by a band of avenging computers, who saw in this harmless exercise a threat to their authority, an outcome which anyone could have foreseen from the opening lines. But still, I had hopes of making this bit fairly gripping and poignant, specially if they allowed me to wear one of those dinky, futuristic Ariel costumes, which, although perhaps I should not be the one to say it, I can modestly claim to have the legs for. Moreover, I had myself made a mental note to plough through a bit of Shelley with rather more thoroughness than the author had troubled to do and see if I could not come up with something slightly more telling than that hackneyed old Bird Thou Never bit.

Altogether, not a bad morning's work, and I felt entitled to a little slackening off during the afternoon. Ellen and I had planned to take a tea picnic, in Matilda's car, to a spot about two miles away known as Stoney Woods, which was just off the Storhampton Road, with stunning views over the valley.

We knocked tremulously on the study door and acquainted Toby with our intention, and neither of us even pretended to be surprised when he came downstairs a moment or two later and said that he had decided to join the expedition. It was one of those days, he announced pompously, when his mind worked better out of doors, but I don't know who he thought he was kidding. When we unpacked the basket we found that even Mrs Parkes, not a very acute student of human nature, had known enough to put in three plastic mugs.

We left him alone with his muse, on a camp stool, in the shade of a beech tree, while Ellen and I advanced in prong-like formation to play the flower game. This is the one where two or more players take parallel paths for a given period of time, picking one specimen of every variety they can find. The winner is he who returns with the highest number of species which no other competitor can match, and it usually ends in a mighty squabble about whether a bud is the same as a flower or whether both are cancelled out by a berry from the same plant.

On this occasion Ellen had penetrated into the heart of the wood, while I had kept to the path which skirted its edge and where the landscape on the other side sloped precipitously down, five or six hundred feet, to the rolling plain. Toby was supposed to call us in after ten minutes, but I knew he would forget, so every second I could spare from scanning each bush and clump was used for checking the passing minutes on my watch. It was for this reason that I stumbled upon Mrs Cornford before I realised she was there.

There was something both outlandish and intimidating about her solitary figure as she stood staring fixedly out over the fields below, and the shock of coming upon her so unexpectedly caused me to utter a small, involuntary scream.

She jerked her head round and her expression, at first blank and bemused, became suffused first with terror and then fury. I had every sympathy with this, as suddenly to find oneself being screamed at while peacefully contemplating the woodland scene was precisely the kind of thing which would have terrified and infuriated me, but as usual her resentment transgressed the normal bounds.

She advanced a pace or two rather unsteadily, but her voice was strident and bellicose as she shouted:

'What do you think you're doing? Get out of here, do you hear me? Get out!'

I should have done so, as fast as my lovely legs could carry me, but it was news to me that she had bought the place and once more her rudeness roused me to retort.

'I apologise for giving you a fright, but I wasn't expecting to meet anyone. However, these are public woods as far as I know, and I have as much right here as you have.'

'Right? What are you talking about rights for? I've got a right to be left alone, haven't I? What right have you got to follow me about, sneaking and spying? You and your fast cars and your actressy goings on. Think you can get away with murder, don't you? But I'll put a stop to you, don't think I won't . . . Following me . . .'

She was clearly getting beyond control of herself, but, stupidly, I still lingered.

'I had no intention of following you, I swear. I've explained that I wasn't expecting to see you, or anyone else. I was just taking a stroll in the woods.'

'Then go and stroll somewhere bloody else,' she snarled. 'Go on, get out of here before I tell you . . .'

I did not stay to hear what further unpleasant things she had to tell me, for she had moved a few more paces towards me, arms hanging down and a threatening scowl on her face, all too reminiscent of our last meeting. As it seemed probable that, in any case, words would soon be replaced by blows, all traces of bravado deserted me. I turned and slunk away, though forcing myself to move slowly, as though the retreat had been of my own choosing.

I risked one quick, backward glance when I had gone a few yards, but it was a very quick one, for she was standing where I had left her, her hands gripping her arms, which were now crossed over her chest, and glaring straight ahead of her like a tormented bull. I stumbled hurriedly on and could not repress a squeak of relief as I flopped thankfully down on the grass beside my dear old normal first and second cousins.

Ellen was tactful about my poor showing in the flower game, and I realised with some astonishment that I was still clutching a wilting dandelion and a spray of green and wizened blackberries. She had at least forty varieties of vegetation laid out on the tablecloth, and, when I congratulated her, gently pointed out that she would have won, anyway, since I had been disqualified by the time clause.

'Where on earth have you been?' Toby asked. 'We were quite worried about you. We decided that you must have fallen into Dead Man's Gully.'

'What's that?' I asked rather thoughtlessly.

'Oh, how should I know? There's always a Dead Man's Gully in every woods, isn't there? And it's just the sort of excuse you would think of. Don't pretend that it has taken you quarter of an hour to collect that squalid little bunch.'

It is probable that I should have recounted my experience anyway, for I was still somewhat unnerved by it and I subscribe to the view that a trouble shared is a trouble halved, or, in this case, trisected, but these aspersions on my sportsmanship made it inevitable:

'I have been studying fauna, rather than flora,' I began, leading up, with slow and suspenseful effect, to my encounter with Mrs Cornford, making a good story of it, the way one does, and had the satisfaction of seeing both pairs of eyes growing larger and more enthralled, as the tale proceeded.

When I had finished, Ellen jumped up, saying:

'Come on, let's get away, before she comes here.'

'I don't think there is any danger of that,' I said. 'As you may have gathered, company is what she seeks to avoid.'

'All the same, she might come by accident, and I don't want to see her.'

She was walking towards the car even as she spoke, and after a moment's hesitation Toby got up and followed her.

'Quite right,' he said. 'We don't want any unpleasantness to spoil our lovely afternoon.'

As I watched them go I almost regretted my undoubted talents. It was one thing to hold such a critical audience in the hollow of one's hand. It was quite another to be left, alone and unaided, to pack up all the picnic things.

EIGHT

(i)

THE most memorable feature about the remainder of that week was the temperature, which soared regularly into the eighties every afternoon, much to the disgust of Mrs Grumble, who, as we were informed with matching regularity, had never been one to care for the heat. She managed to convey that there was something unrefined about those who did and also that she would probably give notice, unless normal climatic conditions were restored forthwith.

We all expected Matilda to come for the weekend, but she telephoned on Saturday morning to say she would be unable to do so. Evidently the Oxford audience had been a trifle more exacting than those in the North and Midlands, and stern measures had to be taken before the Dedley opening. I gathered that they had not actually got the bird, but that it had been a close thing and the director had demanded some drastic cuts and rewrites. All of this meant that Matilda, with the rest of the cast, would be on call for rehearsal on Sunday, as well as for the usual run through on Monday morning.

After commiserating for a bit, I told her of my own plans for that week.

'When do you have to go?' she asked sharply.

'Some time on Tuesday. We rehearse on Wednesday, Thursday and Friday, and it goes out on Friday evening. I trust you have a television set in your dressing-room?'

She was silent for so long that I knew it was not this question which preoccupied her fertile mind. In fact, I was quite prepared for her to tell me that the arrangement was inconvenient and that I should tear up my contract at once. I was marshalling my forces to do battle with her when she suddenly sent them scattering all over the place by announcing that I could borrow her car.

'What car?' I asked stupidly.

'My car. It's in the garage. I gave Ellen the keys and she told me you'd be all right with it because you'd passed the advanced driving test. The battery's down, but you can get that seen to.'

'That's mighty handsome of you, Matilda, but won't you need it yourself?'

'Not next week. At least, the only time I might is for getting home after the late show on Saturday. I believe Dickie means to drive straight over to Brighton that night. I tell you what though, Tessa, why don't you bring the car to Dedley on Saturday? You could see the play and drive home with me afterwards.'

'Fabulous!' I said, resigned to the fact that nothing is for nothing, in this rotten old world of ours. 'Super idea! I should adore that.'

'Right. You can probably have the house seats, if you don't mind coming to the first performance. I'll tell the box office.'

So I was not only to sit through her terrible old play, but I was then to kick my heels in Dedley for three hours while she went through it all again. More than half hoping that she would withdraw the offer, I said:

'But look, Matilda, are you absolutely certain you won't need it yourself? What about the other evenings?'

'Quite certain, or I wouldn't have suggested it, would I? Dickie will be at his mother's all the week, so it's much easier to use his car. It's hardly out of the way at all, and I loathe driving by myself at night.'

There was no way out of it, so I thanked her again and rang off. Moreover, this latest reference to the mysterious Dickie had set up a new train of thought and it had flashed into my mind that I had never been back to the Bull to pay for my telephone call. I have a very strict code about such matters and decided to repair the oversight without more ado.

On second thoughts it occurred to me that Saturday morning was among the more hectic periods of the publican's week and that Marge, being shorthanded anyway, would hardly thank me for bothering her with anything so trivial. This, plus a few other harmless self-deceptions, easily persuaded me to postpone the business until Sunday.

(ii)

I shall not say that I set out on my errand the following morning with high hopes, for I had heard it said that lightning does not strike twice in the same place. On the other hand, I have a saying of my own to the effect that it is not any more likely to strike twice in a different place. Furthermore, having formed the opinion that Fate had intended Mr Robin Price for a major rôle in my life, and knowing how lackadaisical Fate can be in the execution of such business I was prepared to lend a hand whenever the opportunity arose.

The saloon bar was packed, though mainly with the sort of people who only ever patronised it on Sunday mornings. The breed was instantly recognisable, all the men being dressed in a style to suggest that they had left either their horses, or their yachts, tied up in the car park and the patent desire of all the women for their slightest remark to be heard by all the dear ones they had left behind in South Kensington.

Sylvia and Gerry were there and I espied Paul among the screaming melee, but Douglas Cornford was not in evidence and nor, which was more to the point, was Robin Price. When I had transacted my business with Marge I complimented her on the calm competence with which she coped with all this riff-raff, and she told me that her sister and brother-in-law were staying with her, to lend a hand while Leslie was in Canada.

I asked whether she had had any news of Leslie.

'Not a sausage,' she said cheerfully. 'Don't expect any, either. Poor old love, he's not much of a dab hand at letter writing. No, the first I'll hear from him is when he comes staggering in here, Monday week, with feathers on his head and a right old hangover.'

'You've not had any more trouble, since he went?' I asked.

'You mean our friends from the Manor? No, touch wood. Les tore a strip off him after that shindy last Sunday and he hasn't shown his nose in here since. Someone told me he's away, gone up to Coventry to see his old man, or something.'

'That's good. Perhaps he'll decide to go back and live there. That would be a break, wouldn't it?'

'Not half, but I'd say there isn't a snowball's chance in hell. They say he's nuts about this place. Always fancied himself as Lord of the Manor and all that, though he doesn't seem to get much fun out of it.'

'They're a nutty pair,' I said.

'You can say that again,' Marge agreed.

'How about the other man who was in here that day? Has he been back?'

She gave me what I can only describe as a quizzical look. 'Sorry, love, never saw him again. Ships that pass in the night, I expect. He was quite a dish.'

'Oh, did you think so? Well, yes, I suppose he was rather attractive, now you mention it.'

Before I could pursue this interesting topic any further somebody tugged at my arm, and I turned to see Gerry standing beside me.

'What are you having?' he said.

If they were not the first words I had heard him speak, I am sure they were the only ones.

'Nothing for me,' I said. 'I just came in to settle a debt. I'm not drinking, thanks all the same.'

Of course, I could have saved my breath, for he was deaf, as well as mute, and was already relaying a sign-language order to Marge. In a twinkling a large gin and tonic had been set before me.

The main reason for refusing his offer was the obligation, which I knew acceptance would entail, of going over to have a chat with Sylvia, whose beckoning smiles could no longer be ignored. Perhaps the same thought had been in Gerry's mind, for he made no move to follow as I edged through the throng to her table.

'What a crush, isn't it?' she said delightedly. 'Who would believe that our humble little inn could provide such a congenial atmosphere? I'm no snob, dear, as well you know, but it is rather nice, in this day and age, to be able to pop in here and find so many people of one's own sort, don't you agree?'

'No dirty old peasants, to spoil things,' I said nastily.

I confess that Sylvia brought out a mean streak in me, which I had not even known I possessed. I am sure I could have tolerated her fifth-rate prejudices more patiently if she had not always insisted on her immunity from them. Luckily, she was also incapable of recognising a snub, even when it came up and slapped her between the eyes.

'Or even the sort of peasants who fancy themselves to be as good as we are,' she remarked, giving me a knowing little nudge.

'Oh yes?' I said, pretending to be in the dark.

'I hear you had a little brush with just such a person only the other day. It must have been horrid for you.'

'However did you hear that?' I asked cagily. I had guessed that she was referring to the Cornfords and I also now suspected that Gerry had been dispatched on his errand just so that she could pump me, but there was no telling which of two possible brushes she had in mind and I certainly had no desire to present her with some titbit, of whose existence she was as yet unaware.

'Oh, things get around, in a place like this,' she said. 'You'd be surprised. Rather cosy, I always think. I hate gossip myself, but it would be dreadful to live in some nasty suburb where one didn't even know one's neighbours by name.'

'Very disagreeable,' I said, wondering what sort of suburb she could conceivably have in mind.

'And, of course, anything that occurs in this little club of ours, as I like to call it, is all round the place in no time,' she went on, putting an end to my uncertainty.

Nevertheless, I was still puzzled as to how she had come by her information, unless from Mr Cornford himself, for I could not believe that either of the Brocks would have been anxious to publicise the episode. Then, a possible explanation occurred to me.

'Is Robin Price a friend of yours, Sylvia?'

It was a foolish question, because, naturally, she would never have disclaimed knowledge of anything, however unimportant.

'Not a friend, no,' she said vaguely. 'I wouldn't say that, exactly. But, my dear, do give me your version of what happened. You can't think how much I am dying to hear.'

I could think how much and I knew that it was enough to prevent my fobbing her off indefinitely, so I said:

'Well, it was just as you heard, I daresay. Mrs Cornford has this sort of fainting fit. I imagine she staggered in here, when she felt it coming on. Anyway, she rambled on a bit, talking a lot of twaddle and then she more or less passed out. Her husband was here and he gave her a good clip, to bring her round, so he said, and Robin Price, the one who isn't exactly a friend of yours, was here, too, and he got everything sorted out.'

'Well, well, he seems to have made quite an impression!'

Quite what had given her that idea was beyond my comprehension, but it just shows that even someone as obtuse as Sylvia is occasionally capable of an inspired guess. She said:

'I must admit that it is rather a different version from the one I heard, but, there, I admire your discretion, I really do.'

'What did you hear?' I asked, at the risk of forfeiting her admiration.

'Something much more exciting. I was told that Douglas Cornford assaulted his wife, in full view of half a dozen witnesses, including yourself, and would have murdered her if he hadn't been prevented in the nick of time.'

'I think we've got our wires crossed,' I said firmly. 'We must be speaking of two separate occasions.'

'Possibly. Now, where's that man of mine got to all this time, I should like to know?'

I could tell that she had lost interest in me, now that I had failed to provide her with some of the gossip she so much detested, and I seized my chance to escape. It was not very elegantly contrived, because I was in such haste to get away, before Gerry could materialise with my other half, to use the Grimbold vernacular, that I collided with Paul, in the doorway.

'How's the invalid?' I inquired as we covered the short distance to his cottage.

I could as well have been referring to himself, for he looked drawn and haggard, with none of his normal rubicund bounce.

'Not too good,' he answered morosely. 'Foot's still inflamed and giving him gyp. The worst of it is, he's so fed up and bored, being stuck in one place all day. I don't think he'd fret so much, if it were raining, but this fine weather drives him round the twist, thinking of all that needs to be done in the garden.'

'Yes, it must be very trying for both of you.'

'Understatement. They'll be able to sweep me up and throw the pieces in the dustbin if it goes on much longer. What with driving poor old Pete back and forth to the hospital and waiting on him hand and foot, as well as trying to keep up with the garden, I've just about had it, I don't mind telling you.'

'Tut tut,' I said. 'We can't have this. I'll tell you what. Ellen and I will come over and do some hedging and ditching for you when I get back from London.'

I told him briefly about my television engagement and he seemed moderately interested, although still brooding on his own weighty problems, so I said:

'By the way, what news of the building programme. Have they started it?'

He frowned at me, looking furtive and afraid, as though the spies were everywhere. 'Not so far. The stuff's still there, but they haven't used it yet.'

'That's a mercy. Has Peter found out?'

'No, thank God, and I hope he won't. He talks about hiring a wheel-chair, but I've managed to stave it off.'

'It may have been a false alarm. You know what they say? "Don't worry, it may never happen."'

'And I mean to ensure that it doesn't,' he said grimly. 'Not to breathe a word, mind, but I've laid my plans and all I need is the right opportunity.'

'Oh, jolly good! And the best of luck.'

'Thanks. That reminds me: good luck with your show. I'll remember to switch it on. Telly's about the only thing Pete gets any pleasure out of these days.'

Buoyed up by the reflection that I should at least have a captive audience of two, I continued on my way.

(iii)

'Ha! Back from another pub crawl, I see,' Toby said. 'Really, this is a most unexpected side to your character. I wonder who you keep bustling off to meet? It cannot be anyone called Prince.'

'Who? How? What do you mean?' I asked in a great fluster.

'Now she's gone all red. Just look at that, Ellen.'

'I don't know what you're talking about,' I protested.

'Bad luck!'

'He's teasing,' Ellen said. 'It wasn't Prince, it was Price. Someone called Robert Price rang up, while you were out, that's all.'

'Robin,' I said mechanically, struggling to calm myself. 'Why couldn't you have said so?'

'Between us, we have said so,' Toby reminded me.

'Was there a message?'

'No. He said he had telephoned on the off-chance of finding you in. How absurd! As though anyone would telephone on the off-chance of finding you out! Would you care for a drink, or have you had several already?'

'Yes. No. Only one. Didn't he leave a number for me to call?'

Ellen shook her head sadly.

'Oh, in that case, it can't have been anything important,' I said. 'I'm going indoors to look at my part for a bit before lunch.'

They were both gazing at me with wide-open eyes, and I had had my fill of quizzical looks for one morning.

NINE

EVERYONE had retired to bed when Matilda arrived home on Monday night, but I heard the car and went down to see if she wanted a hot drink. She was keen on little attentions of that kind and, besides, I know what a let down it is to return, late at night, to a dark and silent house after a hard slog in the theatre.

She declined my offer of hot milk, but seemed glad to see me and disposed for a chat. She poured herself a large whisky and soda and sat down in an armchair, in the drawing-room. She even offered me a drink, too, though did not press me when I refused.

'How did it go tonight?' I asked.

'Fairly lousy.'

'Bad house?'

'Rotten. You know what Mondays are.'

'Never mind. It'll pick up.'

'Oh yes, we normally play to capacity during the second half of the week. It makes all the difference. I'm glad you'll be coming on a Saturday.'

'I'm looking forward to it, no end,' I said in my polite way.

'I was wondering if you'd like to bring Ellen? I've got you two.'

'She's seen it already, surely?'

'I know, but that was right at the beginning, and a Monday, too. It's improved tremendously since then. Besides, Tessa, how could she be expected to enjoy it with Toby sneering and picking holes in everything? I knew he would spoil it for her, but I am sure she would get a great kick out of seeing it with someone like yourself. It really is fun, now that the dead wood has been cut out.'

'Okay, I'll ask her.'

'From a technical point of view as well I believe it might interest her; to see how much better it works, I mean, now it's been rewritten. For instance, there was a long breakfast scene in the second act which was an awful drag. You know how difficult stage meals are? One of the characters was supposed to have hidden some diamonds in a packet of cornflakes and he was trying to stop everyone else from eating any. It should have been funny, but it never really worked. Anyway, there's a completely new scene there now, which goes beautifully. It got the biggest laugh of all tonight.'

From the sanguine way she related all this I concluded that whatever lines had fallen under the axe they had not been Matilda's.

'And another thing, Tessa. If you bring Ellen you could both go and have dinner at some glam place during the second performance. My treat. She'd enjoy that, wouldn't she? And much nicer for you than hanging around on your own.'

Well, there it was. With all her faults I had always maintained that as a stepmother Matilda rated higher than average, and I was certainly vindicated now. Much of the credit should have gone to Ellen herself, no doubt, for she had a flair for bringing out virtues in the most unlikely people. Nevertheless, the thought of Matilda lashing out with free meals was touching indeed, and I thanked her with tears in my eyes.

She gave a mighty yawn and said: 'God, if I don't soon get some sleep I shall look like a crow tomorrow. Well, that's all fixed then. You'll be using my car, of course, so you can come here and collect Ellen on your way back from London. And you had better allow at least an hour to get to Dedley because parking can be a nightmare.'

I was afraid she would soon be telling me what to wear and to make sure my nails were clean, so I hurriedly thanked her once again and said good night.

She was still decrowing herself when I left early the next morning, but Toby broke the rule of a lifetime by coming downstairs with a cup of coffee in his hand to wish me luck, and Ellen stood by the car to see me off.

'And mind you don't stay in the pool too long,' I warned her. 'I don't want to come back and find a stiff little corpse.'

Grateful tears for my tender solicitude welled in her eyes, so I leant out of the car and gave her another hug before driving off.

No doubt these searing emotions are the price an actress has to pay, but I really felt quite desolate as with tears blinding my own eyes I bumped over the Common, knowing that I should not see the dear child again for four whole days.

TEN

(i)

I SHALL pass rapidly over my stay in London which was in every way unremarkable. The play, which was called *XB 594*, after the protagonist computer, and an unseductive title if ever I heard one, was the least remarkable of all, though I did find something comical in the sight of all those silly actors meticulously shaving themselves all over and then putting on long, blond, silky wigs and beards, to portray Primitive Man.

A few cronies rang me up afterwards to say that my performance had been absolutely marvellous and easily the best thing they had ever seen on television, plus a few more routine comments of that nature, although Toby subsequently informed me that the only amusement he derived from it was in hearing me say: 'Shake me to your Wobot Weeder.' However, since this line bore no resemblance to anything in the script, I did not entirely trust him.

I did manage one plunge down the King's Road, where I blew all my salary on some fancy gear, but I never got a chance to wear it. Nor did I discover whether Robin Price was strolling in Bond Street at the appropriate time. We rehearsed for what seemed like fifteen hours a day, and by the end of each one I couldn't even summon the energy to take Matilda's car out of the garage to visit friends in Hampstead, Islington and other far-flung points on the map who had all been on my agenda.

My agent came down to the rehearsal studio one morning, and we had a brief chin-wag during the coffee break. In the course of it I attempted to pump her about Matilda, without giving anything away in return, but she was a sight more practised in the art than I was. I am afraid she gleaned more information from me than the meagre scrap she handed out, which was merely that Matilda was reputed to be dancing a jig with a millionaire who had a wife and four children. I did not think this sounded very probable, unless of course, a Goring mother was the euphemism for such encumbrances. I asked her whether she knew his name, and she swore on her solemn oath that she did not. Naturally, I did not believe her, because it was exactly this kind of salient detail which she would have set her most accomplished spies to work on. She then asked me if I had any clue to his identity and I said absolutely not one tiny, single hint. So in a spirit of mutual distrust we passed on to other topics.

I slept late on Saturday morning, wasted over an hour on buying and skimming through all the daily papers, none of which had a single word to say about *XB* and, as a result, it was half past two, by the Town Hall clock, as I swept through Storhampton.

(ii)

Twenty minutes later I drove past the Bull and on to the Common where I saw Marge just ahead of me wheeling Jumbo in his push-chair. I stopped to say Hallo to them, complimented Jumbo on his ruddy looks, etcetera, and learnt that they were on their way to spend a lovely, lovely afternoon with Uncle Peter and Uncle Paul. At least, he was. Marge, as she explained, and not very diplomatically in the circumstances, was off to enjoy herself.

She explained that she was being taken to see Matilda's play, by her sister and brother-in-law. It was their last evening and they all considered that they had earned a good old binge for once. The kind Uncle Flyaways had not only volunteered to take charge of Jumbo for the afternoon but also to open up the bar and hold the fort there until Marge returned, sweetie pies that they both were.

'Leslie's not back yet?' I asked her.

'No. Due in tomorrow night. This is my last evening as a grass widow, thank the Lord, and I'm going to celebrate. Isn't that right, love? Mum's going on a cellywellybration.'

'Ellen and I will be there, too,' I said. 'I hope you won't be disappointed in the play.'

'Oh, you bet we won't. My sister was thrilled to the marrow when she heard we had a real live actress living in the village. She can't wait to see her on the stage. She'll be boasting about it back in Luton from now till Kingdom Come, if I know her.'

I sighed, wondering how long it would be before the coffee parties of Luton rang with my name. I had half a mind to go inside with her and say Hallo to Peter and Paul. They might have bolstered my ego with a few kind words about my television. On the other hand, they might not, and it was already nearly three o'clock. If Matilda's instructions were to be carried out to the letter it behoved me not to dally.

It was just as well that my sense of duty overrode vanity; for, as it was, Matilda was in a fine old, foot-tapping paddy when I reached the house.

'Where the hell have you been?' she demanded, flashing her eyes and her diamond wrist-watch at me as I wafted into the hall. 'Do you see what time it is? I have to leave here in precisely two minutes.'

'Beg pardon, I'm sure. You weren't waiting for the car, were you? I thought . . .'

'No, I wasn't waiting for the car, I was waiting for you, to make sure you'd be here and ready to leave on time. I know how scatty you are. It's bloody lucky for you that I haven't got to go all the way round through Goring?'

'Oh, why's that? Has Dickie's part been written out?'

'No, of course not. His mother's going to the show and, as he's not on till the second act, he can easily drive over with her. Do stop trying to be facetious.'

The request was uncalled for, because facetious is not a thing I would try to be in any circumstances, but one must allow a certain latitude for nervous temperament and since nothing was to be gained by working her up into a whiter-hot passion than she was in already I said humbly:

'Terribly sorry, Matilda, but you go ahead and don't worry about us. We'll be on time, I promise.'

'Well, mind you are. You've got the house seats and it's curtain up promptly at five-fifteen. Ellen's resting, by the way, so don't forget to call her in time to change. She's to wear her new dress.'

'Right.'

'I sent her up after lunch and told her to lie still for at least an hour, so see she does. She's got a long evening ahead of her.'

'"Haven't we all?"' I asked myself, as I toiled upstairs with my suitcase.

The door of Matilda's bedroom was open as I passed, and Mrs Grumble was planted in the middle of the room surrounded by coils of vacuum-cleaner flex and presumably waiting for someone to come and be grumbled at.

'Still working?' I said. 'And Saturday afternoon, too!'

'Some people don't have no consideration about such things,' she whined. 'Just their own pleasure, that's all they care for. Couldn't even get here to make her ladyship's bed until lunchtime and, then, the mess! You ought to have seen that dressing-table before I put it all straight and tidy. It's lucky we're not all actresses, is what I say. Some of us have got to do the work, Saturday or no Saturday.'

Since I knew that she was paid beyond the dreams of avarice to work on Saturdays and also that the alternative to dusting Matilda's dressing-table was to sit in her dark, damp and wretched little cottage, grumbling to her unmarried son about the dark, damp and wretchedness of it, I did not bother to commiserate, but said:

'Well, if it lightens your burden, in any way, so much the better, but I should give the hoovering a miss, for once. Ellen's supposed to be sleeping and it might wake her up.'

Mrs Grumble gave an unrefined snort and said: 'Sleeping, is it? I like that.'

'What do you like about it?'

'The young scamp is no more asleep than I am. Her lady-ship sent her up all right, saying she was to have a good rest and no nonsense, and ten minutes later, if she didn't come creeping down the back stairs and out of the house, before you could say knife. Nearly knocked me flying, she did.'

'Did she say where she was going?'

'No. Too much of a hurry to get out of the house before she was caught. But I saw her go to the garage and get her bike out. She's a proper little madam, that Ellen, when she wants to be. I shouldn't want the worry of it, if she was mine.'

This final observation being a little too complicated to reply to in depth, I remarked that fresh air could sometimes be more beneficial to little madams than stuffy bedrooms, and with the parting shot that I must not keep her from her work any longer I drifted on to my own room.

I found a charming picture on the bed, depicting a woodland scene, with elephants and cats, of identical size, gambolling about and encircled with a scroll, in which the words 'Wellcome Home' had been painted in capital letters and a variety of colours. When I had found some drawing-pins and had decided on a suitable place for it on the blue wall, I began to unpack in a desultory and disconnected fashion.

There was no real cause for it and yet I found myself growing steadily more uneasy. I checked my watch with my travelling clock and they both gave back the answer that it was only twenty-five past three. We had nearly an hour in hand, even by Matilda's somewhat generous estimate and yet I knew I should not have a moment's peace until Ellen turned up. I went and stood by the window, like Sister Anne, willing her to come in sight, and thus was ideally situated to witness one of the most chilling little episodes I had ever experienced, although to this day I cannot say exactly what was so scaring about it. Inevitably, Mrs Cornford was right at the centre of it.

My bedroom window faced over the front of the house and commanded a panoramic view of the Common. The first thing I noticed was the demented old Bronwen, approaching from the Bricklayers' corner, on the far side. She weaved slowly across with her usual clumsy gait, head poked forward and arms crossed over her chest, as though in dismal self-communion. I remember how it struck me that she looked even more wretched and hunched that day than usual, and I watched with pity, as well as apprehension, as she came gradually farther into view. Then something caused her to look up and suddenly she stopped dead. I turned my head to see what could account for this, and there, riding along the track from the opposite corner, was Ellen on her bicycle.

Perhaps she rode over a stone, or lost her balance for some reason, but as I watched I saw her front wheel wobble and the next moment the bike tilted over and she fell to the ground. I turned for one more look at Mrs Cornford before running out of the room, and it was her attitude then which temporarily froze me with panic.

She was motionless, with head raised, and there was something unspeakably menacing in her stance. I had the clearest impression, even at the distance of fifty yards which separated us, that her pent-up fury was about to explode into violence and that in a matter of seconds she would rush forward and hurl herself on Ellen. I thought that Ellen must have sensed something of this, too, because she was crouched on the ground, clutching the bicycle like a shield and cowering up at Mrs Cornford.

I pulled myself together and bolted out of the room, down the stairs and across the garden, but when I went through the gate I could see that whatever danger there might have been was over. Mrs Cornford wheeled in a half turn and was walking diagonally away from us, towards the Bull. She had her back completely turned to us by the time I reached Ellen's side, and was covering the last few yards to the road.

Ellen had picked herself up by then. She looked pale but otherwise composed, and her main concern seemed to be for the bicycle which she was methodically examining in every nut and bolt.

'Are you hurt?' I asked.

'Oh, hallo, Tessa. No, I'm okay.'

'Whatever happened?'

'I fell off my bike, that's all. I'm always doing it.'

'I thought when you didn't get up that you must be hurt,' I insisted, stammering a bit in the effort to conceal my silly fear. 'You sure you're all right?'

Her head was bent and she scratched at some dirt on the mudguard, with her fingernail, then looked up at me squarely in the face.

'No, honestly, I'm perfectly okay. What time is it?'

'Not late. We ought to be changing, though. Matilda left half an hour ago. She said you were to wear your new dress.'

'What a bore! I don't even want to go to the silly old play, anyway.'

'Come now, Ellen, if you talk like that I shall really believe you're hurt, after all. It's not in character.'

She did not answer and we walked slowly along, each holding one end of the handlebar. There was a small shadow, as well as the bicycle, between us and to dispel it I started telling her about my new finery and invited her to come to my room and inspect it.

'Shall you wear it this evening?'

'Yes, I think so. Then we shall both have our new dresses on and every eye will be upon us.'

The prospect seemed to cheer her up a little, and by the time we reached the house her spirits were half-way back to normal.

We found Toby on the veranda, reading the latest Nero Wolfe, evidently under the impression that we had already left and that, with the house to himself, all pretence of working could be cast aside.

Sticking to the jocular note I tried to persuade him to come over to Dedley later and join up for dinner, asking if he would not feel very much alone, with both of us out for the whole evening. He admitted that he would, very much alone, indeed, and that nothing could be lovelier.

'What will you do with yourself, all the time?'

'What do I ever do, when I am given the chance of some peace and quiet? Work, of course.'

'All right,' I said, 'I'll accept that. Now tell me what you'll really do.'

But this was going too far and he asked me coldly if it would not be more to the point to remember what I was going to do, namely, go upstairs and change.

Despite my good intentions, I seemed to be in everybody's bad books that afternoon, and I crawled up to my room positively sinking under my burden of vexation and self-pity.

(iii)

It was the darkest hour before the dawn, however, for things bucked up soon afterwards. Ellen was delighted with the placing of her picture and equally rapturous about my new outfit. She possessed an instinctive dress sense, which was one of many qualities which made her so companionable and made a suggestion about the belt, which Yves St Laurent would not have been ashamed of.

No snags or delays attended us on the journey and there was a car park, evidently overlooked by Matilda, right opposite the theatre. We marched into the foyer a full twenty minutes ahead of time.

This was cut down to fifteen, by two old beldams, ahead of me at the box office, who could not decide between two singles in the centre, or two together at the side. When at last I was allowed to state my business, the clerk handed me an envelope. Inside were two tickets and a note from Matilda. With many a dash and an underlining, she had scrawled:

'Tessa – Maddening thing happened and need your help – if time – come round before – if not – interval – without fail. M.'

'Do you suppose her zip's burst?' I asked, showing the missive to Ellen, who read it with pursed lips, giving rather more weight to the matter than I privately thought it merited.

'I've just got time, haven't I? Damn the woman! But I don't think I could stand the suspense of waiting all through the first act. Will you come with me?'

She shook her head firmly, so I gave her one of the tickets and told her to go in, on her own, if I wasn't back by the last bell. Then I scampered off, in search of the stage door. I found it, easily enough, down the usual black and sinister alley and the stage door-keeper was expecting me and directed me to Matilda's dressing-room.

I met with several haughty looks as I chugged up the stair-case and along a series of dirty stone passages. Back-stage visitors are not welcome before the curtain goes up, but Matilda, at least, received me with a veneer of cordiality.

'Oh, bravo, Tessa! Bless you!' she said, when I had knocked and been admitted by her dresser.

She was sitting placidly at her dressing-table, putting the final touches to her make-up, and it was plain that whatever disaster or maddening thing had befallen her it was not of nature to require the services of the fire brigade, ambulance or even her understudy.

'What seems to be the trouble?' I asked. 'Another mix up with the letters?'

I got a warning glare from her reflection in the mirror: 'Don't be silly. I had a blow-out on my way here and the car's a bit damaged.'

'Heavens, Matilda! How ghastly!'

'It's not serious. Luckily, I wasn't driving fast and there was nothing much on the road, but I skidded into a bank. The bumper was crushed and it broke one of the sidelights. It could have been far worse, only, of course, I had to change the wheel and it would bloody well have to happen when I was on my own; and not a telephone or A.A. box in sight, you may be sure.'

'Didn't anyone stop and help you?'

'A couple of people did, but they were both utterly useless. One of them knew even less about jacking up than I did, and the other said he was in a tearing hurry and offered to send a man out from Dedley. Can you believe it? It would have taken at least an hour and I was frantic about the time already. As it was, I was nearly late, wasn't I, Annie?'

'Near as a touch, Miss Spragge, and I was ever so worried, I don't mind saying it. Twenty minutes after your usual time, it was, when you got in and I said to myself, there's something up, you see if there isn't. As I've many times remarked to Mr

Badger, I'd as soon set my watch by you as the man on the wireless, any day of the week.'

Having got the floor she seemed ready to go on extolling Matilda's punctuality indefinitely, but our heroine chopped her off.

'Yes, well, thank God, someone with a bit of sense did come by eventually, otherwise it might have been a disaster. I was almost through by then, but he did tighten up the nuts for me and he got me off the bank. The point is, Tessa, the car's in a garage down the road and Dickie has to take it to Brighton tonight, so I want you to cope. They're mending the puncture and fixing a new light, but they close at seven, so you've got to buzz down there in the interval, check they've done everything properly and pay the bill. Tell them to leave it outside, to be collected and to give the keys to the stage door-keeper. I suppose you can manage that?'

'Expect so. Where's the garage?'

'You'll see a pub on the right-hand corner as you go out. It's a few yards down from there. They're called Watkins, or something . . .'

She was interrupted at this point by a hammering on the door and a voice saying: 'Five minutes, please, Miss Spragge,' and went on, in a rush:

'If you've got it all straight you'd better go. Be an angel, Annie, and show Miss Crichton to the pass door. You've just got time before my entrance. Run along, Tessa.'

It was clear from the way she had us all scooting about at her beck and call that the accident had in no way impaired her morale, and if further proof had been needed she supplied it by calling after me:

'And don't let that garage rook you, Tessa. It was quite a simple job. Shouldn't have taken them more than a few minutes.'

The lights were still up when I went through the pass door into the auditorium, and Ellen was in the third row on the aisle. She moved up a place when she saw me, and I sat down and gabbled off a resume of events. At the same time I was casting an eagle eye over the programme in search of clues to the identity of Dickie. Unfortunately, these had been strewn about too copiously to be of much value. No less than two members of the cast were named Richard and the play had been directed by someone called R.H. Osborn, so he couldn't be ruled out, either.

The house lights went down before I had time to investigate further, and a few seconds later there was Matilda, down centre, stately and erect on a Louis Quinze sofa, filling us in with all the background by means of a dialogue with her maid, Solange, who was attired in black satin with white frills and who responded in a thick, phony French accent.

I have to confess that, although I could not remember a single word of it afterwards, I quite enjoyed all the ensuing nonsense. There were some riotous situations and R.H. Osborn had done a smartish job. Despite a series of complicated movements and lightning changes, the play whipped along at a spanking pace and the entire company played it with a deadly earnestness, which would not have been out of place in the Medea. For my money, that is about all you can ask of a farce of this description and it is a lot more than you often get.

Nevertheless, Matilda had been over-optimistic in her belief that Ellen would enjoy it more, the second time. I did not once hear her laugh, and at one point when I turned to catch her reaction, she actually had her eyes closed.

When the lights went up for the interval I looked around and saw Marge and her party, four or five rows behind us. They were moving out, and I grabbed Ellen and chased up the aisle in pursuit. We caught up with them at the bar entrance and I explained that I had some business to perform for Miss Spragge and asked if I could leave Ellen in their charge until I returned. This was readily agreed to, and I nipped through the foyer and out to the street. It struck me as I went that whenever I had an errand to do for Matilda, which was becoming all too frequent, it always involved me in record-breaking sprints.

I found the garage without difficulty, but then my luck petered out. I was told that the lamp had been mended, but the tyre was damaged beyond repair.

'Lady must have driven a coupla hundred yards, after it went,' the attendant said reprovingly. 'What can you expect? There's a split in the outer casing you could get your arm through. See for yourself.'

I did see for myself, and I was tempted to ask him to put it in the boot so that Matilda could see for herself as well. However, I decided it would be demeaning to us both, so meekly wrote out an enormous cheque and repeated all Matilda's instructions.

'Will do,' he said. 'How about this, though?'

He was holding out a key-ring with a single key attached to it. I looked closer and saw that it was a perfectly ordinary yale key, but the ring was undoubtedly real gold. It was in the form of a snake, curved into a capital D.

'Mechanic found it on the floor in front. He thought it looked a bit out of the way, might be valuable and that, so he handed it in. Want to take it with you?'

Without thinking I dropped it into my bag and cantered back to the theatre. Two minutes later I cursed myself for not having had the presence of mind to tell him to put it in the glove compartment where Matilda would never know that I had seen it, but there was no time to indulge second thoughts, and as the evening wore on I forgot all about it.

Ellen was handed over to me at the stalls entrance, and I was about to embark on the latest bulletin, but she got in first and said:

'They want us to meet up and have dinner together afterwards, so I told them which restaurant we were going to. Is that all right?'

'I expect so, if you think it's a good plan.'

'I do, rather, because, you see, Marge's sister is dying to go round and see Matilda. So I thought if you took her with you, then I could go with Marge and the husband and show them where the restaurant is and all that, and then you can bring the sister with you.'

I had a distinct impression that there was more to this than the words revealed, but before I could get a proper squint at those tell-tale eyes of hers the lights went down and she murmured 'You don't have to take her, if you don't want to, Tess,' which was the last thing I had been worrying about.

As it happened the arrangement suited me well, because however inflamed with rage Matilda might be at having to pay for a new tyre I knew that she would never show it in the presence of a stranger, let alone a raving fan like Marge's sister. In this I proved to be correct.

Back in the foyer we divided into two parties and I led the way down the little dark alley with Marge's sister, whose name rather predictably turned out to be Brenda, positively trilling with excitement at my side.

She told me repeatedly what a thrill it was for her, as she had never before been backstage and had never thought to do so in her wildest dreams.

I warned her not to expect too much, as it was a particularly crummy old theatre, even for the provinces, but there was no damping that ardent spirit and she only said that somehow that made it all the more romantic.

I was afraid the terrible suspense might overpower her as we waited for the stage door-keeper to telephone and announce our presence, but all was well and we were bidden to go up.

Of course, poor Brenda lost her head, her tongue and her nerve at one swoop when she was ushered into the presence, but it did not matter in the least, for Matilda was accustomed to people gurgling and goggling at her; rather enjoyed it, in fact. She was at her most queenly and gracious, and the mask did not slip even when I broke the bad news, although she seized the garage receipt out of my hand and tucked it carefully away in her white jewel-case, so I guessed that we had not heard the last of it.

Fortunately, we could only stay a few minutes as there was less than an hour between performances and Matilda had to change, so I told her that I would be back later with Ellen to collect her and off we went.

Brenda remained in a deep trance throughout dinner. She kept telling everyone how wonderfully natural and unaffected Matilda had been. I have simply no idea what she had expected, but if that was Matilda being natural, then I was Robert Morley.

Meanwhile, a girlish *entente* had been struck up between Ellen and Marge, and it was soon abundantly clear that a fresh scheme was being cooked up between them. Sure enough, as we were drinking our coffee Marge said that the poppet was looking dreadfully whacked and did I not agree that it would be a sound plan for them to take her home, rather than have her wait around for Miss Spragge?

The motivation was not clear to me, but all the signposts pointed in one direction: Ellen was at great pains to avoid a meeting with Matilda. However, whatever her reasons, I took them to be sound ones and acquiesced in the proposal.

I parked Matilda's car as close as I could to the stage door, and when she came out she asked me to drive, saying that she was dead, but dead, and her near escape of the afternoon had temporarily unnerved her. The Lady Bountiful mood persisted, however, and to my intense relief no further reference was made to the garage bill.

Toby was downstairs when we got in and he told us that Ellen had returned, half an hour earlier and was already in bed. Still in her sunny mood Matilda linked her arm in his, kissed the top of his head and said how lovely, lovely it was to be home.

I did not believe I could improve on this happy note as an ending to our day, so I announced my intention of wending my way up the wooden hill to Bedfordshire, and I left them to it.

ELEVEN

(i)

ON SUNDAY we had been invited to lunch by the Grimbolds. Toby had accepted for us all, remarking to me that even the staggering boredom it would entail would be preferable to one of Matilda's garden picnics, but in the end he and Matilda went on their own.

Ellen's bedroom was next to mine, and at nine o'clock in the morning I was creeping about so as not to waken her when I heard some feeble cries from next door. I went in and she told me that she had been sick in the night and was feeling funny. Funny was hardly the word. She was heavily flushed and her eyes, although larger than ever, were dull and lifeless. I took her temperature and it registered a hundred and two.

I busied myself with aspirin, cold sponges and vitamin drinks, and when I looked in again ten minutes later she was asleep. I was more puzzled than alarmed by this development. It had dawned on me long ago that Ellen had urgent reasons for wishing to avoid Matilda and I had often suspected her of possessing magic powers, yet I could not see how she had contrived to become genuinely ill within a few hours of all the giggling and guzzling that had taken place at the restaurant.

It was possible that she had a mild attack of food poisoning, which was the version I gave Toby, playing it down as much as I could because he suffered from an acute form of hypochondria, which embraced everyone under his roof. Nevertheless, as I had feared, his immediate reaction was to call the doctor. I said I thought it would be rather mean to drag him out, on his day of rest, on such trivial grounds and suggested that we should wait and see how she was on Monday.

'Really, Tessa, your logic baffles me. What is the point of getting a doctor tomorrow, when it's today that she is ill? You seem to be more concerned about the doctor's health than Ellen's.'

Nothing could have been further from the truth. I was more than half convinced that Ellen's condition belonged in the psychosomatic class, a fact which I feared might be all too recognisable to the professional eye and, possibly, all too easily cured. In the end we reached a compromise. If Ellen were no better when she woke up, Dr Macintosh would be called in. If she were better, we would postpone the decision until the evening.

A little later I repeated the healing treatment and casually tossed out the remark that if she still felt groggy we would get the dear old doctor to give her some delicious pills, which would soon have her up and about again.

Ellen informed me that she was actually feeling tons better, although still not quite ready to get up. So I took her temperature again and found that it had gone down a notch or two.

I did not have to tackle the problem of keeping Toby out of the sick-room, because the mere sight of a dear one out of sorts was more than his frail nerves could stand, but Matilda was all for going in and cheering up the invalid by reading aloud to her. I deprecated this suggestion on the grounds that peace and quiet were what Ellen needed most. Sleep, I informed them, was the Great Healer.

Matilda said, 'You are bossy, Tessa. It is quite impressive. I had no idea you were such a capable nurse. I shall certainly send for you next time I am ill.'

I believed her, too. One had only to think how much cheaper it would be than going into the Clinic.

They both offered to stay at home and keep me company, but I pointed out that they would get no lunch if they did, and reminded them of the gorgeous victuals in store at Sylvia's. At twenty to one they obediently set forth.

Ellen and I split a tin of nourishing soup between us, and afterwards played a few hands of rummy. The fine weather had broken at last, and at two o'clock it was pelting with rain. At two-fifteen, a police car came up the track, drove through the gates to the Manor and remained there for twenty minutes.

I was perched on the end of the bed and had a full view of all this, but Ellen could not see out of the window and the noise of the thudding rain must have obliterated the motor, for she asked no questions. I was thus absolved from the necessity of telling any lies, although to say that I was agog would be an understatement.

It was Mrs Parkes who filled in some of the details. Ellen had gone back to sleep and I was washing up our lunch things when she popped over, as she put it. Having heard that Ellen was indisposed, she had come, ostensibly, to offer the loan of a hand. Actually, as I soon discovered, she was in quest of an audience for the latest gossip about the Cornfords.

Mrs Parkes detested the Cornfords, as did the whole village, for they took no part in local affairs, refused to lend their garden for the annual fete and bought all their groceries from the supermarket at Storhampton. Needless to say, this did not prevent anyone from giving the closest attention to their activities. How the word always got around so speedily was a mystery to me, but even in this day and age there can be few methods of communication so rapid, or so unreliable as the village grapevine.

'Heard the latest?' she panted, not even giving me time to tell her how much better Ellen was.

'Latest what?'

'Mrs C. done a bunk, that's what.'

'She never!'

'True as I'm standing here. My hubby was having his pint, up at the Bricklayers', before dinner and this policeman came in, asking which was the way to the Manor House. Then he asked Bert, you know Bert, at the Bricklayers'? Asked if he knew a Mrs Cornford, by sight and if he'd seen her at all, today or yesterday. Bert said not offhand, he couldn't say he had.'

'Is that all? That doesn't mean she's hopped it.'

'Ah, you wait! After the Bobby went out they all got talking, as was only natural, and Bert said that last night just before he closed up, about ten o'clock it would be, Mr Cornford come in and asked if he'd seen the missis. Bert thought at the time that it was a bit funny, seeing that neither of them had set foot in there, oh months, it must be, ever since they had a bit of a bust up one evening, and Bert had to ask them to leave. Anyway, he hadn't thought no more about it till then, but someone else piped up, old Tom Wheeler, that was, from over Mancombe way and he said it was a rum do, because he'd been down at the Bull, night before and what do you think? Mr Cornford had come in there, too, asking everyone if they'd seen her. That Mr Dickson, who's such a pal of the Bull people, he was in charge and he come over ever so queer, Tom said, but anyway, he hadn't seen her and no more had anyone else, not a hair nor hide of her. So there you are! Put two and two together and see what you get.'

'About three and a quarter,' I said.

I really cannot account for this tendency, but I invariably try to tone down other people's scandal-mongering, only to play it up, myself, the next time around. I had the uncomfortable feeling that in recounting this stirring tale to Toby and Matilda my total would come to at least five.

'Anyway,' I said, banishing these unkind thoughts about myself, 'I thought Mr Cornford was away.'

'So he might have been. At least, that's what he told everyone, but he must have got back last night and found her gone. And who's to say how long she'd been gone? That's what I'd like to know.'

'What about the children? They could probably tell you.'

Mrs Parkes frowned and I could see her making a mental note to rewrite this part of the script.

'And so can I,' I went on, as memory struck, 'Mrs Cornford was definitely around yesterday afternoon.'

'How do you come to be so sure of that, Miss?'

'Because I saw her with these two eyes, Mrs Parkes, that's how. She was here, walking on the Common, at about half past three, and I could hardly mistake her for anyone else, could I?'

'No, you couldn't hardly do that,' Mrs Parkes agreed reluctantly. She looked distinctly dashed, but rallied quickly and said:

Then, I'd say you were just about the last person, round these parts, that did see her. I should think that Bobby would be interested to hear about it.'

'And so he shall, any time he cares to ask me.'

'You don't think you ought to go down to the station and report it?' she asked hopefully.

'I don't think it is at all necessary,' I replied, and nor did I. If every policeman in the vicinity wasn't in possession of the news within a couple of hours, with Mrs Parkes on the job, then they must be a dud lot and I should never bother to look at *Z Cars* again.

'Which way was she walking, when you thought you saw her?' Mrs. Parkes asked, in a feeble attempt to undermine my confidence.

I was saved from making an undignified retort by sounds of the master and his wife returning from their luncheon party, whereupon Mrs Parkes said that if I was sure there was nothing else she could do to help she'd be off home, and streaked through the back door like a sheet of lightning.

(ii)

Having satisfied herself about Ellen, Matilda went directly to her room to lie down for an hour or two and Toby said that since he had wasted a whole morning and the best part of an afternoon he must drag himself off and do some work. He then went directly to his room to lie down for an hour or two.

I took some tea up to Ellen's room and we had a session with the ludo board, but during the second game she pushed it away saying that she did not feel like playing any more. I took her temperature and was dismayed to find that it had climbed back to a hundred and two.

Naturally, I impressed upon myself that this was nothing for a child and that fevers always got worse in the evening, but all the while another me was telling myself that I had taken a sight too much on my own shoulders and would have done better to listen to my elders. I effected a compromise between these two clamorous voices by telling Toby that while Ellen was not worse, neither was she a great deal better and we should ask the doctor to call in the morning. He agreed with alacrity and I got to work on the telephone.

Dr Macintosh asked if we would mind his paying an early visit so as to fit it in before his surgery, which was usually heavy on Mondays. He would be over at eight-thirty, if I had no objection. I had none whatever, for I knew that no other member of the household would be stirring at that hour, and if I were in for a scolding for not having called him earlier I preferred it to be held *in camera*.

I warned Ellen of the impending visit, but of course with the perversity of all invalids she was already looking much brighter and even wanted to get up and have a bath. I talked her out of this idea and having tucked her up for the night and feeling in need of some fresh air I put on some gum-boots and walked on to the Common.

The rain had stopped and the air was fragrant, as though it had been washed in expensive bath essence. I sniffed it with pleasure as I plodded down to the Bull.

There were several reasons for making this my destination, but if the hope of meeting Robin Price lurked somewhere among them it lurked exceeding small. My principle object was to ascertain whether Marge, or her relations, had suffered any upsets during the night, since there was always an outside chance that my secondary diagnosis of a mild form of food poisoning had been the correct one. Another motive, which it was not my intention to reveal, was to learn of any further developments concerning the disappearance of Mrs Cornford, which I assumed would form the main topic of conversation in the saloon bar.

I was disappointed in both quests. Marge was extremely cut up to hear about the poor poppet, but assured me that she had suffered nothing of the kind herself, and that Brenda and Jack had both been fit as fiddles when they drove off to Luton that morning. She also said Not to Worry, because kiddies of that age went up and down like one o'clock and Ellen would doubtless be as chipper as I pleased by the morning.

It was plain that she was not giving her full attention to the subject, because Leslie had arrived back from Canada and neither of them was willing to talk of anything except the marvellous old thrash which had taken place on the other side of the Atlantic.

I even sank so low as to introduce the subject of Mrs Cornford myself, but to no avail. Marge turned to serve a customer just as I spoke and I was not sure whether she had not heard me, or was indicating that such topics were bad for business. It was mystifying, but I felt it would be unseemly to press the point, so I listened attentively while Leslie told me some strange tales about the licensing laws of Toronto, observed that we were a lot better off than some and, in due course, drifted away again.

The reactions of Matilda and Toby were scarcely more rewarding when we all assembled for dinner. The story I had heard from Mrs Parkes fell on stony ground, because they knew it already. Sylvia, inevitably, had been to church that morning and the news had been poured into her no doubt reluctant ear by several of the congregation immediately after the service.

Toby expressed the devout hope that Mrs Cornford had run off, a very long way, and that Mr Cornford would run after her and never catch up, and Matilda mentioned that Sylvia could vouch for Mrs Cornford's having been on the Common the previous afternoon. Gerry had been taking his afternoon walk and had seen her.

I had left this part of my tale until the last, believing it to be the *bonne bouche* and I was most put out to find that Sylvia had stolen my thunder. From being a key witness in the affair I was reduced, by her officiousness, to the vulgar ranks of the crowd.

Inspired by the urge to recapture my lost prestige I remarked knowingly that poor old Bron would doubtless turn up at the bottom of Dead Man's Gully and it would be one hell of a job to find out whether she had fallen, or been pushed.

It was a flippancy which I soon had cause to regret.

TWELVE

TOBY was a great admirer of Dr Macintosh, an attitude which was not shared by many in the neighbourhood. There were numerous people who would have gone to their graves, or to his partner, which almost amounted to the same thing, sooner than consult him.

The aversion cannot have been on account of his medical skill, which bordered on genius, but he did possess two characteristics which, to put it mildly, accorded oddly with his profession. He was amazingly indiscreet and he was as confirmed a hypochondriac as Toby himself. He was always asking for glasses of warm milk to help his ulcers along, and while slowly sipping them would regale one with hair-raising details of the mental and physical maladies of his other patients. Apart from the milk, he appeared to subsist exclusively on pep pills and free samples from the pharmaceutical firms, all of which he conscientiously tried out on himself.

These two eccentricities, while undermining the confidence of many people, naturally endeared him to Toby.

Ellen was eating cornflakes, when, true to his word, he bowled up at half past eight on Monday morning, and he helped himself to some milk from her breakfast tray, downed it with a couple of pills and began to tell us about a new Swedish cereal which was supposed to contain pretty well everything ever invented in the way of proteins and vitamins.

He clamped his fingers on Ellen's pulse, for about half a second, asked me what her temperature was without bothering to verify it, pushed her tongue down with a teaspoon and then borrowed a pen in order to write out some prescriptions. It was cursory in the extreme, but I knew from experience that she could consider herself cured.

Walking out to the gate to see him off, I thanked him for coming so promptly:

'No trouble at all,' he said, 'I've got another patient up here and I'm taking him down to the hospital this morning for some X-rays. Funny chap, name of Dickson. Expect you've come across him?'

'Oh, Peter? Yes, rather. Is his ankle worse?'

'Worse? No, healed up beautifully. We just want to get the plaster off and take a few snaps, but he should be as right as a trivet.'

'You don't say? I understood it was a multiple fracture and that he'd be in plaster for months.'

'Stuff and nonsense. Silly little crack, that's all it was. He's a fearful fusspot; screams for anaesthetics if he splits a thumb-nail. Still, we all have our funny ways, don't you know? You've got those prescriptions? I'd run down to Storhampton and get them made up right away, if I were you.'

'Yes, I will. There's nothing seriously wrong with her, is there? I mean, you won't need to come again?'

'Oh, I'll look in tomorrow. Can't promise when, but you keep her in bed till I come, no matter what she says. I'll try and get over in the morning.'

Nevertheless, he was back at five o'clock the same evening. I immediately took this as a sign of some threatened complication in Ellen's illness, but he reassured me, saying that he had been called out for a job of work, only a mile or two away and had thought to save himself two journeys, by coming to us as well.

Matilda had driven off to Brighton some hours before, but Toby was at home and delighted, though not in the least surprised, by this development. I think, if he could have chosen, he would not have let a day go by without at least two visits from Dr Macintosh, or, better still, have had him to live in the house with us.

He gave us a good account of Ellen and said that she could get up for a bit the next day, but must keep on with the medicines. He was then easily persuaded to stay on for a chat and even consented to take a little soda-water in his glass of milk. He and Toby enjoyed themselves, swopping symptoms for a while, until, growing bored and hoping to break it up, I asked what had brought the doctor out to Roakes twice in one day.

To my amazement he looked at me sternly, just as though I had committed some breach of etiquette. Then he said:

'Oh well, no doubt you'll be hearing all about it sooner or later. I was up here doing a bit of work for the police, as it happens.'

'How very interesting,' Toby said. 'Do tell us about it. I always thought they lived such healthy lives. Although, of course, some of them do drive much too fast.'

'I wouldn't know about that. I was called in in my capacity as police surgeon. It's a job which is largely confined to motor accidents, I grant you, but not this time. I had to go and view some remains.'

'Oh, how frightful for you! Remains of what?'

'Your neighbour, no less. Mrs Cornford. Not a patient of mine, as it happens.'

'Oh, has she turned up?' I asked stupidly.

'Turned up is one way of putting it. She was face down when I saw her. In a ditch at the bottom of Stoney Woods. Know where I mean?'

'Was she dead?'

'Oh, very. Been like it for twenty-four hours, too, by the look of it. We'll know more about that, when we've done the post-mortem.'

There cannot be a doubt that if I had heard this news only a few hours earlier I should have rivalled Sylvia in my burning curiosity to learn all the gruesome details, but coming when it did it made singularly little impact, for my circumstances had changed to an unprecedented degree. My agent had telephoned during the morning to say that there was the chance of a film part in the offing. Some superannuated French actress had been lined up to star in an Anglo-French production and I was being considered for the part of her daughter. I had asked if a French accent would be required, as I was good at it, but my agent said she knew nothing at all, except that I was required to be at the film studios for a camera test on Thursday morning, and she thought she could wangle me fifty a day.

It was thus a very fraught period for me, with my big chance dangling just beyond my nose and the knowledge that it might yet be snatched away and it would have taken more than the death of one unlovely, unloved female to rouse me to my normal inquisitive heights.

Nor was Toby's reaction any more encouraging. He loved to hear about other people's minor ailments; their death was quite another matter. The mere mention of it was abhorrent to him and he turned pale and stared at Dr Macintosh, with dislike, disbelief and apprehension on his face. We must have been a very stodgy audience and rarely can one of his indiscretions have been so sadly wasted.

Out of sheer sympathy I exerted myself and said: 'Poor thing! How ever did it happen?' and simultaneously Toby blurted:

'Did she fall, or was she pushed?'

I really thought the shock must have unhinged him and I spoke sharply:

'Really, Toby, how can you? It wasn't even funny at the time and I certainly don't care to be reminded of it now.'

Not surprisingly Dr Macintosh was casting appraising looks at both of us and I was all too painfully aware that we were supplying him with a splendid store of raw material. 'What are you both on about?' he asked.

'Oh,' I said feebly. 'It was nothing, absolutely nothing. Just an idiot remark I made last night. We'd all heard that Mrs Cornford was missing, you see, and she wasn't much liked by people around here, well, I mean, you know, I made this daft sort of joke.'

I limped off into silence, not daring to ask what had happened, being convinced he would say it was not yet known whether she fell or had been pushed, but Toby, who seemed bent on destroying me, said glumly:

'I suppose it was one or the other?'

Dr Macintosh glanced at him reflectively. 'Interesting theory, but I wouldn't care to give an opinion myself. I was simply called in to estimate what time she kicked the bucket and so on. Don't know what ideas the police may have. They'll keep an open mind until after the postmortem, I shouldn't wonder.'

'I suppose suicide is the most likely,' I said. 'She was more than a trifle cracked.'

I thought from his expression that he was about to utter a rebuke, but evidently he thought better of it, for all he said was:

'There'll be no end of twaddle flying around before long. Only to be expected. You can say what you like to me, I'm in a privileged position, but I wouldn't advise either of you to broadcast your jokes and theories outside these walls. In fact, I'd keep a watch on it if I were you.'

Having stirred up this unpalatable mixture of insinuation, threat and innuendo and flung it in our faces, he left us. Not liking the look of Toby, who was sunk in gloom and liable to snap my head off, I went upstairs to tell Ellen the glad tidings about getting up in the morning.

She had just emerged from her bath and was brushing her hair at the dressing-table. Her reflection in the glass as I stood talking to her from the doorway was angelic in its purity.

I said: 'Oh, by the way, Ellen, Mrs Cornford has had an accident and I'm afraid the poor thing is dead.'

I meant it for the best, but I should have been shot. Ellen closed her eyes and the hairbrush clattered down. She swayed forward over the dressing-table and thinking she was going to faint I darted forward and caught her by the shoulders. However, she was rigid in my grip and recognising in a bemused way that this was incompatible with loss of consciousness, I let go one of my hands and tilted up her head. Her face was pale, but her eyes were open again and I said:

'Come on, now, love, you've been overdoing it. Hop back into bed and I'll sit with you for a bit, until you go to sleep.'

She obeyed without saying a word, and as soon as she was in bed, closed her eyes again and lay still.

'Would you like me to read to you?'

She shook her head.

'There's nothing wrong, is there?'

She answered with another head shake, and I said with forced brightness: 'You see how it is? Darling old doctor was quite right when he said you weren't to get up today. You've been smitten by a beastly bug and it's knocked the stuffing out of you. You'll be as right as anything by the morning.'

This time she did not even bother to signify that she had heard me, and I could hardly blame her. There was little hope of convincing her that her malaise was of a purely physical nature when I only half believed it myself.

THIRTEEN

(i)

'YOU!' I said dramatically and with justification, I consider, for it was a truly dramatic moment.

I had been passing through the hall with a pile of books for Ellen, part of my campaign to keep her in bed for the day, when I heard the front door-bell ring. I put the books down and went to open it, and there, on the doorstep, stood Robin Price.

There was another man with him, and Robin himself looked sleeker and more formal than he had in his Sunday morning, pub-crawl outfit. Elucidation was soon forthcoming.

'I do apologise for bothering you,' he said.

'No bother at all. I was right by the door, as it happens.'

'I should explain that we are here in our official capacity. This is Sergeant Baines and I am Detective Inspector Price.'

'How do you do?' I said with commendable aplomb. 'My cousin must have been parking on an awful lot of double lines, for both of you to have come.'

'We aren't here to haul him in for that, although I should be most grateful if he could spare us a moment or two.'

'Of his valuable time?'

'Precisely. I should also explain that we are from the Dedley C.I.D. Would it be possible for us to come inside, do you think?'

'Oh, please do. How rude of me! Kindly step this way.'

I led the way into the drawing-room, composing my features and running through my part as I went. I was just the merest bit rattled, though not so seriously as anyone else might have been in my place. Having just completed six episodes of a crime serial I was pretty well up in police procedures and jargon, and, apart from the initial shock, nothing outside my experience had so far occurred. It was a relief to find Life travelling on parallel lines with Art.

'Please be seated,' I said. 'And I will fetch my cousin.'

'Just a second, Miss Crichton. Before you go I wonder if you would be so kind as to answer a few questions yourself?'

'By all means.'

'Won't you sit down?'

I did so and he went on: 'We are making some inquiries about the death of your neighbour, Mrs Cornford, and I understand that you may have been one of the last people to see her.'

'Yes, I may. Ought I to telephone my solicitor?'

'I am sure that won't be necessary. Sergeant Baines is only taking some notes for our records. We want to try and narrow down the time when the accident occurred.'

'So it was an accident?'

'Had you reason to think otherwise?'

'Oh no, no. None at all.'

'Quite sure?'

It was on the cards that he had talked to Dr Macintosh and so I said: 'Well, she might have done herself in. I mean, she was as whacky as a glue-pot. You ought to know that.'

'My personal knowledge of her has no bearing. And in any case it is not her state of mind we are concerned about at present. What I would like you to tell me, if you possibly could, is when exactly you saw her and what she was doing at the time.'

'Not to the absolute minute, no, but I can tell you this much. It was around half past three on Saturday afternoon when we – when I saw her. Could have been five minutes earlier or later, not more.'

'Well, that's most helpful and you're positive about it?'

'Yes, I am, and in case you're asking yourself how I can be so precise, the answer is that my cousin and I were due at the theatre in Dedley at five-fifteen. We had to allow an hour to

get there and park the car and so on, and I was watching the
time rather carefully.'

'Well, that was very fortunate for us. Thank you so much.
You didn't happen to pass her on the road later, or anything
of that kind?'

'No, we didn't. She was travelling in the opposite direction,
for one thing.'

'Yes, I see.'

'Of course, dozens of other people may have seen her after
three-thirty.'

'They may, but it does not appear that anyone did. What
made you say that she was going in the opposite direction to
Dedley?'

'Because that's what she was doing.'

'You must forgive me. I seem to have been misinformed.
We were given to understand that you saw her from this house
and that she was walking on the Common.'

'That is correct,' I said. Everyone in the television had said:
That is correct,' when they were hauled up for questioning,
and I thought it had the right ring about it.

'Nevertheless, something gave you the impression that she
was making towards Storhampton. I wonder if you can tell us
what it was.'

'Well, you see, she came on to the Common from the
Dedley side, up by the Bricklayers'. She crossed over, well,
not straight over, but the result was the same and she went off
the Common at the other end, by the Bull. Unless she meant
to make a complete circle, by road and get back to the beginning again, the assumption is that she was walking towards
Storhampton and had used the Common as a short cut.'

'Except that it wouldn't be, would it?'

'Wouldn't be what?'

'A short cut. It would have been quicker to stick to the
road. You don't think she had some other reason for being on
the Common?'

'Well, now you mention it, when I first saw her I concluded she was going home, but if so she must have changed her mind. She was pretty erratic, by all accounts.'

'You may be right and you've been extremely helpful. It is lucky for us that you are so observant. I take it that your cousin saw all this, as well?'

'My cousin?'

He said apologetically: 'When you started to tell us about it, you said "we", then changed to "I". I assumed you were including your cousin, but then quite rightly decided to speak only of what you had seen with your own eyes?'

'That is correct,' I said.

I was jolted, but not unduly so. Inspector Margetson, in the play, had behaved exactly like this, always appearing to miss every trick and then pouncing on the unwary out of the blue, and showing that he had known all along which cupboard the skeleton was concealed in. The pattern was familiar, but nevertheless I resolved to be on my guard.

'Well, that's that, then, and thank you again, Miss Crichton.'

'It was nothing at all,' I said. 'Shall I fetch Toby now?'

'Your cousin? Oh no, I don't see that we need to trouble him, just at present. Perhaps, later, it may be necessary, but you have been most exact and I have no doubt he would corroborate everything you've told us. He can hardly have anything to add to it, since you both left for Dedley together. I think that is what you said, isn't it?'

I can be as bright as the next person on occasions and I saw exactly how the misunderstanding had occurred. The English language being ambiguous in this respect, two separate cousins had been woven into my narrative and he had taken them to be one and the same. I am not quite sure what decided me to leave him in the dark, for as motives go mine were a trifle mixed. The main one, undeniably, was to keep Ellen out of it as far as I possibly could, and by contributing unwittingly to this end he had persuaded me that it might continue to be feasible; yet there was an element of concealment, for its own sake, too, and even a third factor.

I realised that he was under no obligation to tell every female, on meeting her for the first time, exactly how he earned his living, but I felt obscurely that he had owed it to me to do so. The interrogation, so polite and relaxed on the surface, had, in its undertones, been something of a sparring match, and I was not altogether displeased to have come out of it with one thumping, unspoken, undetected lie to my credit.

'I can't think why you need Sergeant Baines at all,' I said gaily. 'Your own memory is quite reliable enough, I should say, without all those notes.'

'No, not always,' he replied, getting up. 'Which reminds me; if you should remember anything else, anything at all that you've overlooked, we should be most grateful to hear about it. Here is my card and you can telephone this number at any time and leave a message if I should be out.'

'Yes, of course, but won't you both have a drink before you go?'

'No, thank you very much.'

'Not while you're on duty?'

'That is correct,' he said.

(ii)

I stood in the doorway and watched them go down the garden path. There was a brief parley at the gate and then Sergeant Baines turned and walked away towards White Gables. The Inspector came back up the path, towards me.

'Forgotten something after all?' I asked.

'No, remembered something.'

'Like?'

'Like telling you how much I enjoyed your play the other night. You were superb, honestly. I'm off duty, at the moment.'

'In that case, come in and have a drink while the moment lasts, and you can tell me all over again.'

'It must be wonderful to have a talent like yours,' he said, when I had stocked him up with gin and bitters.

'It is kind of you to say so, but it's not all that clever, really. It's in the blood, for one thing. I come from a long line of pros. Apart from the fact that our training started in the nursery, I spent two years at a Drama school and three more in provincial rep, so I ought to have learnt something, by now. When it comes to natural talent, I put you far above me.'

'I've never been on the stage in my life. What on earth makes you say that?'

'I said "natural talent". If I'd been asked to guess, the other morning, what your job was, I think policeman would have come about a hundred and third on my list. I might have said the Navy, but that's as near as I'd have got.'

'That was just the pink gin?'

'That and a sort of blue-eyed, outdoor look about you.'

'I can see you're pulling my leg.'

'No, honestly, I'm only laughing because I've just remembered how you smiled, when Marge said they didn't get the coppers around on a Sunday. You see how good your disguise is? Psychiatrist was my guess, but flatfoot, never!'

'I expect you're like a lot of people and have all sorts of preconceived and largely erroneous notions about policemen.'

'Oh, I daresay. Just as people have all sorts of preconceived notions about actors.'

'Which usually turn out to be false?'

'On the contrary. Which usually turn out to be dead accurate. That's the whole trouble. It's like all the crude jokes about mothers-in-law and seaside landladies; they're mostly just a grotesque version of the truth.'

'But you'll admit there are exceptions to every rule?'

'Yes, I'll admit that; and, pending evidence to disprove it, I am prepared to say that we are two of them.'

He seemed relieved to hear this and we raised our glasses, in a toast. Then he looked at me warily, as though there was still something on his mind which he did not know how to express, and to help him along, I said:

'But you didn't come back here to do a public relations job for the police, or even to tell me what a brilliant actress I am?'

'No, you're right. There was something else, something I wanted very much to ask you.'

'I see. Have you gone back on duty again?'

'Far from it. In fact, if this case is cleared up by then, which seems probable, I shall have a whole twenty-four hours off-duty, starting at midday on Thursday. I've been trying to summon the courage to ask if there's a chance of your spending part of it with me, like lunch, for instance?'

I sighed. 'It's a lovely idea and I'd have said yes, like a shot, only we're box and cox, I'm afraid. Thursday is my working day, this week.'

I told him briefly about my forthcoming camera test, and, professing complete ignorance of such matters, he questioned me closely on what was involved. When he had got it straight, he said:

'But you'd be through by about six in the evening, whatever happened?'

'Oh, sure. Most likely, hours before that, only I couldn't make any appointments, in case of delays; but they certainly wouldn't pay overtime rates on my behalf, and it's a very strict union.'

'So, if I were to come to your studio some time after six, to collect you, we might be able to have dinner? Or would you be too tired by then?'

'Not a bit too tired.'

'Oh, marvellous! So may I do that?'

'With pleasure,' I said, and told him how to get past the watch-dog on the main gate and where and when to meet me.

He said: 'I'll be there at six. It's wonderful of you. Now I must go and retrieve poor Baines. Till Thursday, then, and I'm looking forward to it most awfully.'

So, indeed was I, the most cheering aspect of all being that Thursday's ordeal no longer held quite the same terrors. However badly I flopped, I should still have the prospect of an agreeable evening in store, to compensate. How thankful I was, after all, to have made that trip to the King's Road boutique.

FOURTEEN

MATILDA had driven her own car to Brighton and was spending the week with friends who owned a mansion known as Otterway Cottage a few miles from Haywards Heath. So Ellen and I were reduced to the bicycle once more. However, the weather was no longer inviting enough to tempt us out on excursions and we both had a horror of the local woods and meadows at this time. Neither of us mentioned it, but I am sure that, like me, she pictured a corpse, face down, in every ditch.

There was no visible activity, either on the part of the police, or the inmates, at the Manor. So far as we knew, Douglas Cornford was still incarcerated there, but a car had arrived shortly after Robin's visit to us, and an hour or two later had driven away again with the children inside. The house was gaunt, silent and secretive as ever.

We also learnt from Mrs Parkes and similar sources that there was to be an inquest at Dedley on Thursday morning and that the funeral would take place at the end of the week, in Birmingham. The latter news came as a mighty relief to everyone, for had it been held locally, whether to be or not to be present would have been the question, indeed.

Sylvia had sent out invitations for a Bring and Buy Coffee Party in aid of the orphans on Wednesday morning, and it was a measure of the suspicion and hostility which surrounded the Cornfords that it occurred to no one that she would cancel it.

These semi-commercial, semi-social coffee mornings had been an unknown phenomenon to me until I visited Roakes, though, for all I knew, they may be commonplace in all rural communities.

Admission was strictly by invitation, but card holders were still required to pay to go in and each was expected to bring some contribution to the value of at least a pound. This entitled them to a cup of weak coffee, the run of the hostess's drawing-room and garden and the privilege of buying some article priced at at least a pound, although preferably not the same one as they had brought with them.

Attendance was normally high, as most people seemed to enjoy wasting a morning chatting to acquaintances and spending money, so long as it was done in an aura of charitable endeavour.

Having nothing better to do, Ellen and I decided to patronise Sylvia's effort, and at a quarter to eleven we walked up the track to her house, clutching, respectively, a bottle of sherry which I had whipped from the store cupboard and a bunch of roses which Ellen had snaffled while Mr Parkes' back was turned.

There were about forty cars parked outside the house and Sylvia received us on the doorstep, blessing us for coming and begging us to sample some of her little macaroons which she had slaved over for hours the night before. All of which indicated that we were about to be fleeced in the most ladylike fashion.

There was a flurry of irritable women in the hall, all asking each other what they had done with the scissors and what price to put on that talcum powder, with the Boots label on it. These were the working bees; the drones were sampling the macaroons and droning away in the drawing-room, but before we could join them we had first to hand over our offerings and then to pay our entrance fee.

Peter was in charge of this department, very self-important behind his trestle table, with his money boxes and different coloured rolls of tickets spread out in front of him. His foot was ostentatiously propped on a stool, but I noticed that the plaster had been replaced by bandages.

'Five shillings for you,' he said, holding up the purple roll, 'Kiddies half price.'

Ellen strongly objected to being called a kiddie, but I thought it was worth it to save half a crown, so requested one of each.

'Oh dear, haven't you got any change?' he groaned. 'If anyone else gives me a pound note, I shall go raving mad, I know I shall.'

'How's the ankle?' I asked to pacify him, as he reluctantly counted out twelve and sixpence change.

'Not too good. Still under the doctor. He thinks it'll be weeks, before it clears up.'

'You've got the plaster off, though. That must be a relief?'

'Yes, they had to take that off. I was in agony. Nobody knows what it was like.'

This I doubted, but there was no time for further medical bulletins, because people were pressing up behind us with more pound notes to drive him mad.

'Paul's on the clock golf,' he called after us. 'Do be lambies and go and help him out.'

We had to run the gauntlet of two raffles and the home-made cake stall before we could get there, but we finally ran him to earth on Sylvia's newly shaven lawn, handing out putters at a shilling a go.

'What's the prize?' I asked.

'Oh, aren't you mercenary? You aren't here to enjoy your-selves, you know. Come on, Ellen, have a go and see if you can't trounce Auntie.'

I suppose that Peter and Paul were uncles to so many, that they could not envisage any other relationship between the generations, but he was so much more chirpy than when I had last seen him, practically dancing on air, in fact, that I did not risk dashing his spirits by correcting him. In any case, if Ellen could get through the morning as a kiddie, it was not for me to grouse about being an auntie.

We played a couple of rounds to oblige him, and then moved on to the bowling pitch where Leslie was in charge. Still no prizes, and it was rather hot work, so when I had sent my first ball charging into a lavender bush and set an Ena Harkness tottering on her roots with my second I gave up and left Ellen to play on her own.

I had noticed Miss Davenport among the bevy of women in the drawing-room. She looked more bizarre than ever in her dusty, black cape in that throng, all of whom had evidently collected their pastel cashmeres and light blue hair from the dry cleaners that very morning. I took my coffee cup and sat down beside her.

'I hear you were on the box, the other evening,' she said. 'First-rate, so they tell me. Didn't see it, myself.'

'You didn't miss much.'

'Oh, I'd have looked, you can bet your boots, only I don't happen to have a set. Just as well, I daresay. Better things to do with my time than stare at all that tosh. No offence, you know.'

'None taken,' I said, and instantly began working out a scheme whereby Toby should give a coffee party in aid of the broken-down-scriptwriters' fund and that the first prize in the raffle should be a television set, to be won by Miss Davenport.

I recognised that there were certain obstacles to be overcome before the fulfilment of this neat plan, but I was only able to give half my mind to them because she was saying: 'Give me the live theatre, any day, don't you agree?'

'Yes, any day. Do you go often?'

'Hardly ever. But I like to know it's still there, if you know what I mean? Read all the reviews, you know. Some of this modern stuff in the West End doesn't sound much in my line, but I saw a rattling good one, last Saturday. Your cousin's piece, it was. Tophole.'

'Oh, really? Not the early performance, by any chance?'

'That's the one. Don't care much for being out late at night. Pooch gets worried and sets up a howl if he's left on his own. Annoys the neighbours.'

Taking Pooch to be the current alias for Fido and picturing the reactions of Peter and Paul when the howling started, I could easily see what she meant.

'Funny we didn't see you,' I said. 'Ellen and I went to that performance.'

'Nothing funny about it, my dear. I didn't see you either, but, then, you probably weren't in the upper circle.'

'No, my cousin was able to get us free tickets. How did it go from where you were sitting? I mean, was everyone around you enjoying it?'

'With knobs on. We were all convulsed. Friend who'd taken me in her car practically had to be carried out when he kept running round the breakfast table changing all the plates. He's a real corker that John Headley, don't you agree?'

'Jimmie,' I said automatically, 'Jimmie Headley.' Part of my mind was still grappling with the problem of doing good by stealth, in providing her with a television set for her lonely evenings and I must confess that I had only retained the vaguest recollection of the scene in question, but I politely agreed that it had been highly risible.

Ellen appeared in the French window, looking round for me, and I waved to her. She came across to us, carrying a bunch of pansies.

'Ho, Ellen! What's the meaning of this? Not at school, today?'

'Would you like these?' Ellen asked, sighing patiently and holding out the flowers. 'They would look pretty in the little pottery vase you got when you went to Cornwall with your governess.'

Miss Davenport looked suitably taken aback. 'Bless me, what a memory the child has! Very kind of you, my dear. Sure you don't want them, yourself?'

'They are a present,' Ellen said reprovingly.

'They were a present for you really, Tess,' she told me, as we were walking home.

'But you gave them to Miss Davenport to create a diversion?'

'What's that?'

'To divert her away from questions about why you weren't at school and why you don't join the Brownies and all that jazz?'

'She's dotty. Nobody goes to school in August.'

'Is it all genuine dottiness, do you think?' I asked. 'Or does she rather overdo the eccentric spinster act?'

I do not know why this thought had occurred to me, for until then I had never suspected Miss Davenport of affectations of any kind. Plainly, Ellen still did not and she said:

'Oh, she's as mad as the march hare; mad, bad and dangerous to know, that's what she is.'

I reflected that she might be so retarded in Eng. lang. as not to know the meaning of diversion, but she was certainly well up in her Eng. lit.

FIFTEEN

(i)

I HAD been severely exercised in my mind over the problem of getting to the Studios punctually on Thursday morning.

I had to be made up and on the set by nine o'clock, so it was a right puzzle, but Toby came to my rescue. He insisted on hiring a taxi at his own expense, and it had been settled that the driver would call for me at seven o'clock.

Everything went according to plan and none of the horrors I had anticipated came to pass. I had never worked with, or even met the director before, but he had the reputation of being an actor's director and deservedly so in my opinion. He gave me plenty of time to study my two scenes and told me that I could have as many rehearsals as I wanted. None of that alarming improvisation for him, thank goodness. I have always thought that sort of thing should be reserved for amateurs, when it can be effective; for actors who have been trained to project a character from the inside out it is a method which requires immense practice to be convincing.

I read straight through the scenario and then concentrated on the two short scenes for my test. One was with an actor whom I knew slightly, who was being considered for the part of the family solicitor, and the other with the young Frenchman who had been cast for the girl's brother.

The situation was that an ageing French actress had been married in her obscure youth to an Englishman, but had tossed him away like a worn-out *gant* as soon as she became a celebrity. They had been parted for fifteen years before the opening of the story. The son of the marriage had stayed in Paris with his mother, but the daughter, quite rightly in my opinion, had elected to be brought up in England by her father. The plot, such as it was, hinged on the efforts of the now remorseful and hard-up French lady, aided and abetted by her son, hampered and hindered by her daughter, to bring about a reconciliation.

The first session went without a hitch, but the second was less successful owing to some unprofessional larking about by my opposite number. He was a popular performer, in his own back yard, with the looks of an angel, but he patently resented being called on to the set so early in the morning and for such a purpose. He told me repeatedly, as we waited for camera angles to be set up, that in France such practices were *inconnus* and *inouïs* and to demonstrate his contempt for them used every trick in the book to trip me up and to keep his left profile in camera. It would have been no surprise to me if he had whipped out his handkerchief and flapped it in front of my face. However, I have nerves of steel when it comes to a crisis, and the director and cameraman were both on my side, so I resisted the urge to push his beautiful face in and came through it with feathers comparatively unruffled.

After it was over he switched on another André and became the jolly, friendly *copain*, even offering me a lift back to London, in his hired Daimler. This encouraged me to believe that he was resigned to my getting the part and had therefore reasoned that to kiss and make up would now be the intelligent move.

I thanked him profusely, but said that I had my own transport laid on. I did not go into details, but, in fact, if it had been laid on for me by anyone else but Robin I might have jumped into the Daimler without another thought, for things had gone so smoothly that it was still only one o'clock.

However, faced with five hours to waste, I would as soon waste them in a film studio as anywhere else on earth, for the simple reason that it is normally half full of other people, who are doing exactly the same thing. Between frenzied bursts of activity, there are prolonged, yawning lulls, when to the naked eye nothing whatever happens and, should a real hitch occur, as it does with monotonous regularity, an actor may be on call from eight in the morning until four or five in the afternoon without ever needing to leave his dressing-room.

I found one or two familiar faces in the Commissariat and lunched in the company of a dowdy trio who were filming on Stage One. It was an adaptation of a D.H. Lawrence story, and the Art Department had transformed the entire stage into a coal-mine, complete with pit-head and lift-cage and a mock-up of the underground section, where the leading man was shortly to be walled up. They told me that they hadn't much to do that afternoon except to stand around, moaning a bit and twitching their blade shawls, as they waited for the bad news, but invited me on to the set, to watch for a while, and inspect the wonders of the re-created Black Country, *circa* 1920.

So I mooned away a couple of hours in this fashion and then returned to the make-up department to get my face and hair attended to and to put on my new dress and coat, which I had brought with me in a suitcase.

At five-thirty I presented myself, according to instructions, at the little projection theatre beside the cutting-rooms, where I was joined by the director and a few of his henchmen and women and we saw the rushes of the morning's shooting. This is always an ordeal and I was rigid with tension before the screening began, and limp with disappointment by the time it was over. However, I got a friendly little hand from some of the technicians and a big, friendly kiss from the director, so I walked out with my head high, ready to fight another day.

At two minutes past six I stationed myself at the entrance to the artists' car park, thinking how rare and splendid it was to have the time, the place and the person, all combined, not to mention the clothes.

(ii)

Half an hour later I was still standing in the same spot, but my thoughts had taken a different turn. Sackcloth and ashes would have been overdressing for the mood I had sunk into by then.

Various acquaintances had sauntered out and none failed to inquire, with varying degrees of jocularity, whether I had been stood up, was waiting for their autograph or wanted to cadge a lift to London. I had vowed to accept the very next offer in the last bracket, which might come my way, when at long last I saw the Sunbeam bowling up the concrete drive towards me.

I would not consider myself to be especially volatile, yet in the ten or twelve seconds which elapsed before the car came level my mood had passed from despair, to relief, to delight, to wounded pride, to cool indifference; and yet when it drew up beside me I heard myself saying:

'Oh goodness, I have been so worried.'

'Not half so worried as I've been, on my honour. The last half hour has been a nightmare, wondering if you'd still be here. You're an angel to have waited and I'll spend the rest of my life making it up to you.'

I climbed into the car, saying: 'That will do nicely. There may even be times, during the next fifty or sixty years, when I shall be forced to keep you waiting. I shall try to prevent it.'

'Please do. I could never stand the strain.'

'Where are we going?'

'If you've no objection, I'd like, first of all, to find somewhere near by where it's quiet and we can have a drink, which I badly need, and while I tell you what has held me up, which you may or may not want to hear.'

'Oh yes, I'm interested in every tiny thing.'

He leant across to kiss me and tell me how wonderful I was, and I directed him to a pub in the village where we could have a drink in the garden and watch Old Father Thames go rolling along, Down to the Mighty Sea. I explained that it was always crammed to the lid with studio people, at lunch-time, but silent as the grave, in the evening.

It turned out even as I had promised, but when we had installed ourselves in deck-chairs, with every prospect pleasing, the thoughtful frown remained.

'Tell me the bad news,' I said.

'It's not too good, I'm afraid, Tessa, and the worst of it is that I'd so much like to discuss it with you, and naturally I'm not supposed to do that, even though it affects you, in a way.'

'It's about your work?'

He nodded.

'Something to do with the Cornford business, in fact?'

'Yes. That's why I was late. I had to cancel my day off. I couldn't think of any way of letting you know, short of requesting the local station to send a constable to dig you out, and I was afraid you might not care for that.'

'Oh, I don't think I'd have minded. Stranger things have happened.'

He smiled, looking more relaxed.

'But, Robin, I thought you banked on having the whole case sewn up and tucked away in the files, by this time?'

'We did, but things have turned out differently. You know the inquest was this morning?'

'Yes. What was the verdict?'

'We had assumed it would be either misadventure or suicide while the balance of the mind, etc., and naturally we hoped the Coroner would go all out for the first. It was true that she was full up to the neck with tranquillisers, but it was an even chance that she had slipped, then passed out, rolled down the slope and eventually died from exposure. The odds were against her having deliberately killed herself, and in the event we didn't get a suicide verdict.'

'Why are you so worried, then?' I asked, and, for all my care and deliberation, my glass slithered as I put it down on the table. 'What was the verdict?'

'None. They've adjourned until next week. So it's all sixes and sevens again. Don't worry, I'm not being indiscreet in telling you this much. The inquest was public and you can read all about it in the local papers if you've a mind to.'

'I'd rather you told me.'

'Well, that's it. The inquest was adjourned for lack of evidence, and we start again from scratch.'

'But do explain one thing to me. Do the police usually fix everything up with the Coroner in advance? I mean, is it rigged to get exactly the verdict you want?'

'Certainly not. What an idea! But the point is we're in on it from the beginning. We see the body, we have a complete set of photographs and, as you know, we take statements from everybody who might conceivably know anything relevant. Most important of all, we have the medical report on the post-mortem. There's usually not much guesswork needed, with all that.'

'Was it the medical bit that came unstuck this time?'

'How did you know?' he asked sharply.

'I didn't know, I inferred. But I do know Dr Macintosh.'

He sighed. 'I wish I'd thought of asking you about him. I've not worked with him before. Storhampton is only a part of our district and we've not had an event of this kind since I came here. What about Dr Macintosh?"

'Clever as a cartload, but unconventional in some departments. What happened?'

'He gave his report in a perfectly straightforward way and the Coroner took him through a few of the details which he wanted expanded. That's a normal routine and it's really just a way of thumping the point home to the jury in terms they can understand. It seemed to me that Macintosh began to go a bit out of line at that point because he enlarged on some facts about the contusions and bruises on the skull which the Coroner hadn't even asked him for, but I wasn't specially bothered. They often like to show off a bit. It wasn't until right at the end, when he was asked formally to state the cause of death, that he dropped his tiny bombshell.'

'And said she'd been knocked off?'

'Really, Tessa, your inferences are pretty near the mark. Are you sure you haven't been reading it?'

'How could I? But did he really say that?'

'Not in those words, but it amounted to much the same thing. He calmly announced that he'd given some thought to the matter after submitting his report, which was most unethical of him, as I hardly need to tell you, and had reached the conclusion that these bruises could equally well have been inflicted before she fell and could therefore have contributed to her death.'

'Meaning that she'd been killed first and then chucked over?'

'Or else knocked unconscious and then been pushed, which is a very different cup of tea, as you can see, from being in a half-drugged state, tripping over a root, or something of the sort and then pitching headlong. It's a goodish way down and it had seemed reasonable to suppose that she would have collected quite a few bumps and bruises on the way.'

'If you had known what he intended to say, could you have stopped him?'

'Lord, no. It's a mystery to me where you get your ideas about police methods. All the same, we could have prevented his blurting it all out in the witness box at this stage of the game. We could have had things postponed for twenty-four hours and got it all sorted out. The way he's played it, we have to treat it as murder, till proved otherwise, whether we like it, or not.'

'And you don't like it?'

He looked at me speculatively and said: 'How about another drink?'

'Good idea.'

'When he returned a few minutes later with our refilled glasses, I said: 'I assume that my last question was indiscreet?'

'More inferences? No, it wasn't that at all. It was simply that I hardly knew the answer myself, and I still don't. In this job one is apt to get pulled in half from time to time.'

'I believe you.'

'This time I am pulled in three ways, which makes it even more dodgy. As a human being I hate the idea of murder or violence in any form, come to that. As a policeman, well, this is the first time I've been in charge of a murder case, or even suspected murder. I've worked on them before, as a humble sergeant, but this is the first since my promotion. It would be hypocritical to pretend that I'm not ambitious enough to get a certain satisfaction out of it.'

'Why did you choose to be a policeman?'

'I'm sure you don't want to hear all about that.'

'I'm sure I do,' I said.

'Well, let's go and get some dinner, shall we? While I was waiting for the drinks I booked a table at the White Swan at Storhampton. Do you know it? I'll tell you all about my life and times as we go along, and then when you're bored you can look out at the rolling countryside.'

'Besides which,' I said. 'You feel less self-conscious, talking about yourself when you have to concentrate on driving, as well.'

'That's not inference,' he said, taking my arm. 'That's bloody witchcraft.'

(iii)

It took us just thirty minutes to drive to Storhampton, which proved to be enough for the story of Robin's life, because, despite some hesitations at the start, once he was fairly launched into it there was really no stopping him. I threw in a question or comment from time to time, but this was mainly to assure him that I was still listening.

He told me that he was thirty years old, had been born in London, but spent most of his childhood in Herefordshire, where his mother had retreated to when the bombing started. His father had been in the Navy and had been killed when his ship was torpedoed in 1941. He was their only child, and he and his mother had remained in the country until she remarried two years after the war ended.

He had intended to read law at the university, but had decided to do his national service as soon as he left school so as to get it out of the way. If he had gone straight to the university the national service law would have been repealed while he was there, which would have got it out of the way even more effectively, but that, as we agreed, was the way the cookie crumbled; for it was the year and a half he had spent in the army which had shaped his future.

As the result of some string-pulling by a military uncle he had joined a Guards' regiment and after six months had been commissioned. Then he had spent a year with the regiment in Kenya, where there was some bother going on at the time. This experience convinced him that he could never be happy with city life and he decided to apply for the Colonial Service as soon as he had a degree. However, before this came about he realised that there was a rapidly diminishing number of colonies left to serve and he was back to the beginning again.

He had toyed with the idea of going into forestry, but the opportunities were few and promotion slow, and, I gathered, the prospect of tending the saplings of the New Forest was not half so attractive as tramping through Colonial swamps and jungles, or dispensing rough and ready justice in the shade of the banyan tree.

Ultimately he had chosen the police force, which he admitted had earned him some cruel jibes and sneering glances from many of his contemporaries; but it was a largely outdoor life, and so far as he was concerned still offered a challenge in a world where such a commodity was getting hard to come by.

'You have to commit yourself, you know,' he told me very seriously, as we slowed down for Storhampton bridge. 'At least, if you're like me, you've got to plump for one side or the other. It's no use hiding your head and hoping all the nasty crooks will go away. And it's no good whining about them when you get hurt, and adopting bits of their morality when it suits you. You have to be for or against, and, smug as it may sound to you, I'm against. This is the only job I know which gives me the chance to do something about it.'

I watched his profile as he manoeuvred us through the town traffic and marvelled that anyone so beautiful could be such a prig, paying a passing tribute to Nature on the side. It was one of her subtler tricks to have me fall, like a dead sparrow from a tree, for a man whose philosophy of life was so alien to my own.

'Well, that's enough about me,' he said, when he had ordered the dinner and we were sitting at a window table looking out over the river. 'You've been most patient, but you have an unfair advantage now and it's time to even up the score.

Kindly begin by telling me everything that has happened to you since the hour of your birth.'

I knew better than to do so, of course, but I did tell him a few things about my career in the theatre, past, present and future, winding up with an account of my morning's experience at the Studios.

'It sounds thoroughly nerve-racking to me,' he said. 'Are you nervous still, or have you got over it ages ago?'

'No, and I am sure I never shall. It gets more intense, if anything, as one becomes more experienced. I think most people would tell you the same, and the odd thing is that secretly one has a kind of jealous attitude to one's nervousness. It's hell at the time, but I believe it would be even worse to wait in the wings one evening and find that all the nerves had vanished. It's an occupational disease and without it you'd feel like a surgeon who'd lost one of his fingers. He might still know everything there was to know about surgery, but he'd no longer be able to perform the really tricky operations. My cousin Matilda, for instance, has no nerves at all, but she'll never be anything but a very limited actress.'

'Tell me about Matilda,' he said.

So, almost without realising it, there I was, filling in all the details about Toby and Matilda and Ellen, and explaining how I came to be staying with them. All the time, I was studying the way his hair grew and the set of his eyes, and all the time the river flowed by and the wine flowed down and a tiny, inner voice warned me to be careful; but it was such a cautious, carping little voice that I chose to ignore it.

By tacit consent we did not refer again to Mrs Cornford's death until right at the end of the evening, when he was driving me back to Roakes and I said:

'By the way, there's something that's been bobbing about in my mind. You said something about being pulled three ways. Remember?'

'Yes, and I meant it.'

'Well, you mentioned two of the ways and they were fairly obvious, but you never told me what the third was.'

'Did I not? I suppose I took it for granted that you knew. I told you that this might be my first chance to handle a murder case. I could have added that it's the first time I've been in love, believe it or not.'

'Oh, Robin,' I drooled. 'How could you have left that bit out? It's the most important of all. Please don't do such a thing again.'

'I promise I never will,' he said.

We drove some way in silence while I watched the magical floodlighting effect of the headlamps hitting up the beech trees on either side of us and then I said:

'I'm wrapped in a kind of cosy mental blanket and I still don't get it. Why should your being in love present any conflict?'

He turned off the road and drove slowly round the Common.

'You being so intelligent, as well as beautiful, I've been expecting that question, Miss Crichton, although you might have worked it out for yourself. The simple answer is that, if this does turn out to be murder, a fair amount of unpleasantness is going to be stirred up and I can't see any way for you and your family to avoid getting mixed up in it.'

I liked him even more for that, as I am all for being treated as a tender and sensitive plant, but I did not share his pessimism. Both Toby and I were tough as old boots at rock bottom, and Matilda was rock the whole way through. So long as none of the unpleasantness rubbed off on Ellen, I saw no cause for concern.

He stopped at the gate, then turned to me and said: 'My instinct is to suggest that you pack your bags and get as far away from here as you can. Unfortunately, it might be just about the worst advice I could give you.'

'Why? You surely don't imagine that Toby or I would be suspected of having any part in it?'

'No, of course not, nothing like that. Luckily, you were both miles away when it happened. But you might be called as a witness, which would be no fun at all, I can assure you.'

'Oh dear me, yes, I am sure I should hate that,' I said, and fell to wondering what I should wear in the witness box should the disagreeable necessity arise.

'When shall I see you again?' he asked as I was getting out of the car.

'Who knows?'

'Who indeed? But I'll ring you up tomorrow; about midday, if I can.'

I walked into the dark house and fumbled my way up the stairs in a happy, idiotic daze. It was only when by a series of disconnected, dreamlike movements I had got my night-dress on and was climbing into bed that a nasty little thought cropped up to break the spell.

So divided were my loyalties by this time that before I fell asleep I offered up two short prayers. The first was that Robin would be given a lovely murder case to solve and would unravel it so beautifully that he would be decorated by the Queen; the second that he should never, never discover that Toby had not been miles away from the scene of the crime.

SIXTEEN

(i)

I HOVERED round the telephone during the whole of Friday morning, blocking all Ellen's attempts to get me out in the bracing air. With something less than my usual candour, I pretended to be expecting a call from my agent. She immediately understood the gravity of this and agreed with me that it was the perfect day for spring-cleaning the dolls' house.

By a strange coincidence the telephone rang on the stroke of noon and, what is more, it was my agent. She told me I had got the film part and suggested that I should go to London on Monday to look through my contract and have a celebration lunch.

As soon as the strength had returned to my legs I tottered back to relay the news to Ellen who fell into raptures of excitement. We forgot all about the boring old dolls' house and danced out on to the lawn, for a festive game of croquet, laughing and shrieking and twirling the mallets round our heads; making such a hullabaloo, in fact, that poor old Toby was quite distracted from his work and had to come downstairs and join in the game.

It was an odd state of affairs that with so many threads running through my life at that time they so rarely overlapped. On first hearing my agent's voice on the line I had been ready to sink from disappointment. Ten minutes later I had become the full, dedicated film star, attending premières, with diamonds in my hair and white mink down to the pavement. If I hadn't known better I could have been excused for suspecting that my emotions were rather shallow.

At all events, my interest in the question of whether Robin would or would not remember to ring me grew steadily more tepid as the minutes passed, and by the time he did so, at half past one, I had almost achieved a state of indifference.

He may have mistaken this for injured pride, for he apologised abjectly for not calling before and begged me to show my forgiveness by dining with him that evening. I graciously consented and he said he would call for me at seven o'clock.

We had been in the middle of lunch when he rang, so Toby and Ellen were still in the dining-room and I could speak freely:

'Could you make it a bit later, Robin, say eight? The fact is, I've just had to neglect Ellen for a whole day and I would rather stay here until she is in bed.'

'What time is that?'

'She has a bath at seven, then comes down again for supper and half an hour of telly. Toby will be here, so I can leave as soon as she's in bed.'

He agreed to it all and as I rang off the film, running through my head, switched to a new sequence, with me at the centre of it counting the hours until I saw him again.

(ii)

'Will I see your swain?' Ellen asked, when I had outlined the programme.

'My what?'

'Your swain. Don't you know what that means?'

'I do, actually, but it always conjures up a vapid sort of swoony swan. I don't think I should care to go out to dinner with one of those.'

'No, but will I see him?'

'Most unlikely. He seems to have no idea of time. He's bound to be late and you'll be in bed.'

'Couldn't I just stay up till he comes?'

'I think it would disconcert him. The whole plot hinges on your being in bed by the time he arrives.'

'How jolly mean! I just hope he comes early, that's all.'

I might have guessed that her wish would be granted and I should certainly have known that people without a sense of time are just as likely to be ahead of it as behind. He arrived just before seven-thirty, in time to see the gang rounded up and to hear the screams of the arch criminal as he jumped from the eighth storey window smack into the posse of bluebottles.

I switched off and performed the introductions.

'Does it really happen like that?' Ellen asked him.

'Oh, rather! Sometimes, that is.'

'Come on,' I said. 'Time for beddy byes.'

'Oh, Tessa, I haven't even finished my banana yet.'

'Finish it as you go upstairs. Buck up.'

'You're not going out in that dress, are you?'

'What's wrong with it?'

'Nothing much, but I saw you ironing your pink one, so I thought you meant to wear that.'

'So I do, clever cuts. I shall change while you're brushing your teeth.'

'I think she looks very nice, as she is,' Robin said in a distinctly soapy voice, 'but it's my fault that she hasn't had time to change because I came too early. So I'll tell you what; why don't we let her go up and I'll stay here with you while you eat your banana?'

She rewarded him with the full, wide-eyed, benevolent gaze.

'What a clever idea! I'll eat an apple, as well, Tess, and then I won't need to waste time cleaning my teeth.'

'Brilliant!' Robin said.

So the battle was joined. I was prepared to believe that Robin was only trying to curry favour with Ellen, either because he was charmed by her, or hoped to charm me, in the process, but there was also just the chance that he was angling for a few minutes private talk with her and I was very sure that the only way he would get it would be over my dead body.

'Enough of this foolery,' I snarled. 'You know very well that I can't zip myself into the pink dress, without your help. Bring an apple and a banana and a bunch of grapes, as well, if that is your wish, but come along upstairs before I lay about me.'

(iii)

'Even the best child in the world,' I said, when we were in the car, 'and no one can deny that Ellen is far and away the best child in the world, tries to drag out the moment of going to bed. It was very wicked, thoughtless and foolhardy of you to encourage her.'

I was trying to keep it jokey, but I could hear my own voice sounding governessy and aggrieved, just as it would when we had been married for fourteen years.

However, since we had not been married for fourteen years Robin took the wind out of my sails by accepting the rebuke very contritely, adding that he could well believe that one might search the world without turning up a nicer child than Ellen.

'What became of her mother?' he asked.

'Well, she wasn't murdered, if that's what you're thinking, although she certainly went about asking for it.'

'It didn't occur to me that she had been. What else?'

'Well, she was an actress, of course. Rather a dud one, too. Toby has a genius for picking that kind. She went to America in a play which opened and shut on Broadway in the twinkling of an eye. Then she wrote to say that the separation had made her realise what an empty shell her marriage was and a lot more twaddle of that sort. She was a frightful ass and a frightful liar, to boot, because it turned out that she had managed to lasso some rich Canadian and, as soon as the divorce was through, she married him and went to live in Canada. As far as I know, she's still there. It's rather a coincidence, in a way.'

'What is?'

'Oh, just that I heard of someone else the other day who was a rich Canadian. Still, I suppose one would expect there to be more than one in a country of that size.'

'She didn't try to get custody of the child?'

'No, thank God. She said she wanted to make a clean break. You bet she did. She knew damn well that it would have slowed things up if she'd tried to get her claws on Ellen, because Toby would have fought till Kingdom Come to keep her.'

'Quite an unnatural woman?'

'Oh yes, all Toby's wives are unnatural. Why are we always talking about them? Where are you taking me?'

'To Dedley.'

'I guessed that much. Is that where you live?'

'Yes. Over a shop in the High Street, but we're not going there. It's not your style. I've booked a table at the Red Lion.'

'Would you say that was my style?'

'Not really. You probably belong in a mink bathrobe beside your serpentine swimming pool, but the Lion is the best that Dedley can produce. The other will have to wait.'

'Not for long,' I said incautiously. 'They can start digging the pool, any day now. I got the part. I noticed you hadn't asked me.'

He excused himself on the grounds that it would have been tactless if it had fallen through, and compensated for the omission by congratulating me very warmly and asking for every imaginable detail. When I told him how much I would be paid, he looked incredulous and deeply dismayed.

'Fifty pounds a day,' he repeated, in a stunned voice. 'My God, that's as much as I earn in a week.'

'I daresay it is, but you don't have all the upkeep of the swimming pool. Furthermore, yours comes rolling in, every week of the year, including three weeks' holiday, I shouldn't wonder. In my job I'm lucky to tot up five or six working months out of twelve; and don't forget that I have to pay my agent ten per cent of every shilling I earn. Not that I grudge it. God knows she works hard enough for it, and she's the best friend I've got.'

'All the same, fifty pounds a day! It doesn't make sense.'

'It makes a great deal of sense. I'll pay for the dinner if you like, and then you'll begin to see just how much sense it does make.'

'No, thanks. Poor I may be, but I still have my pride.'

The Red Lion was a large, solid building in the centre of the High Street, furnished in the early Waring and Gillow style, and the clientèle was made up about equally of muttering American tourists and groups of English people who looked as though they were dressed for the wedding of a couple they faintly disliked; sour expressions and tasteless finery. The food was respectable, though uninspired and the wine excellent. It was all vastly expensive and I was rather relieved that my offer to pay had been so chivalrously rejected. It was a mystery to me how Robin could afford a Sunbeam and meals of this category if his salary was as meagre as he claimed. I hoped the answer was that he had private means and not that he was taking bribes, but was rather at a loss to phrase the question.

'Tell me about your unhappy lot,' I said. 'Is the case solved yet?'

'We haven't made an arrest, if that's what you mean.'

'But you do know the culprit?'

'Technically speaking, there isn't one. We await the Coroner's verdict, on Monday.'

'And non-technically speaking?'

'Oh, we peg away at it, under cover. Not making much headway, though.'

'Perhaps I could lend a hand? There must be all sorts of odds and ends I could dig up for you without anyone guessing what I was up to.'

'That is a kind thought,' he said. 'I suppose you're well up in detective work?'

'You're dead right, I am. I've already told you that I had a prominent rôle in six episodes of a crime serial and, furthermore, we had a real, live, retired superintendent from Scotland Yard in attendance to keep us straight on the technical details. I can even tell you about French police methods if you like, because at one point the action switched to Paris and we had a marvellous, pipe-smoking *"Vite, Gaston!"* scene, at the Quai des Orfèvres. No location shots, unfortunately.'

'Too bad! Though I doubt if your French law would be applicable in this case. It might only add to the many confusions. What we could really do with is some evidence.'

'I suppose you've given some thought to the husband? It nearly always does turn out to be the husband, I believe. If I were you I should arrest him now and drag out a confession later.'

'That may be your French way of doing things, but it is a method which would be frowned upon by my superiors here. Besides, he's in the clear as it happens.'

'You're positive of that? Alibi? Witnesses?'

'The whole lot. All sewn up, nice and tight. As you say, it often does turn out to be the husband, so, naturally, he was the first to have his movements scrutinised.'

'Well, let's see?' I said. 'Who has next priority? First, husband; second, lover. Except I don't think it's likely she had one. Wait a bit, though . . . now, there's a thought!'

'Where?'

'Supposing all that zigzagging about the countryside and psychotic behaviour were all a blind? But, yes, I see it all. There she was, that afternoon, off to meet her lover at the usual trysting-place, and of course he's been trying to wiggle out for ages, but she made such terrible scenes; so along he comes at the appointed time and bumps her off. What could be more obvious?'

'Most ingenious. You may well be right and we should be delighted to pin it on him, except for one or two minor objections.'

'Such as?'

'That no one has ever seen or heard of such a person and, until we can prove his existence, it is going to be rather hard to prove that he is a murderer.'

'Well, I confess I am stumped for the moment,' I admitted, 'but don't despair. I shall bring my mind to bear on it and make a few discreet inquiries here and there and I feel sure I shall come up with the solution.'

It was the waiter, who came up at this point, wishing to know whether we were ready for our desserts.

'God forbid!' I moaned, but he did not see the joke and Robin told him that we would finish our wine and then have coffee. He then turned his attention back to me, saying:

'I know this is all just for fun, but I do hope you would never be seriously tempted to meddle in this business.'

'Oh, certainly not meddle, that is not a thing I would ever do,' I said in an offended tone. 'My intention was simply to keep my eyes and ears open and to bring any facts to your attention, which you might not be in a position to discover for yourself. Do you call that meddling?'

'Yes, I do, and for God's sake don't get the idea that you're Miss Marple, and start asking all and sundry what they were doing between four and six o'clock, on Saturday, 3rd August. It could quite conceivably lead to your being whacked on the head yourself.'

'I wouldn't be so crude. Is that the vital time?'

'What? Oh, I see what you mean. No, that was just a figure of speech.'

I did not believe him for a second. The phrase had come out much too pat not to have been engraved on his heart and, furthermore, it was compatible with the facts I already possessed. Dr Macintosh had doubtless been able to establish the time of death within an hour or two, and my having seen Mrs Cornford alive and kicking at three-thirty inevitably made the period between four and six o'clock the crucial one.

It was the single fact I needed to make a start on my investigations, and having snapped it up I diplomatically let the subject drop and allowed myself to be steered to other topics.

I was perhaps a little too complacent, however, in thinking the wool had quite covered his eyes, for on the way home he said:

'Look, Tessa, I hate to say this and I hardly know how to put it without giving you the wrong impression, but I think it might be better all round if we didn't see each other for the next few days.'

'Better all round what?'

'There! I knew you'd misunderstand.'

'No, honestly, Robin, I understand perfectly. You are finding out that business and pleasure don't mix and at this precise moment of your life, business has to come first. Aren't I right?'

'It's an awfully blunt way of putting it, but I suppose that's the gist. It wouldn't matter if you were living somewhere else, but we're bound to centre all our inquiries in and around the Manor House, and with you there smack in the middle of things it would be rather too delicate an operation to keep our private relationship in a separate compartment. To be frank it has come to matter so much to me that I dread something happening to spoil things between us. On the other hand, I do know that my feelings are quite strong enough to withstand a few days, or even weeks of separation. How about you?'

'I agree with you and I am sure your motives are highly laudable. You did say there would not be the same difficulty if I were living somewhere else?'

'Yes. You must see what a difference it would make.'

'Then I have news for you. By all means let us meet as strangers when you come to Roakes, but on Monday night I shall not be there. I shall be temporarily under my own roof, which happens to be situated off the Fulham Road. If you meant what you said, you may come to dinner with me.'

'Why, that's marvellous. Terrific, in fact. What a wonder you are, Tessa! But I shall take you out to dinner. Anywhere you like.'

'The only place I like,' I said, 'is my own flat. You see, our relationship, as you call it, is rapidly getting on to a footing of mutual understanding and one of the things I have learnt about you is that, through no fault of your own, you are liable to keep me waiting for about two hours. If I must languish, I prefer to do it in comfort and not in a public restaurant.'

'Very prudent of you, if I may say so. And can you cook, in addition to all your other virtues?'

'Just you wait!'

'Very well,' he agreed. 'I suppose I'll have to. It will be the hardest thing of all, but it must be done, somehow.'

SEVENTEEN

TRUE to my secret resolve, I spent every free moment of the next forty-eight hours in a concentrated effort to untangle the puzzle of Mrs Cornford's death. It was a labour of love and altruism, for personally I should have preferred it to remain unsolved for all time, with the memory of her death as much as her life, rapidly fading into the mists, so far as everyone at Roakes was concerned.

However, since I could hardly expect the authorities to view things in this light and since they would inevitably continue to dig and delve until they had wrapped up the case to their own satisfaction, I saw no reason why, with a little help from myself, Robin should not have the credit for it. I could hardly doubt that my success in this sphere would bind him to me with hoops of steel.

I had intended to begin by drawing up a list of every person in the vicinity who was known to have a grudge against Mrs Cornford and then to eliminate all those for whom it would have been physically impossible to be present in Stoney Woods at the time of her death. This had appeared to me as an extremely simple exercise, which I had fully intended to dash off in about twenty minutes, leaving myself with the *bona fide* suspects narrowed down to three or four.

It proved to be a far lengthier undertaking and the final result emerged as a much less tidy document than I had foreseen. I wrestled with it in spare moments throughout the day, and by dinner-time on Saturday evening the final draft had materialised, with no less than ten names, to each of whom I had awarded points, under three separate headings, which I labelled thus: M. (Motive), O. (Opportunity), PP. (Psychological Probability). This was how it looked:

1. Douglas Cornford

    M. Usual husband's – otherwise unknown (8)

    O. Cleared by police (Worth further check? Yes, but how?) (2)

    PP. High. Known to be sly and subject to fits of violence (9) Total 19

2. Toby

    M. None known, apart from Oscar thing, but wouldn't let on if he had one (2)

    O. Plenty. 4-6 p.m. working at home, but no proof (9)

    PP. Minimal. Hates violence, or even movement, of any kind. Frightened of death (1) Total 12

3. Matilda

    M. None known, apart from general high-handed attitude to anyone who gets in her way (3)

    O. None, if story true. On road to Dedley 4-4.30. Thereafter in theatre. Confirmed by dresser (Could check also with stage door-keeper) (2)

    PP. Medium. Might not hesitate, through scruples, though probably not often guilty of unpremeditated action (5) Total 10

4. Sylvia

    M. Strong; snobbish and practical. Ready to wipe out entire Cornford family, if necessary, to make Roakes better place to live in and improve value of own property (7)

    O. Whereabouts unknown 4-6 p.m. (Reputed to spend every Saturday visiting prospective adopters. Could check whether she did so on 3rd) (5)

    PP. Not sure (say 5) Total 17

5. Gerry

    M. Possibly none, personally, but all Sylvia's could apply, at second hand (5)

    O. Claims to have seen victim at same time as Ellen and I. Could have followed, on foot, or by car (7)

PP. Unknown, but definite signs of subnormality. Also capable of blindly carrying out Sylvia's orders, regardless (5) Total 17

6. Paul

M. Obsessive hatred of victim, both on own and Peter's behalf. Situation exacerbated by threat of new building to spoil garden, privacy – possibly livelihood (7)

O. Unknown. Ostensibly at home, as co-guardian of Jumbo, between four and six, but could easily have been absent part of the time (7)

PP. Highly strung and impulsive. Showed unmistakable jubilation after victim's death (Be fair, though – this would be even more natural, if conscience clear) (5) Total 19

7. Peter

M. Same as Paul, with reservation that he was conceivably still ignorant of building plans (5)

O. Ostensibly out of running, owing to injured foot, although hints abound that this not such a handicap as he pretends (4)

PP. Medium. Less impulsive than Paul, but perhaps more calculating (5) Total 14

8. Marge

M. Strong. Victim was constant threat – both to business and for spilling beans about unmarried status (7)

O. Practically nil, if at theatre, at time stated, though not actually seen there until first interval (2)

PP. Low. Good-natured, kind-hearted and fundamentally easy going (2) Total 11

9. Leslie

M. Same as Marge (7)

O. Nil, if – as claimed – did not return from Canada, until hours after event (1)

PP. Dubious. Presumably shot down dozens of enemy flyers, during war and no mental scars to show for it. May have affected attitude to life and death (6) Total 14

10. Miss Davenport

M. None known, though undoubtedly suffered inconvenience and persecution from Cornfords. Perhaps more so than most, owing to proximity (5)

O. Nil, if story true, though not actually seen in theatre, during relevant period. Could verify from M. whether breakfast scene occurs in first or second half. (Reminder: known to take solitary walks, armed with suitable weapon, i.e. heavy dog chain) (4)

PP. Rather moot. Reputed to be eccentric and arrogant (by some). (Dotty enough to confuse ancient *droits de seigneur* with *droits* over life and death of lower orders and/or imposters in family home?) (5) Total 14

This modest contribution was the result of hours of labour and in the course of it I became reconciled to Robin's view that policemen were grossly underpaid, although I considered my task to be heavier than theirs, in so far as I had been obliged to wrestle, all the way through, with my conscience. By far the greatest stumbling block had been the temptation to award unfairly low marks to those I liked personally and to whom I felt a sense of loyalty. It was not until my third and final draft, for instance, that I succeeded in committing to paper the fact that it was Toby who had the best opportunity and the flimsiest alibi. I only stifled my reluctance at last by reminding myself that the alibi, such as it was, had been provided, unsolicited, by myself and that he had never attempted to fabricate his own, as he surely would have done, had there been anything to conceal. Nevertheless, it was a relief to be able to reduce his score to something below the average, by an equally honest assessment of his P.P.

Furthermore, this tussle between candour and equivocation revealed how mistaken I had been in treating the highest scorer as the most likely suspect. Without a doubt, the murderer would show a high rating in both M. and P.P., whereas, so far as O. was concerned, his first object would naturally have been to falsify it out of existence. Only the innocent would have left themselves unprotected in this area.

Buoyed up by this cheerful reflection I drew up a new list, in which I added together the points scored by each candidate, under the first and third headings, omitting the second, in which I now realised that low marks were irrelevant if not positively incriminating.

My second analysis came out like this:

Douglas Cornford 16
Toby 3
Matilda 8
Sylvia 12
Gerry 9
Paul 16
Peter 9
Marge 9
Leslie 10
Miss Davenport 9

It was a mighty relief to discover that by this method Toby earned himself such a clean bill that I could virtually strike him out. Moreover, with Mr Cornford and Paul coming, neck and neck, up to the winning post, with Sylvia in third place and Leslie about a length behind, my next step was obvious. All that remained for me was to train every gun on each of these four people in turn until I had accumulated enough evidence against one of them to pin the crime on him, or, if necessary, her.

Precisely how to set about this simple task was not immediately clear to me, but I decided that I had done enough work for one day and would postpone further brain-cudgelling until the morning.

EIGHTEEN

(i)

I REMEMBER reading somewhere that when Sir Walter Scott became stuck over a passage, which it is hard to imagine he often did, he used to slide the problem into the seven o'clock slot, this being the witching hour, between sleeping and waking, when all his best ideas came to him, so that he had only to wait for it to find a firm path through the morass.

I had frequently attempted to apply his system to the problems in my own life, though with only limited success. Not being a person of such regular habits as Sir Walter, my dozing period did not infallibly occur every morning at the same hour, and, moreover, I had seldom achieved the perfect balance between sleep and wakefulness. I was either torn from the first, into the second, by the telephone or alarm clock, or else, on those rare mornings when I awoke naturally, with time to spare for the business of organising the day ahead, it would happen that a bare two minutes of this exercise was enough to send me straight back to sleep again.

Nevertheless, I persevered in my efforts to acquire the knack, and when I opened my eyes on to the sunshine streaming into my blue bedroom that Sunday morning I was rewarded, for once, with an answering gleam lighting up the dark patches of my mind. This visionary state was soon blotted out by returning waves of sleep, but it lasted long enough for me to grasp the premise and, when fully awake, an hour or so later, I found that it still made sense.

The solution to my difficulties may not have been the profoundest ever arrived at, but perhaps some of Sir Walter Scott's struck him as a bit obvious, when he came to write them into the story. The special problem that had confronted me was that, since Mr Cornford was the hot favourite, my first task was to investigate his relations with his wife, his psychological potential for murder and his precise movements during the period when it was known to have been committed. The only trifling obstacles to an immediate start on this programme were that I had barely exchanged half a dozen words with him in my life, and secondly, if he were as guilty as I supposed, however tactfully I might phrase my inquiries, there was a risk, as Robin had so shrewdly pointed out, of their being answered with a bash on the head and another body dumped in Dead Man's Gully.

However, the way out of the impasse, which had been vouchsafed to me during those few lucid daybreak moments, was that there are two ways of winning a race. One is to ride faster than anyone else and the other is to be the only jockey to finish the course. It was a logical step, from this flash of inspiration, to decide to concentrate on the rest of the field, starting with the closest rival and going on down the runners until, by a process of elimination, only Mr Cornford remained. Time enough, after all that, to work out his unmasking.

I consulted my list again, but only to confirm that a visit to Peter and Paul was the first duty. As it was then nearing ten o'clock, there was not a moment to be lost.

I went downstairs to make coffee and cook bacon and eggs for myself and Ellen, and as we ate them I mentioned that it would be a Christian gesture to call on the Flyaways and offer to pull up a few of the weeds in their poor, neglected garden. I could see that the idea held small appeal, but she was too kind-hearted to refuse, and having put my hand to the plough I was prepared to be merciless.

(ii)

Drawn, as he claimed, by the heady smell of coffee and the sound of our merry chatter, Toby joined us at our kitchen breakfast table. It must, however, have been the smell and not the sound which chiefly attracted him, because he complained that it was mean of us not to have taken a steaming cup up to his bedroom.

'You could have made some and brought it to us,' I pointed out. 'I read the other day that ninety per cent of the men of this country take early tea to their wives, every morning.'

'Do they?' he asked, with a gleam of satisfaction, and I realised that I had taken a foolish line. Toby had only to hear of large numbers of people behaving in a certain way to be instantly thrown on to the opposite course.

'I'm going to make my bed now,' Ellen said, getting up. 'I'll do yours for you, Tessa, if you like.'

'Mine, too, while you're about it,' Toby called after her, adding, as he turned to me with a stony glare: 'And please don't tell me that ninety per cent of the men of this country make their daughters' beds, because I don't wish to hear about it.'

'Console yourself,' I said. 'I feel sure you are in the majority there.'

'Speaking of family cross-currents, your step-cousin by marriage telephoned while you were out last night.'

'Do you refer to Matilda?' I asked, thinking that things had come to a pretty pass if he had to go to such lengths to avoid mentioning her name.

'The same.'

'How is she? How did the play go in Brighton?'

'Riotously, I understand. Packed out and three deep in the standing room; but, then, you know Brighton! People would go anywhere to get away from the howling gale and all those pebbles.'

'Will she be back today?' I asked. Brighton was the last point on the tour and the company had three days' rest, before the London dress rehearsal and opening night. We had assumed that Matilda would be spending them at home.

'Not until tomorrow,' Toby said. 'They've talked her into opening the Church Bazaar, or some such Sussex beanfeast and she will spend an extra night there.'

'Do they have Church Bazaars on Sunday?'

'I don't see why not. It seems an appropriate day.'

'Well, so long as she'll be back tomorrow. I'd planned to go to London, as you know, and I rather thought of staying the night, or maybe two. Does that conflict with any plan of yours?'

'Do as you please,' he told me graciously. 'Your life is your own, in a manner of speaking.'

'And in the manner of which I am speaking I should be grateful to hear your views on this life of mine. You may not think it desirable for me to return here at all. I suppose that Matilda will be able to come down most nights, at any rate, for the next few months?'

'I haven't the slightest idea. I wash my hands of it.'

'Oh, Toby, your Pontius old hands must be so clean, after all these years. Couldn't you sully them, just this once and tell me what you'd honestly like me to do?'

'I thought you were starting on this film?'

'Not immediately. I'll be given the exact date tomorrow, but I gather it's not due to go on the floor for a week or two, and in the meantime I am at your disposal.'

He affected enormous, incredulous astonishment. 'Can you be serious? Two or three weeks without any work and you actually contemplate spending them in London? In August? What extraordinary taste.'

'That is what I'd call a breakthrough,' I said. 'You have talked me into it. Subject to Matilda's approval I shall be delighted to accept your pressing invitation to remain here until the demands of my career compel me to take up other lodgings. Furthermore, I shall now have some more coffee, to seal the bargain. Allow me to refill your cup.'

I crossed to the stove to fetch the coffee-pot, and in doing so passed by the open window.

'Crumbs!' I said, stopping in my tracks. 'That police car is outside the Manor gates.'

'I know that. It has been there for about five minutes.'

'Do you think they have come to arrest Mr Cornford?'

'I sincerely hope so.'

'On second thoughts, it can't be that. They wouldn't leave the car here and drag him, handcuffed, all the way down the drive, would they?'

'They might, on the other hand, have left it here in order to take him by surprise. They may even now be tiptoeing from laurel to conifer so as to surround the house before he is aware of his danger.'

'It sounds so pointless. He is bound to find out in the end.'

'The point would be to forestall his arming himself with a shotgun and firing on them from an upstairs window, or swallowing cyanide, or making his escape through Miss Davenport's garden. Such tricks are commonplace, I believe.'

'Really, Toby, you are the limit! Do you mean to tell me that you have been sitting there all this time pretending to listen to me while you quietly worked out everything that's going on next door?'

'Well, not all of us have your one-track mind. I have sometimes noticed that you are limited by the fact that your right hand always tells your left hand what it is doing.'

'My left hand does not always approve, however. Well, I wonder if your devious mind has hit on the truth this time? We shall know that it has if one policeman comes out on his own to fetch the car.'

By a curious coincidence, as I spoke, one policeman did come out on his own although he ignored the car.

'Cripes!' I said. 'He's coming here now. What does your left hand make of that?

'It is no time for conjecture. You had better let him in and allow him to tell us himself.'

It was the freckly Baines and I had the door open before he had time to ring.

'Excuse me, Miss, but I wonder if I might have a word?'

'With me?' I asked nervously.

'If you please, and with Mr Crichton, too, if he should happen to be available.'

'Oh, certainly, if you don't mind coming into the kitchen and seeing him in his dressing-gown.'

'I could call back at a later time, if that would be more convenient, Miss.'

My confidence was building up by the minute, for I did not believe that if he were about to arrest us he would offer to do so by appointment, when, presumably, we should have the shot-gun, the cyanide and the escape route all fixed up, and I said:

'Don't bother. My cousin works far into the night, so he is a late riser, but he is quite accustomed to receiving callers in his dressing-gown.'

'I shan't have to take up much of your time,' Sergeant Baines said, when he had been introduced to Toby and waded through all the preliminary civilities. 'I was wondering whether you had been the recipient of anything in the nature of an anonymous letter?'

I quite expected Toby to ask how anything could be in the nature of an anonymous letter without being an anonymous letter, but I saw from the blank and innocent look which he immediately assumed that the question had jolted him beyond the point of pedantry. At the same instant I was mentally trans-ported back to another Sunday morning just two weeks earlier, and a picture rose up before me of Toby scuffling through his desk drawer, with me on my knees beside him holding a sheet of torn off notepad.

There was a long hush, and Sergeant Baines began to fidget and clear his throat.

'Might I have your answer, sir?'

'Yes. No.'

'Am I to take it that your answer is in the negative, sir? You have not been troubled by anything of that kind?'

'Certainly not,' Toby said with great firmness. 'Had that been the case, I should have informed the police.'

'Very sensible and public-spirited, if I may say so, sir. It is to be regretted that more people do not pursue that course. There is – er – um – often some embarrassment in showing these things to a third party.'

'Is that so? I can assure you that it would not embarrass me in the least. May I know what prompts this inquiry?'

'There is no harm in your knowing that, sir. In the course of some investigations concerning the late Mrs Cornford some threatening letters have come to light. They are of an illiterate character and unsigned. They may or may not have a bearing, but we are anxious to ascertain whether anyone else in the district has received missives of a similar nature.'

'All that you have found so far were addressed to Mrs Cornford?' Toby asked casually.

'That is so, yes.'

'What did they say?'

'I regret, sir, that I am not empowered to divulge such information. I am sure you understand?'

Whether he did or not, it was plain from his bland and incurious manner that Toby was badly shaken and my suspicion that his right and left hand were working flat out was confirmed by an unexpected change of tactics.

'You are not going to like this, Sergeant, but when I told you that I had not had any letters, I may, unwittingly, have misled you.'

'Indeed, sir? You wish to convey that something has since come to mind?'

'Exactly. It has come into my mind that I may have received some, without being aware of it.'

'Ah!'

'You see, I very rarely read any letters at all, and in no circumstances any in an unfamiliar hand.'

'Am I to take it that you destroy them, unopened?'

'Yes, you are. Unless, of course, they are obviously bills, and then I put them away in a safe place until I have time to deal with them.'

I could not but admire Toby for so adroitly steering the interrogation on to lines where he could give truthful answers, but I also gave full marks to Sergeant Baines for recognising a plain statement of fact, however improbable, when it was handed to him. Instead of pursuing the subject he turned to me.

'And how about you, Miss? Do you read your letters?'

'Oh yes, always, but I know so few people locally. I'm only on a visit here, you know. When are they supposed to have been sent?'

'All within the last three weeks, it seems.'

'Posted in the village?'

'They bore the Storhampton postmark, but all mail from the outlying districts is conveyed there for sorting, so there's no telling exactly where they were posted.'

'Finger-prints?'

He looked at me thoughtfully and allowed himself a brief respite from the flowery phrases. 'Dozens. Well, thanks very much. Sorry to have troubled you. You won't forget to let us know if you remember anything, will you?'

'Don't call us,' I said. 'We'll call you.'

He gave me another of his suspicious looks as he went out, and, when I had shut the front door, I bolted upstairs to find out what Ellen had been up to while all this was going on.

I found her in Matilda's room, experimenting with some boxes of eye shadow.

'Who were you talking to?' she asked.

'How do you mean?'

'I could hear you and Daddy talking and giggling, and then I heard some other man, as well.'

'Must have been the radio.'

'Oh! I thought it might have been one of the policemen, because their car was outside the Manor.'

'Really? Is it still there?'

'Don't know. You can't see, from this window. Was it one of them, Tess?'

'Well, yes, it was, to be honest. He just came in to ask for a glass of water. I wasn't going to mention it, in case you might be scared.'

'By a policeman?'

'Ridiculous, I know, but some children are scared of them.'

'Why are they?'

I felt a momentary impulse to jerk a reaction out of her, by stating the real purpose of Sergeant Baines' visit, but at the same instant she looked up and her eyes, as Mesdames Parkes and Grumble would have put it, gave me quite a turn. One was heavily shadowed with deep purple, the other with brilliant, iridescent green. I was temporarily speechless and she said placidly:

'I don't know why you thought I would have been. I wasn't scared of your swain.'

Nineteen

(i)

'WHAT have we here, a Council of War?' I said gaily. It was a fatuous question and quite uncalled for, but it heralded my first venture into the direct approach in detection, and my nervousness had been sharpened by the unexpected sight of a conference apparently in progress between three of my principal suspects.

Nothing had gone according to plan. No sooner had I recovered from the shock of Sergeant Baines' intrusion into the quiet, domestic scene than another hitch occurred. Ellen and I, having set out to pay our delayed call on Peter and

Paul, she had elected to take her bicycle and had ridden on ahead. I had fully anticipated finding her at their gate when I arrived, but there was no sign of her, either there or on the back terrace. Instead, I found Sylvia in earnest conversation with both Flyaways.

There was absolutely no reason why Peter and Paul should not have entertained anyone they chose on a Sunday morning, but I was annoyed because it was a contingency I had not reckoned with. The scene, as pictured, had consisted of Ellen safely snipping away at the dead heads in the rose bed, which is a job she enjoys, while I, my kind offer to perform some similar light task having been brushed aside, indulged in some profitable chit-chat with our hosts.

My intention, naturally, had been to get them both talking at once, since there was a fair chance that at least one of them would let fall some revealing remark, even while the other rattled on obliviously, on some totally different subject.

None of those present took me up on my idiotic greeting, although I noticed a slight hardening in Sylvia's expression. Peter smiled ruefully and pointed to his foot, to explain why he could not get up, but Paul bounded forward and somewhat to my embarrassment embraced me warmly.

It was news to me, and in the circumstances unwelcome news, that we had grown to be such dear friends. However, I soon saw that his humour was such that he would have bestowed loving kisses on the Vicar, the milkman, or three strangers collecting for the Salvation Army, if they had chanced to drop in. He was in an even more exuberant mood than when I had last seen him. He pulled another chair into the circle and at once began plaguing me about what I would drink.

'I am not here to enjoy myself,' I said, 'but to do some work. Ellen is on her way, too. I promised we would give you a hand with the garden and I am sure you can find some jobs for us.'

'Too late, my dear,' Sylvia said patronisingly. 'I sent my gardener over, only yesterday. Silly boys, if they'd only told me before what a fix they were in . . .'

'And Pete can manage a few light jobs himself now,' Paul said. 'So long as he doesn't stand on it too . . .'

'. . . dreadfully tired, though. Doc says I oughtn't . . .'

'. . . don't want to boast about my old faithful, but I always say he gets through more work in a day . . .'

'. . . wouldn't believe the torture . . .'

'. . . One of the last of the good, old-fashioned country people . . .'

'Couldn't even persuade him to knock off for elevenses. Coffee, I said, or tea, whichever . . .'

'. . . no idea when I'll be mobile again, just have to grin and bear it . . .'

'When one's been brought up with the old-fashioned type of servant . . .'

All three of them talking at me simultaneously was one more than I had bargained for, so I dammed the flow by saying, loud and clear, that what I wanted most in the world was a long, cold drink.

Paul must have been the spark who set all this loquacity blazing away, for as soon as he had scuttled off to fulfil my heart's desire, a complete silence fell upon the other two.

I addressed myself to Sylvia. 'Not at church this morning? I thought you made a point of going every Sunday?'

'I certainly try to do so. I count it as one of my duties, if only to set an example.'

'An example of what?'

'Now, my dear, you are just being clever. We leave that sort of thing to your cousin. I suppose we have to put up with it, from him. All literary people, especially the English, I daresay, have their little quirks.'

I was interested to hear that she regarded Toby in this light. As a genuine, all-purpose, Anglo-Saxon eccentric, he no doubt had his niche in her romantic conception of rural life, a fact which might have accounted for her imperviousness to all his snubs.

'Anyway, you didn't go today?' I said, as Paul came skipping back, with a tall glass of lemonade.

'Through no fault of mine. Gerry and I were just setting out when this policeman turned up. I was telling these two about it when you arrived. I popped over to ask whether they'd had a call from the law, too.'

'About the anonymous letters, you mean?'

'Oh, he's been to you, has he? It's what they call a house to house inquiry, I suppose.'

'Yes, and he was at Miss Davenport's before he got to Paul and me. I happened to notice, because I was giving the old foot a bit of exercise on the Common. I'm supposed to practise using it, as much as I can.'

'He was quite polite and well-spoken, for a person of his class, I will say that,' Sylvia said, saying it.

'Quite a charmer, I thought,' Paul said.

My sympathy for the constabulary was increasing by the minute. If they had to wade through such a stream of irrelevancies at every interview they conducted, it was small wonder that the crime figures were going up.

'What did you tell this well-spoken old charmer?' I asked.

'Tell him?' Sylvia repeated in shocked tones. 'Why, nothing at all. What should I have told him? I am certainly not in the habit of receiving anonymous letters. None of us is, I should hope.'

'Ah, but that's not the point. Surely, what he was really after was not whether we'd received any, but whether we'd sent them?'

'What an extraordinary idea! How could he possibly have thought such a thing?'

'Simple. The police discover that Mrs Cornford was receiving threatening letters. What more natural than that they should have come from one of the neighbours. And whoever it was could have been the same one who bumped her off. Ergo, as they say.'

Sylvia did not seem prepared to say anything of the kind.

'You must have taken leave of your senses, Tessa. The idea of the police imagining for one moment that people of our sort could be mixed up in anything so sordid simply passes belief. I should say it is far more likely that they were written by someone who knew her in the past and nursed a grudge of some kind. Goodness knows, there must be plenty of those. Gerry and I have always thought that the reason why they came here at all, where they don't know a soul and have no ties of any kind, was because they'd made so many enemies in Bradford, or wherever it was they came from. If the police take my advice, they will look for the letter writer up there.'

'They won't take it, though, because they have already found part of the answer down here. All the letters had a Storhampton postmark.'

'How do you know that?' Paul asked, in a croaky voice.

'The Sergeant told me. It's no secret.'

'Some wretched shop assistant who'd suffered some of her rudeness, no doubt. Besides, if she was killed by one of those hit and run drivers, which is what most of us believe, it couldn't possibly have any connection with these stupid letters.'

'Most of you may believe it,' I said smugly, 'but the police don't. They think she was murdered.'

'Indeed? You seem to know a great deal about it,' Sylvia said furiously. 'Or is this some sort of a joke?'

'Not at all. I happen to have an inquiring mind and there is no law against asking questions.'

'Then there ought to be. It is exceedingly mischievous to go around, spreading tales of this sort. I advise you to say no more about it.'

'The subject is now closed, in any case,' I said. 'We have two more visitors.'

I referred to Gerry and Ellen who were walking towards us. The conversation, which had been terminated by their arrival, had not turned out as I had hoped, for such information as had been bandied about had all been bandied by me. However, their reactions had not been without interest and I filed away for future reference the fact that my needling had aroused a fury of indignation in Sylvia, on exactly that territory where she would normally have exploded with curiosity; whereas the effect on Peter and Paul had been even more marked. They had barely uttered a word, but had stared at me like two unhappy rabbits who asked themselves whatever the nasty old snake was going to come out with next.

'The chain came off my bike again,' Ellen said. 'And Mr Grimbold put it on for me.'

Paul instantly jerked into action again, like a puppet whose master had returned from the coffee break and started all the usual fuss about plying the newcomers with refreshment. After this storm had subsided, Ellen announced in a clear voice:

'We've been watching the policeman, too. He's gone back into our house now.'

'Has he?' I asked, sitting bolt upright. 'How do you know?'

'We saw him. We were over in that little dip, opposite White Gables, where you can see out without being seen, and as soon as you were out of sight he popped up and went back to our house.'

'Did Toby let him in?'

'I couldn't see that because he didn't go to the front door. He went round to the side. I expect he left something behind when he came for his glass of water, and wanted to go in and fetch it without disturbing anybody.'

'Which side? The kitchen?'

'No, the nursery. Probably, he saw the windows were open there.'

Sylvia's anger had evaporated, but had been replaced by a new emotion, and the label I put on this one was apprehension:

'Speaking of kitchens, my dears,' she said, in a high, flustered voice, 'I must fly. What can have possessed me? I have left our Sunday joint in the oven and it will be frizzled if I don't run and take it out. Are you ready, Gerry? Yes, I can see that you haven't finished your drink, but never mind that. I know what these good people are. They'll get you talking and you'll forget all about the time, just as I did.'

At any other time, I am sure we should all have been glad to witness this minor miracle, but the thought of Sergeant Baines prowling round the house made me quite as impatient to be off as Sylvia was. Nor was there much sign of Peter and Paul wishing to detain us and, with the most perfunctory of goodbyes, we both scuttled away, followed in a more leisurely fashion by Gerry and Ellen.

There was no police car outside the Manor gates when we reached them, and I slowed down, saying to Sylvia:

'The birds have flown from this nest. Do you suppose they have gone to perch on yours?'

'No, certainly not. We should see the car from here. Besides, I shouldn't be surprised if Ellen had made the whole thing up, just to tease you. It is the kind of little game she does get up to.'

I was so incensed by this aspersion that I almost provided the police force with another murder to solve on the spot, but controlled myself and said with quiet dignity that I trusted it was not the kind of game that Gerry often got up to.

'I expect he didn't want to spoil her fun, but he's a naughty man and I shall scold him for giving you such a fright. Are you all right, my dear? Not nervous any more? You wouldn't like me to come inside with you just to make sure everything's in order?'

'Very kind of you, but what about your joint?'

'Oh, a few more minutes won't hurt. Besides, what's a bit of overcooked meat compared to giving a helping hand to one's neighbours? That's what I always say.'

It sounded an exceptionally pointless thing to be always saying, and sooner than risk a repetition I firmly declined her offer.

(ii)

I padded round to the nursery side of the house, moving like a thief in the night. The French windows were wide open just as we had left them and I could hear voices inside the room. I pressed myself up against the wall and peered inside. There was no one there, except Toby, who was watching a cartoon film for the under-fives on television.

He looked up as I stepped over the sill, then motioned me to sit down and be silent. After a few boring minutes the programme ended and, sighing gustily, he got up and switched off the set.

'Very, very fascinating,' he announced. 'It is a pity that my favourite programmes are shown at such an inconvenient time.'

'I expect they try to fit them in before you eat your bicky pegs and go to bye-byes.'

'Very possible,' he agreed, 'and I certainly mean to snuggle down in my karri kot this afternoon. It has been a most restless morning.'

'More visitors?'

'Yes, your freckly friend came back. It was quite a drama.'

'Why?'

'To begin with, I must tell you that I don't believe he is a policeman at all. Just a burglar dressed up as one. It is quite an old trick, you know.'

'It is? I always thought they dressed up as gas-meter readers.'

'That's for weekdays. Even you and I might be expected to know that we don't get the gas-meter read on Sunday. Specially,' he added thoughtfully, 'if either of us happened to remember that we have no gas here.'

'Did you manage to apprehend him before he pinched anything?'

'Oh, certainly. I could see him hovering furtively about, do you see? I watched it all from my study window. When he came creeping round to this side of the house I guessed what he was up to and I bounded down all ready to greet him red-handed, so to speak.'

'That was plucky of you.'

'Just quick thinking. Some people's brains do work faster than others, and it is bound to be an advantage.'

'I still think it was brave of you to confront him, knowing he was a burglar in disguise. I would rather have expected your quick thinking to have sent you diving under the bed. He might have been armed, for all you knew.'

'One does not stop to consider personal danger in such emergencies.'

'Does one not? And what excuse did he make for this breaking and entering?'

'The uninspired one of having left his gloves behind. Can you imagine anything more banal? I suggested that they might be in his pocket, which would be the natural place for one of his profession to secrete them; but he said he might have left them in the kitchen, but would have a look round outside first, in case he had dropped them on the path. Puerile, really, but I pretended to fall into the trap and said that meanwhile I would conduct a search in the kitchen.'

'Who won?'

'It was a dead-heat. We both left the room, counted to ten and came in again. He then said that the gloves were not outside and I said that comb the kitchen as I might they were not there either. I also said that he was welcome to go and look for himself, if he chose.'

'Which he didn't?'

'Of course not. It was a ruse, pure and simple; a thought too simple, one might even say. He saw that the game was up and retreated, without a shot being fired.'

'Well done! You showed great aplomb and it's no wonder that you felt the need for a little escapist television after all that real life excitement.'

'I did not turn it on immediately,' he admitted thoughtfully. 'It occurred to me, after he had gone, that it would be a sensible measure to cast an eye round and see if I could discover what he had been after. You never know, do you? They are a ruthless lot, these modern, high-powered burglars.'

'Very true. Did you find it, whatever it was?'

'Oh, I think I did, you know,' Toby said, in his blandest manner. 'I think I have taken all the necessary precautions.'

'I am relieved to hear that,' I said. 'Although I suppose we might even consider ringing the police next time we have a burglary?'

'It is an idea. Let us hope it won't come to that. One wouldn't wish to exaggerate.'

TWENTY

(i)

AT THE conclusion of a mutually satisfactory session with my agent on Monday morning we strolled out into sunny Shaftesbury Avenue, the only cloud on my horizon, and it was not half so big as a man's hand, being the obligation which now confronted me of breaking it to Robin that my fifty quid a day would be worth almost twice that figure, since out of a ten-week schedule six weeks would be spent on location in Spain with all expenses paid.

'Why Spain?' I had wanted to know. 'I had the fixed impression that this story had a French background.'

'Oh, you know how it is,' she had answered. 'It's cheaper in Spain and I expect the company has a few million frozen *pesetas* lying around.'

This sounded to me more like the surplus stock of a deep-freeze factory than a method of financing films, but so long as it paid my salary mine was not to reason how.

We crossed Regent Street and entered the grander of the two restaurants in which she habitually treated her clients to lunch. Not more than seven minutes had elapsed since leaving her office, but it hardly needs to be said that, even as we revolved ourselves through its illustrious doors, a panting attendant sprang forward to announce that my agent was wanted on the telephone.

I proceeded onwards to the bar, a crimson-padded cell of great magnificence, to place my order for champagne cocktails and saw to my surprise and pleasure that Leslie and a female companion were seated at a table at the far end of the room. I flapped a friendly greeting which he did not acknowledge, and as I hoisted myself on to a bar stool I noticed that he had slightly shifted the position of his chair so that his back was turned towards me. I also perceived that the woman with him was not Marge as I had automatically assumed but a brassier female altogether. He did not once turn in my direction, either during the ten minutes I spent on my own, nor in the even longer period, after I was joined by my agent, although I could tell, from the appraising glances of his young lady, that my presence had not gone unnoticed.

I found his behaviour singularly fatuous, as it would never have occurred to my guileless nature that he had any but the most innocent reason for being in such company and it was purely on account of the ostentatious cut that I began to question it. If he had set out to convince me that he was conducting a secret *affaire*, he could not have done so more effectively by standing up on the table and announcing the fact at the top of his lungs.

However, the distasteful impression which this incident had created was soon swept away by more agreeable encounters. By a lucky chance, numerous old friends and acquaintances were dotted about in the restaurant and, thanks no doubt to that sixth sense with which so many actors are blessed, I was greeted with all the courtesy and kindliness due to one who had just signed a whacking film contract.

Basking away in the first rays of success I forgot all about the oafish Leslie until much later that evening when I was presenting my analysis of suspects for Robin's approval, and by then so many new trains of thought were flying through my head that the episode appeared too trivial to be worth mentioning at all.

(ii)

The evening got off to a fine start because Robin was half an hour late, which is exactly what I require of all my dinner guests. It is a delicate balance because five minutes' mistiming, either way, can spell disaster. As it was, when the bell rang I was not obliged to go to the front door in my dressing-gown and with my hair uncombed, while still safely on the right side of that depressing stage when the preparations are complete and nothing remains but to sit and wonder whether the guests have forgotten they were invited. There can be no hope of a successful outcome to this mood, because it inevitably degenerates into a passionate boredom at the prospect of meeting them, accompanied by mounting and all too often dashed hopes that they really have forgotten.

Robin's arrival, on the stroke of eight, spared me all these emotional complexities, and I earned some unmerited praise for the airy way I assured him that the dinner would not be ruined and that he might linger for as long as he chose over his reviving pink gins.

I had not spared any trouble, or expense, to make myself attractive to the man of my dreams and we started with smoked salmon, followed by tournedos rossini and a bottle Haut Brion and finished with raspberries and cream.

He was so appreciative that I fancied him to be on the brink of proposing, even before the last mouthful was down. However, I was relieved that he did not, because I had still to break the news of my forthcoming six weeks in Spain and also because there might have been some indelicacy in reverting, immediately afterwards, to the more prosaic subject of murder.

I had naturally asked him how the inquest had turned out and he had replied gloomily that the verdict had been murder by person or persons unknown and that he would really prefer not to discuss it.

Relying on my fortifying dinner to engender a more expansive mood, I had delayed my next question until I was ladling out the coffee and brandy.

'Tell me about this person, or persons. Are they equally unknown to the police?'

'Yes and likely to remain so. We have explored every avenue and left no stone unturned and much good it has done us. If it really was murder most foul, then we have a most foully clever and lucky murderer to deal with.'

'I have been doing some exploring and stone-turning of my own,' I said modestly. 'I don't suppose you would be interested to see the result?'

'Why not? It could hardly make the situation any more confusing than it is already.'

I had spent most of the afternoon typing out my two lists. They now looked impressively neat and business-like and Toby's name had been expunged from both.

Robin glanced at them casually at first, then gave a second, closer look. After a minute or two he discarded the shorter, condensed list, leant back in his chair and perused the longer one with intent and flattering attention.

Finally, he put the typewritten sheets down on the table, saying: 'Well, clever boots, I have to hand it to you. You have certainly come up with some items that were news to me.'

'Oh, good!'

'Unfortunately, they are all connected with motives. You are more hazy in the department you call Opportunity.'

'That's really your job. I cannot very well go around nagging people about what they were doing that afternoon. I don't mind risking a little unpopularity in the cause of truth and justice, but there are limits.'

'I know and I hope you'll remember that. Meanwhile, elucidate a few of these cryptic notes for me. What for instance is meant by that bit about Peter and Paul: "new building, spoil garden, etc."?'

I explained it all to him, adding some comments concerning Peter's lameness, which might have more of malingering in it than met the eye, quoting Dr Macintosh as my authority. He seemed faintly interested, but almost immediately passed on to the subject of Leslie and Marge, asking if I had any substantial grounds for believing they were not legally married.

This reminded me of Leslie's odd behaviour in the restaurant, and I was on the verge of telling him about it when he said:

'It's all quite good background stuff, but it doesn't get us much farther. We've been sifting and checking, twenty-four hours a day and I must tell you, right off, that some of your suspects are definitely ruled out. Their alibis are what you would probably call cast iron.'

'As you know, I regard that as incriminating rather than otherwise, but who, for instance? I'll bet I find the fatal flaw.'

'Well, try and trip up your number one favourite, the husband. Listen to this: he left his parents' house, outside Birmingham, about tea-time on the previous day, drove to London and spent the night in an hotel. Verified. The following morning he went out early to do some shopping; presents for his wife and children, so he said. Duly arrived back at hotel at midday complete with parcels, which he left with hall porter. Went upstairs to pack. Came down half an hour later, asked for luggage to be put in his car and for any messages which came after he left to be relayed to a Slough number, where he would be at a Board Meeting from four o'clock onwards. He then drove to a pub near Sloane Square, where he stopped for beer and sandwiches and passed the time of day with the landlord, who remembers him. Left there at two-ten. By his own account he reached Slough just after three and spent the next forty, or forty-five minutes poking around various sections of the factory floor. One or two people vaguely remember catching sight of him during this period, but he went out of his way to be as unobtrusive as possible and there's no absolute proof.'

'It sounds just the sort of sly and snoopy thing he would do, though.'

'It's fairly immaterial, in any case. The point is that he was in the board-room a few minutes before four o'clock and remained there continuously, in full view of eleven pairs of eyes, until the meeting broke up, at five-fifteen.'

'Yes, that is a tough one, but allowing for even a little inaccuracy on Dr Macintosh's part, he could still have just had time. At the rate he drives, you could do it from Slough in half an hour.'

'There's worse to come. As he was leaving the meeting he found that another member of the Board had arranged to be driven home in one of the firm's cars and he offered him a lift.'

'Cutting down on the overheads, no doubt.'

'No doubt. At all events, the man accepted and Cornford made a detour to drop him off at his house, in Maidenhead. In spite of this he was back at the Manor before six, which is pretty smart going, even without stopping off to commit a murder on the way. Agreed?'

'Who says he was back before six?'

'Everyone. Every bloody person you can think of. Not counting the children, there was an old crone who goes in daily and was giving them their tea, plus old Miss Daven-port who was exercising her dog on the Common and says the animal was damn near run over when he came charging down the lane at seventy miles an hour. There was also a lout of a boy who does odd jobs outside and was hoping to knock off ten minutes early to catch the bus to Storhampton, in which he was thwarted by the unexpected return of the boss. Knock some holes in that, if you can.'

'I'll do my best. Any remote chance that he could have done it, after all that?'

'Not one. You can take my word for it.'

'I will, but I'm strangely disappointed in you. It would have been so nice, if he'd been the one. Well, who else has to be eliminated? Might as well hear all the bad news while we're about it.'

'There's your man at the Bull, Leslie Brock. He's out.'

'Out and up, in an aeroplane?'

'Right. We checked with the immigration people on this side and with the airline passenger list. Also two of the cabin crew identified him from a photograph. They had good reason to remember him because he was pretty thoroughly stoned when he came aboard and they thought they might be in for some trouble. However, he quietened down and slept it off all the way across the Atlantic.'

'That sounds conclusive. I suppose you have taken into account the difference between London and Canadian time and all that sort of thing?'

'A good point, but one which had occurred to us.'

'Too bad. Still, I don't much mind about losing Leslie. He's not a bad sort really, and his being a murderer would have been a nasty blow for poor old Marge, whether she's married to him or not.'

'Emotionally speaking, I sometimes wonder if you're quite cut out for police work.'

'I sometimes wonder the same about you, but we'll let that pass. Who's next?'

'I suppose you do realise that you have no right to ask me all these questions and that I have even less right to answer them? Shall we talk of something else before I jeopardise my career irrevocably?'

'Splendid idea!' I said, tipping some more brandy into his glass and flashing on one of my captivating smiles. 'I have been meaning to tell you all the evening that the weather is getting a little warmer, which is a blessing, indeed, although I do not care to think what Mrs Grumble will have to say about it and I am not perfectly sure that I enjoy London in the heat. What is your opinion about that? You may speak freely.'

'Ha ha!'

'No, not ha ha at all, my darling Robin. I was merely pointing out, in my winsome fashion, that if we are prohibited from talking about this rotten old murder, which is naturally uppermost in both our minds at present, the weather is about the only safe and neutral topic that is left to us. Every other will inevitably lead us back to the forbidden one.'

'I believe I know of one that wouldn't, although I do agree with you that there is nothing very neutral about it.'

'In any case,' I went on, choosing to ignore this, 'I am not really asking you to be indiscreet, you know. I shouldn't dream of questioning you about the people you do suspect, or what evidence you had against them.'

'Nor should I dream of telling you.'

'Exactly. But there can be no harm in establishing a person's innocence and producing evidence to support that, can there? It seems to me that it would be almost your duty, in fact, to clear the name of someone whom you knew to be wrongfully suspected. So I'll do the wrongfully suspecting and you can dutifully name clear.'

'I don't know,' he said in a puzzled voice. 'You're a terrific actress and I've been thinking of you as dedicated to your job, but I begin to wonder if you shouldn't have gone into law. You remind me of some wily old Counsel for the Defence.'

'Perfect! I'll be the wily old whatever it is and you can knock holes in my case. It will be good practice for you and in that way we shall make a splendid team. For instance, who else on my list deserves to be crossed off? You mentioned the Grimbolds, I think?'

'Did I? It is true that all the evidence, so far, points to their innocence.'

'There now! And what were they both doing at the crucial time?'

'Mrs was at the house of a couple named Robbins in Storhampton. She arrived there, just after three, had tea and stayed for over an hour. She was driven there by a colleague from the same committee who remained throughout the visit. Between twenty and half past four Mr arrived in their own car to collect her, as they were going on to an engagement party in Harrow.'

'In Harrow?' I repeated. 'That doesn't sound like Sylvia.'

'Nevertheless, it is where she lived for fourteen years before they moved to Roakes.'

'Well, the old faker. My word, you have unearthed some disreputable things! Did they get to the party?'

'Yes, before six; the first guests to arrive, so the time was engraved on the hostess's mind. How long would it take you to drive to Harrow from Storhampton?'

'Allowing for some fairly thin traffic on Saturday afternoon, I should say one could do it in an hour and a half.'

'So should I and they did not start out until four-thirty. There are three unprejudiced witnesses to prove it.'

'Better and better! So now you have cleared the Grimbolds. I confess I am sorry to see Gerry go. All the stamping about on the Common and muttering to himself ought to have had some sinister significance. Still, I suppose he can be moronic without being a murderer.'

'Not so moronic, either, I must tell you. He owns a couple of carpet factories, among other things. Semi-retired now, but still principle shareholder and director of half a dozen companies. The muttering bit is probably his system of working out the takeover bids.'

'You do surprise me, although one sees why Sylvia finds him so fascinating. Anyone else?'

'Just one. Your cousin is also in the clear, which will please you.'

'Toby? I knew that already.'

'Your cousin's wife, I should say; the celebrated Spragge.'

I sighed. 'You mean that far-fetched story of hers was true? Wouldn't you know? But how could you begin to check it?'

'No great problem. Both the dresser and the stage door-keeper agreed, to within minutes, about the time she arrived in the theatre that afternoon. And we found the man who helped her on the road. He confirmed that not only was she there at the stated time but also could not possibly have been there for less than twenty minutes when he stopped.'

'How on earth did you find him? By advertising?'

'No, Miss Spragge gave us his name and address. It was as simple as that.'

'Oh, come now! People don't go around handing out their names and addresses just because they've helped you change a wheel. I'm surprised you swallowed that.'

'I know, but there was a reason for it this time. When he arrived on the scene she'd already got the punctured wheel off and the spare one on, but she was worried about the nuts not being tight enough; also she'd run the car into the bank and couldn't reverse it out again. He described her as being in a fair old taking, about being late, so he gave the nuts a final yank and then he climbed up on to the bank and helped to heave her off. He got his coat in a bit of a mess and she was bothered about that and of course grateful, as anyone would have been.'

'Ha! You obviously don't know Matilda. I'd have expected her to take it as her just right and dues.'

'Well, this time she didn't. He'd already mentioned, when he first stopped, that he was on his way back to Worthing, and when they got the car moving again she told him she was in a play that was opening in Brighton the following week and would like to send him tickets, by way of saying thank you. So he gave her his card and that was how we found him.'

'Sounds fishy to me. Are you sure they didn't cook it up between them? She has loads of friends in Sussex.'

'Not of this ilk. He works for the Council and is a model husband and father, not to mention an impeccable witness. He told us he'd had a dim idea, all along, that he'd seen her somewhere before, but he couldn't place her until she mentioned the play. He also said he hadn't expected to hear another word from her, but sure enough the tickets turned up.'

'For Monday night?'

'No, the Wednesday matinee, as it happens.'

'Well, that figures,' I said. 'They wouldn't have cost her anything. Probably, half the house was papered at that performance. Ah me, it's a sad business to see all these lovely suspects going down the drain, but it does prove my point. By a process of elimination we shall eventually get back to the husband again. Keep at it and you'll break him down in the end.'

'You're more optimistic than I am. When are you going back to Roakes, by the way?'

'Tomorrow morning. Want me to do some more sleuthing for you?'

'On the contrary, I want you to keep your beautiful nose out of it; but it's not the same seeing you there. I'd hoped you might be staying up in London for a bit.'

'The thing is I've more or less promised Toby to go back. Wild horses wouldn't make him ask me outright, but things are a bit sticky at the moment with . . . what I mean is, he's got a load of work to finish and it's Ellen's holidays and all that.'

That my near blunder had not gone undetected was obvious, from the odd, inquiring look he gave me, and to cover my tracks I went on rapidly: 'Incidentally, how did you come to collect all those facts from Matilda? Did you send Freckles to beard her?'

'No, I did the bearding myself, right in the lioness's den.'

'Go on! You never told me. When?'

'Last Saturday. I drove to Brighton in the morning. She'd already consented to be in her dressing-room twenty minutes early and to receive me there. She was most gracious.'

'I'll bet she was. But just think! I saw you on Saturday evening and you never breathed a word about it.'

'Rotten of me, wasn't it? But you know, Tessa, you're apt to be a bit touchy where your family is concerned. I wasn't quite sure that you'd take kindly to my ferreting about in their affairs. It was funk, more than anything.'

'I see. Then what has made the brave boy own up now?'

'I'll tell you some day. Right now I'd like to talk of something else.'

'Nothing doing. Tell me now.'

He sighed. 'It was something you did, yourself, or rather, wrote. That *dramatis personae* list of yours made me think again. It struck me that you had referred to Matilda in exactly the same terms as all the others; not hostile, but just as detached and open-minded about her potential guilt. It opened my eyes to the fact that she is not included in your category of relatives to be protected, at all costs. Was I right?'

'Could be. I should love to think I was detached and open-minded in all circumstances, but I'll concede you three-quarters of a point.'

'Good. Now that we've got that settled, could we please talk of something else? Like how much I still love you, in spite of this relentless inquisition?'

This time I willingly complied. Once again he had shown himself to be more perceptive than I had allowed for, and there still remained some awkward gaps on my side in our free and frank exchange of views. It had been driven home to me that I needed time to prepare my ground before embarking aloud on further speculations about the murder. I told him I was all ears.

(iii)

Nevertheless, when a few hours had passed, caution was brushed aside and I could not resist asking:

'Did you see the play?'

'What?'

'Matilda's play. Did you see it when you were in Brighton putting her through the hoops?'

'Oh, that! Yes, I did, as a matter of fact.'

'Enjoy it?'

'Not bad. Certain *longueurs*, but I laughed quite a lot.'

'What did you think of Matilda's performance?'

'She was all right. I wouldn't put her in the Bernhardt class.'

'You're just saying that to please me.'

'I know I am.'

'How many curtains?'

'If that means what I think it means, I can't tell you. I didn't stay for the end.'

'Oh, really? So you weren't laughing all that much?'

'Yes, I was, I was in paroxysms, but I had a very pressing appointment for the evening and I didn't intend to be late.'

'You mean you actually left before the end because you were dining with me?'

'What do you think?'

'I don't know what to think,' I said. 'I expect you're a frightful liar.'

'That should make us rather compatible. You did say you were going to marry me, by the way?'

*

Later still I was blinded by the first of two Walter Scott flashes, although he might not have rated them as *bona fide*, since they were not so much the voices of inspiration as of total recall.

I said: 'Listen, Robin, this is important. When you saw the play do you remember a breakfast scene, with Jimmie Headley running round the stage swapping over all the plates?'

I had to repeat the question three times, in different forms, before I could get his full attention and then he said drowsily:

'Sorry, very sorry, no bells ring. It must have happened after I left.'

'I don't believe it did,' I said, on a note of triumph and fell asleep again.

When I awoke for the last time, Robin had gone, and with him all my typewritten notes.

However, by then I had the satisfaction of knowing that the last word was still with me. It was not written anywhere on the papers he had filched. It had not even been spoken.

TWENTY-ONE

(i)

IN ACCORDANCE with Toby's instructions I caught the ten-thirty train to Dedley. I had armed myself with the *Complete Works of Osborne* to sustain me through the ordeal, but I hardly spared them a glance so obstinately did my thoughts go leaping ahead to my next task.

I knew precisely what end was required, but as usual the means continued to elude me. One course of action after another had to be rejected, either for its impracticability or because it required more courage than I possessed.

By the time we lumbered into Dedley Station I was no nearer the solution than when I had set out on the journey.

The moral of all this, as I was soon to learn, is that life provides its own answers for those who are patient enough to wait for them, and that I should have been far more profitably employed in the company of Jimmie and Alison Porter than in bashing my brains to a pulp over hypothetical problems.

The first indication of this came with the fact that Toby was not on the platform to meet me. He had sent, instead, the chauffeur who had driven me to the film studios. He said that this was on account of all the family being obliged to spend the day with some friends. Somewhere over Goring way, he believed he was right in saying it was. Mr Crichton had asked him to apologise for them.

'Quite all right with me,' I said. 'You're a much better driver than he is, and frankly the set-up suits me down to the ground.'

He looked faintly mystified by this, but I did not trouble to explain that I had a small but essential task to perform, whose safe and successful accomplishment ideally required the absence of the entire Crichton household.

As though to spur me on and stiffen my resolve, I found a note addressed to me on the hall table. It was fastened down in four places with gold sealing wax, and inside was written:

> 'Dear Tess, Dad says sorry not to wellcome you (Me Too) but M. has fixed us all to go out to lunch, Werse Luck, but weel be back after tea (Hope so) Longing to see you. E.'

Nevertheless, even the sternest spirit cannot indefinitely deny the pangs of hunger and, having ascertained that there was no one in the house and no lunch left for me, I made a sortie down to the Bull. I estimated that there was ample time for this as I did not envisage my business taking more than an hour or so to complete, and besides I was curious to see what effect my arrival would have on Leslie so soon after the dubious encounter in London.

I anticipated a certain sheepishness in his manner and was even prepared for him to draw me aside and mutter warnings about mum being the word, etcetera, but, in fact, nothing of the kind occurred. He was back in his old place behind the bar, looking as jaunty as ever, with no remaining traces of the slick city gent of the day before. Even his hair seemed to have grown in the interval and he was as friendly and welcoming as I had ever known him.

There was no one else in the saloon bar, all the regular clientèle having doubtless decamped to its midday dinner, but, at a summons from Leslie, Marge appeared and got to work with the fresh, crispy, farmhouse bread, in its plastic wrapping, opened a tin of home-baked, hand-smoked, perfectly square ham and knocked up a plate of nourishing sandwiches. I called for drinks all round and having savoured my wine, sold over the counter at two and a tanner the glass, I said:

'Ah me! How are the mighty fallen! This time yesterday, believe it or not, I was seated at the bar of one of Regent Street's most gilded halls, lashing into the champagne.'

Even then Leslie did not flinch, and Marge said:

'Hark at her! Was it your birthday, love?'

'No, but a celebration all the same. I haven't dared mention it before, but all can now be revealed,' I said, and proceeded to reveal it.

Marge declared herself to be thrilled to the marrow and I had real hopes that the tidings would soon be spreading through Luton like wildfire, but, alas, her interest evaporated all too soon. She was burning to tell me the local news and as soon as she could decently get a word in edgeways asked me if I had seen about the inquest.

I was undecided whether to say I had, or not, but she surged on without waiting for my answer:

'Honestly, it's the sensation of the year in these parts. Murder, if you please! And the police haven't a clue who did it. Fact is, we've got a homicidal maniac on the loose and we're all likely to be murdered in our beds. Fat lot they care!'

'Pity they don't spend less time and money on their precious breathalysers and get after the real criminals,' Leslie said virtuously.

I could not let this pass. 'Well, we don't actually know what they're doing about it, do we? And it needn't necessarily be a homicidal maniac. Some murderers turn out to be quite ordinary people and they're much more difficult to catch.'

"Quite true, love, and always stick up for your pals, that's the ticket,' Marge said amiably.

Not best pleased by what I can only describe as a twinkle in her eye, I said craftily:

'Did either of you go to the inquest?'

'Les did, lucky old bastard. He had to be in Dedley all day yesterday, seeing the brewers about our rotten old toilet and that, but he managed to get away in time to take in some of the fun, didn't you, Les? Poor little me was stuck here all day on my ownsome, you may be sure.'

'And was it fun?' I asked Leslie, giving him a long, cool look.

'So so,' he replied, giving me a long, cool look back. 'Bit boring, really. The Coroner was a dried-up old stick. He mumbled so much that I doubt if the jury were able to hear half he said. I certainly couldn't.'

I saw that I should never shake him and I had important work to do, so I asked a few more random questions for politeness sake, refused their offer of a second drink and got down from my stool.

'Cheerioh!' they both said with dazzling smiles, and calling Cheerioh back I walked out to the lane in a state of near despair.

It must always be daunting to the professional to find the amateur beating him hollow at his own game and the perfidious Leslie had carried off his act with such consummate ease and skill that I began to feel distinctly foolish in taking such pride in my own achievements. It also induced some depressing speculations as to what other aspects of his life and character were based on fake. Perhaps he had never been in the R.A.F. at all? Had he really a brother in Canada? . . . brother in Canada . . . brother in . . .

The thoughts went on whirling around in my head, but my feet had ceased to function. I stood stock-still on the track and was probably only saved from certain death by Miss Davenport's dog. At least, I presumed that it was the memory of that near disaster, which induced Mr Cornford to sound his horn and crawl round the bend, at half his usual speed. Even so, I only just had time to jump aside as he passed and my wild, open-mouthed expression may have reminded him of his wife, for he looked scared to death all of a sudden.

I tramped on mechanically, went into the house and upstairs to my room. The plan I had fixed on now seemed empty of purpose, but, since I had the premises to myself for at least two hours, I apathetically set myself to perform it. All the same, if the things I was searching for had not been practically staring me in the face in almost the first place I looked, it is doubtful whether I should have persevered, so obsessed had I now become with my new theory.

As an afterthought I took the gold snake key-ring out of my bag where it was still lying and dropped it on Matilda's dressing-table, for I no longer cared whether she knew I had seen it or not.

After that I sat on my bed to ponder the situation. At the end of twenty minutes I had reached a decision and I went back to Matilda's room and picked up the telephone. I had mislaid Robin's card, but I dialled 999 and the operator connected me with the Dedley C.I.D. without a murmur.

There was much more hanky-panky involved in getting through to Robin, and when at last he did come on the line he sounded worried and impatient.

'This is Theresa Crichton speaking,' I said, cutting him short, 'And this will only take a minute. I apologise for insisting on speaking to you personally, but you asked me to let you know if I remembered anything which might be helpful and I think I have.'

There was a pause and then he told me to go ahead. So I made two suggestions to him which used up the rest of the minute and rang off.

'Was it Dickie boy that you went to have lunch with?' I asked Ellen. It was not that I was profoundly interested, but it seemed a natural question, and with this diabolically clever murderer in our midst I reckoned that our best chance of survival lay in behaving as naturally as possible in all circumstances.

'Yes; and his old mum.'

'No wife?'

'Didn't see one,' Ellen said. 'Perhaps she is kept locked in the attic, like poor Mrs Rochester.'

'Yes, I expect she would be,' I said.

Despite my preoccupation, I experienced a faint sense of triumph in the anticipation of informing my agent how far at sea she had been on the question of Matilda's paramour.

I was also awestruck by the colossal insolence and lack of taste in taking the husband and stepdaughter to lunch with the lover, even if he did have a mother in evidence and a mad wife in the attic.

'I suppose he and Matilda jabbered on about the play all the time?'

'Oh no, they hardly mentioned it. He only has a weeny part. He's the goofy one who keeps trying to deliver a parcel and nobody wants it. Remember?'

'Vaguely.'

'Anyway, he doesn't seem particularly interested and I should think he's got loads of money, even without working. It was mostly because of Daddy that we went.'

'You amaze me.'

'I know, but when Matilda was here before you remember how he was on about selling the house and moving away from here?'

'Vividly.'

'Well, Dickie's mother wants to let her house for six months and move into London so that Dickie can be near the theatre, and Matilda thought it would be marvellous if Daddy could rent it while he was looking around for something else. That's why she fixed it all up for us to go to lunch and see the house.'

'I see; and what's it like?'

'Not bad. Not half so nice as this one, though and Daddy wasn't a bit keen. He only went because Matilda made such a fuss. You see, Tess, he really did want to leave here when the Cornfords were living at the Manor. Now that Mrs Cornford's dead they'll probably all go away, so we haven't got to move after all.'

It was precisely this faculty of hers for going straight to the root of the matter which had made me so strenuous in preventing direct contact between her and Robin, or Sergeant Baines.

(iii)

Robin rang me back in the evening. Luckily, I was able to take the call myself, as Matilda was upstairs in her room and Toby and Ellen were in the nursery, beating their brains out over *The Times* crossword.

'Was I right?' I asked, speaking in a low voice.

'Quite right. God knows how you stumbled on it, but it was just as you said.'

'No stumbling about it,' I said huffily, forgetting to keep my voice down. 'It was straightforward, logical deduction.'

'Well, never mind about that now. Why I'm ringing up is to impress on you the need to be careful. Will you please try? A few more logical deductions like this one might get you into real trouble. Do you understand, Tessa?'

'Yes and thanks for the warning.'

'You promise?'

'I promise.'

'That's a good girl. I'll see you very soon.'

'I trust so,' I said, 'although you don't sound too sure of it.'

'This is no joke, my love. Believe me, I'm deadly serious.'

'I know you are, and I'll be very, very careful. Guides' honour.'

A sound made me look up and I saw Toby watching me morosely from the doorway. I said goodbye to Robin and rang off.

'Who was it?' Toby asked.

The direct question was so much out of character that I found myself floundering.

'A friend of mine. We are just good friends, as the saying goes. Did you finally master nineteen down?'

'What?'

'Ten letters, beginning with C. "Hoffman was more daring" question mark.'

'Oh, that! It was cautionary, funnily enough. Feeble but obvious, when you think of it.'

He started to walk slowly upstairs, stopped at the half-way mark, to peer down at me and added sternly: 'I am sure you agree.'

TWENTY-TWO

THE following morning Matilda was at her most governessy as she rapped out her orders across the breakfast table. Toby, as usual, was in hiding upstairs, so Ellen and I took the brunt.

The job which had been earmarked for me was to take Matilda's car down to the Storhampton garage, where she had made an appointment for servicing. She said that since she would have to drive it back and forth to London every day, when the show opened it was essential to have it in tiptop condition, and she cautioned me to emphasise that both the steering and the brakes needed special attention. She added, in hectoring tones, that there must be no hanging about, or last-minute telephone calls to agents, as the garage could only guarantee to have the car ready on time on condition that it was brought in before ten o'clock.

'How is Tessa to get home again?' Ellen asked, voicing the question which had been uppermost in my own mind.

'Well, I don't intend her to walk, if that's what you are implying. I shall follow down in Toby's car. I have some shopping to do and can drive her back afterwards.'

'I'll go with you, if you like,' Ellen told me, 'and keep you company.'

'You had better come with me,' Matilda said. 'I'm not too happy about those brakes for one thing, and also there's the fruit and vegetable market at Storhampton this morning, so you can carry one of the baskets.'

No one who had ever accompanied Matilda to the fruit and vegetable market and watched in anguish while she prodded the oranges and tried to get twopence knocked off the price of a damaged cauliflower would willingly have repeated the experience, and I did not at all blame Ellen for immediately backing out.

She gulped and turned a deathly pale and then mumbled something about having an important poem to write.

Shortly afterwards she darted an apologetic grin in my direction and left the room. Perhaps she took after her father, in that inspiration flowed more easily in the open air, for a few minutes later I saw her go past the window on her bicycle. On the other hand, she might have considered it prudent to get as far away as possible from Matilda until the Storhampton cortege was safely on its way.

This was achieved with masterly generalship and only one trifling delay. Mr Parkes duly brought both cars round to the gate and stood by while we got in, Matilda taking her place behind the wheel of the Mercedes which was parked in front.

'Bloody hell,' she said, and got out again. 'I forgot to tell Mrs Parkes about the lunch and it's half past nine already. You'd better go ahead. Can you get past all right?'

'Oh yes, easily.'

'Go on, then, but take care.'

She waited while I edged past, probably to make sure that I did not graze her car, then turned and went back into the house.

It was an agreeable and attractive drive down to Storhampton, especially on a sunny morning, with the dew still misting the hills and the beech trees fresh and green against the sky. I enjoyed it all the more for knowing that Matilda was not close on my heels, noting my every move and liable to harass me with peremptory blasts on the horn if I drove too fast.

The road climbed up and down, over a series of small hills, for the first few miles of the journey and I was able to test the brakes on some of these. It was true that they were not all they should have been and I decided to be extra cautious and go into third gear for the last two miles of the road, which descended for several hundred feet in a steep and winding slope to the outskirts of the town. There were three hazardous bends following sharp upon each other just before the road straightened out again for the last lap. I manoeuvred the first of these without difficulty, although at a slightly greater speed than I had actually intended, but as I approached the second everything began to go wrong. I jammed my foot on the brake and swooped on, even faster than before. I groped for the handbrake, and a second later was tugging with both hands at the wheel. It spun round as easily as the hands of a watch when the spring is released, but the direction never wavered. The car and I shot diagonally across the road and crashed, head on, into a tall beech tree, which it seemed to me in my panic and despair had been waiting there all its life to receive us.

Indeed, it is astonishing what a number and variety of thoughts can fly through the head in the course of a few terror-stricken moments. I remembered to be grateful that Ellen was not with me, but the shameful truth is that what might have proved to be the last deliberate act of my life consisted of damning Matilda to hell for having economised once too often.

I do not know how long I remained unconscious, although I was told afterwards that it cannot have been more than a few minutes. When I did open my eyes I found that, whereas I could not move a muscle, I retained a distinct and detailed recollection of everything that had occurred, although this merciful awareness soon brought its own snags. Through the left-hand side of the shattered windscreen I saw with a fresh onrush of fear a familiar car winding up the hill towards me. It did not appear to be travelling at great speed, but I can remember begging the driver, in a shout or a whimper, to slow down . . . slow down . . . please, slow down . . .

I shut my eyes and waited for the crash to come. It did so sooner than I had believed possible, and with far more impact than the first one. This time I blacked out completely and stayed out for several days.

TWENTY-THREE

(i)

FOR A time I swung about between dreams and distortions which merged into bouts of drowsy awareness, when faces, both strange and familiar, loomed up and receded again before I had time to ask any of the questions which kept struggling to the surface.

The return to lucidity coincided with a visit from my agent, most of whose statements were so far away from any point that I could latch on to that they started my head aching, even more painfully than before.

She began by telling me that there was not a thing to worry about, as darling doctor had given his solemn word that I would be fit to travel to Spain as per the terms of my contract.

'What's the date now?' I asked her.

'The eighteenth, my darling, so you see, you've got loads of time to get yourself into one piece again. He says you are very severely concussed, but the skull wasn't fractured, which is so marvellous.'

I couldn't see anything so marvellous about it, or even why it should have been fractured, but before I could voice these objections she went on:

'They've even agreed to release you for a couple of days and fly you home, if you should be needed to give evidence, but of course we all hope it won't come to that.'

I assumed she must be referring to some insurance claim and I said sharply:

'You're so right, it won't. I'm not intending to sue Matilda for criminal negligence, if that's what you're thinking. I know a lost cause when I see one.'

She looked at me a bit oddly and said: 'Let me peel you a grape, doveikins. They're delicious.'

'Are they? Who sent them?'

'Your blond admirer, the one Ellen calls Swain. He's very dishy, isn't he, darling? Do you think we could persuade him to give up the beat and become a pro? There's this tremendous thing going at the moment for actors with educated voices, and we simply can't lay our hands on any.'

'Not a chance in the world. He's only interested in moral channels, I mean challenges.'

'Oh well, that must be fun for you. It does seem a waste, though.'

'Was he in the car?'

'No, my darling, you were quite alone in the car, don't you remember?'

'I don't mean that car, I mean the car that crashed into me and brought on this very severe concussion. Was he in that?'

'In a word, no, but you're not to worry about a thing. You'll be as sound as a bell in a day or two.'

'What I'm getting at,' I said, making a painful effort to insert a clear-cut question before she could slither off the point again, 'is this: I have a vivid memory that the car I saw, just before all the lights went out, was a police car. It had one of those blue bobbles on top. I've been trying to ask people for ages whether Robin was in it.'

'Well, he wasn't.'

'Thank you. But it was a police car?'

'Luckily for you, yes, it was.'

'There you go again,' I said petulantly. 'I can't see what was lucky about it. Were any of the people in the police car hurt?'

'Listen, my darling, I think you've been chatting for long enough and that hammy old Scotsman will accuse me of sending your temperature up. I shall leave you now and you can have a nice little kip.'

'No, please don't go,' I implored her. 'People always go away the minute I start asking questions, and there's so much I want to know. It's the Chinese torture.'

She consented to stay, but had evidently been placed under orders to thwart my every attempt to obtain a straight answer to a plain question and I was never within miles of getting under her guard. I should say that we were both equally relieved when a middle-aged woman in nurse's costume barged into the room, thrust a thermometer down my throat, remarked that someone she knew was getting a wee bit over-excited and that my agent was wanted on the telephone.

(ii)

Ultimately, it fell to the lot of Dr Macintosh to give me an outline of events. He may have decided that the point had been reached where ignorance would retard my convalescence, rather than allow it to proceed in bliss, but knowing him as I did I incline to the view that he had expressly forbidden everyone else to break the news to me in order to preserve that pleasure for himself.

I listened silently to his tale, bewilderment, horror and disgust succeeding each other, as it proceeded, though, inevitably, the principle emotion which inspired me at the conclusion was the sense of personal outrage.

'I simply cannot get over it,' I complained to Toby later that evening. 'The way she made use of me, all the way through! It beats everything. Take that spurious alibi, for instance, and her planting me there so carefully, to establish it. If I had not gone about insisting to the police and everyone else that Mrs Cornford was alive and walking on the Common at half past three that afternoon when really she was miles away and dead as a doornail, there would have been no mystery at all. It is her callousness in involving me in every beastly move that I simply cannot get over.'

'You should count your blessings,' Toby said mournfully. 'You might not have been able to get over the way she had killed you.'

'Yes, I know, although for some inexplicable reason I don't find myself resenting that quite so much. At least, it was cards on the table.'

'Oh yes, it was that, all right.'

'Not a deceitful pretence that she was really doing me a favour, if you see what I mean?'

'I do.'

'And why did she want to kill me, anyway? I still haven't got the hang of it.'

'Neither have I. It is all much to distasteful to be endured. Swain has some theory about it, I believe; something about a key-ring and a telephone call, which gave her the idea that you were getting on her way. You'll have to ask him. Personally, I prefer not to talk about it.'

I had heard these words before, but never with the same sense of remorse. They recalled me to the agonies he must have suffered during the past few days, and also to his heroism in actually coming to visit me while I was lying in bed, with my arm in a sling and a bandaged head.

'I won't nag you about it any more,' I said contritely. 'Just tell me one small thing and then I'll shut up. How is Ellen taking it?'

'More placidly than you might expect. After all, poor darling, she was living through the horrors, long before the rest of us had an inkling. I daresay the *denouement* came as something of an anti-climax.'

'You mean she knew all along it was Matilda on the Common, dressed up as Mrs Cornford?'

'It seems she did.'

'How incredible! And yet, you know, Toby, I sensed at the time that there was something off-key about that scene and about Ellen's reactions, too. What a dolt I was, not to have got to the bottom of it, there and then!'

'I thought we had agreed that you would not try to get to the bottom of it, here and now?' he said reproachfully.

'Yes, and I'm very sorry, but it's so hard to push it out of one's mind.'

'You had better thrash it out with Swain. He probably won't be nearly so squeamish. In fact, he has been hanging about for days, waiting for permission to talk to you. It will be a relief to us all when he is allowed to do so. Ellen doesn't seem to mind so much, but I find he is rather getting in my hair.'

'Is he here now?'

'Bound to be. One trips over him in every corner of the house, these days. Shall I send him up?'

'Oh yes, please, but give me ten minutes. I must try and do something about my face. If that old nurse is anywhere about, tell her the patient needs her. I can't manage my make-up, single-handed.'

'I'll send her to you,' Toby said, bending over to kiss the tip of my nose, 'but it's a waste of time, believe me. Poor Swain is in no condition to care what you look like, and you will never convince the rest of us that you are not made-up for a horror film.'

TWENTY-FOUR

(i)

'YOU'RE not going to believe this, Robin, but I had the solution in my grasp, and, like a fool, went and threw it away. I lost the wheat through chasing after the chaff.'

'I am sure you did, my love,' he said, looking rather puzzled.

'If only I'd followed up the theory, I'd soon have found out how it was worked, in practice. I had all the evidence at my finger-tips.'

'What evidence was that?'

'Why, Matilda's letters. You see, on that celebrated occasion, about a hundred years ago, when you and I spent an evening together at my flat, I had a vision from above about a letter. It was the full Walter Scott and one ignores them at one's peril. Let it be a lesson to us.'

'It shall be, but listen, my angel Tessa, wouldn't it be better to leave all this until another time, when your poor old head's not so muzzy?'

'Nonsense. My poor old head is not muzzy at all. Bloody but unmuzzy.'

'Very well. Tell it in your own words, as we always say, and I'll do my best to keep up with you.'

'It's quite simple, but I must explain that when I first came to stay here Matilda got in a tangle about two letters she had posted. It's a longish story so I'll cut it down to the essence, and the point is that in her usual estimable fashion she got round me to help her out of the jam. Got that? Well, in the process of carrying out her instructions I accidentally learnt the identity of the other person she had written to, although it didn't register at the time. In other words, I not only saw the letter I was meant to retrieve; I also saw the letter I was not meant to see. Are you with me?'

'Every inch of the way, but please don't tire yourself.'

'I saw the letter and it was addressed to D. Cornford, Esq. Not D. for Dickie, mark you, but D. for Dougie. It was in Matilda's handwriting and Mrs Cornford was clutching it in her crazy little paw. The trouble was, though, I only saw all this with my subconscious, which failed to pass it on until the evening when you and I were together. Naturally, when the truth dawned my conscious told me exactly what I should do. Can you guess what it was?'

'I think it may have told you to search through Matilda's belongings until you found more letters, or some other evidence, to indicate that she was Cornford's mistress and that they intended to marry as soon as all the inconvenient obstacles had been removed.'

'Oh, how wise and wonderful you are?' I sighed, sinking back on my pillow, in an ecstasy of relief. 'I was so afraid you were just humouring me.'

'As if I would! And, no doubt, you found exactly what you were seeking.'

'You bet. No trouble at all. I went straight to that white jewel-case of hers and there they were. Four or five letters from him to her, two of them on Manor House paper, which is printed, by the way, not engraved, and the rest from some dinky little love-nest they'd set up in London. I didn't read all through them, you know. In fact, I hardly spent five minutes on them, but if only I'd had the sense to ring you up about that instead of Leslie and his twin brother, I might be alive today. But I'd gone completely round to the Leslie-for-culprit idea, by then. Perhaps, in my heart of hearts, I welcomed the chance to pin it on someone outside the family and it did seem to fit so neatly. It was true, as far as it went, wasn't it?'

'Quite true. Leslie actually arrived in England twenty-four hours earlier than he admitted, travelling on his brother Rodney's passport; Rodney followed the day after, on Leslie's. Apparently, like a good many identical twins, they'd made a habit of impersonating each other when they were young and thought it would be rather a lark to try it on again. Of course, they were as high as kites when they planned it and there was no ulterior motive, but when Leslie heard about the murder and discovered it had happened after he arrived in this country he naturally decided to keep quiet.'

'Pity I didn't do likewise.'

'He's been very jumpy ever since, poor fellow.'

'I suppose that's why he went to the inquest. Of course, the Leslie I saw in London was really Rodney. And another bloomer I made was to cast poor old Miss Davenport for the villainess, at one time. She was for ever stamping around the countryside, brandishing that whacking great iron dog lead and she definitely hadn't been in the theatre that afternoon, as she claimed. The breakfast scene she enjoyed so much had been cut out by that time. My Walter Scott voices put me on to that bit, too, only they spoke with false tongues, then. I soon saw that she was much too well brought up to kill anyone, and Ellen had drawn my attention to the fact that she couldn't tell the difference between India and Russia, so a slight confusion over Oxford and Dedley was quite in character, specially as she was driven there in a friend's car. Now, I'm digressing again. Tell me how you came to unmask those two fiends in human form? I do think it was brilliant of you.'

'I couldn't have done it without your help.'

'Oh, Robin, you must be joking. Tell me you're not.'

'No, I'm not. You and Ellen between you supplied all the missing bits. You must remember that we were up against a murderer who was either fantastically lucky or exceptionally daring, resourceful and controlled. Everything you had ever told me about Matilda indicated that she possessed those qualities to an unusual degree. Unlike you, I had her at the top of my list, right from the start.'

'You're a genius!'

'Without a doubt, but it was you who put me on the right track. Do you remember telling me that she had nerves of steel, but was not a particularly gifted actress?'

'Vividly.'

'Well, that walk across the Common in broad daylight dressed as Mrs Cornford and knowing that the wretched woman was even then being bundled into a ditch by her husband was a pretty cool performance, you must admit.'

'I do admit it.'

'On the other hand, as a piece of acting, it seems to have lacked something.'

'Well, it certainly fooled me,' I said, 'to my everlasting shame, but I gather Ellen saw through it?'

'She did, indeed, and of course Matilda had been aware of that contingency and thought she had taken precautions against it. Ellen was supposed to be safely in her room with the curtains drawn. Her suddenly turning up on the Common when she did very nearly put a real spanner in our heroine's works.'

'Why on earth didn't Ellen say anything to the rest of us?'

'Fright, I think. She was in awe of Matilda and she'd been expressly told to go and lie down. Children of that age can rarely distinguish between large crimes and small ones. And, then, when she heard about Mrs Cornford's death she sensed there was some connection and became more scared than ever. There was also the little matter of some anonymous letters to add to her terrors. Of course, you knew she'd written them?'

'Yes, Toby and I both guessed that much. I gathered that Freckles had some notions about it, too. Toby whipped round the house and destroyed the remaining evidence just in time.'

'I guessed as much, but you'd have saved us a lot of delay by telling the truth.'

'You might have got the wrong idea. Ellen's always writing letters to everyone under the sun. It's a perfectly harmless occupation, in the normal way. I didn't want you to nag her about it and make her out to be some kind of juvenile delinquent.'

'Oh, what a tangled web, etcetera. You're fond of quotations and you ought to add that one to your list. I refer now, of course, to the way you tried to mislead us over the movements of Cousin Toby. You won't deny that you did your damnedest to imply that he was at the theatre with you that afternoon?'

'Not very convincingly, it seems. How did you catch on?'

'By the simplest means imaginable. You overlooked the fact that you spent most of the time with Marge and Co. They had no reason to pretend that Toby had been among the party and they didn't. In fact, in their innocence they all spoke in such glowing terms of Ellen that it didn't need a master-mind to detect which of your cousins had been in Dedley with you, that evening. Unfortunately, your machinations made us believe that Toby might really have something to hide and we wasted a lot of time back-pedalling over that ground.'

'What was he really doing?'

'Ten minutes after you and Ellen drove away, a gent from a Storhampton estate agency called by appointment, and he and Toby spent the next three hours inspecting properties for sale in the neighbourhood.'

'Well, I'm damned. He never mentioned it.'

'Perhaps you never asked him. He hadn't made up his mind about any of them, as it happened, and before any decision was required of him he'd heard of Mrs Cornford's death and the incentive to move house had gone.'

'What a dark horse he is! I wonder if he had inklings about Matilda and Douglas Cornford, all along?'

'Possibly. I daresay he could have given us quite a lot more information, if he'd had a mind to.'

'I expect it was one of those things he preferred not to talk about. Anyway, you seem to have managed quite well without his assistance. I suppose the deed was actually done by the male half, while Matilda just rigged up the alibi?'

'That's about it. The wretched Bronwen was a sitting duck for that ruthless pair. She was dreadfully jealous and neurotic, as you know, though not by any means insane. It turns out that he'd tried everything to get her certified and put away. When that failed he saw to it that she was plugged to the gills with so many tranquillisers and different kinds of dope that the poor devil didn't know whether she was coming or going, half the time.'

'Yes, she kept confusing me with Matilda. That was mainly on account of the car, I suppose, but she must have had a glimmer, somewhere, of what Dougie boy and Matilda were up to, and our both being actresses didn't make it any simpler for her.'

'I don't think she can have been particularly strong in the head, even before those two got to work on her. She was a poor simple girl whom he'd taken up with in his student days and then outgrown; but she saw him as a paragon of all the virtues, fending off pursuing women, left, right and centre. It was a pushover to get her to a rendezvous at that spot in the woods, where she so often went wandering off on her own. All he had to do was clock her over the head, roll the body down into the valley and beat it, back to the board-room, making sure he was seen by several people, on his way through the factory workshop. Meanwhile, the other half of the partnership was carrying out its own programme, up here on the Common.'

'And all she had to do was to park the car, off the road, where it was hidden by the trees, put on her Bronwen costume and go for a little walk. Is that it?'

'Not quite. She also had to slash the spare tyre and loosen the hub screws on one of the wheels.'

'Don't tell me that puncture was a put-up job, after all?'

'Well, naturally, she had to invent some reason for the gap in time. You knew to the minute when she left here, and she was so celebrated for getting to the theatre dead on time that the smallest discrepancy would have stood out a mile. She had about twenty minutes to account for, so the wheel was punctured in advance, and, as soon as she was on the main road, she rammed the car into the bank and hailed the first motorist who came along. It was sheer luck that he happened to be a Worthing man, but she'd have found some means of getting his name and address, you may be sure.'

'Yes, I am sure she would,' I said dejectedly. I was beginning to feel as tired as everyone assured me I ought to be, but there was one more thing I had to know before I could sleep peacefully.

'Why did she have to attack me?' I asked.

'She believed you were on to her.'

'She did me more than justice.'

'Not entirely; I think it was a correct assumption, in so far as you were getting closer all the time. Unluckily for her you were not part of the original plan, and for once she allowed herself to be panicked into acting without enough premeditation. She guessed that you'd read the letters and she thought you'd left the key-ring on her dressing-table on purpose to show that you knew about the London flat, as well. Also, she overheard our telephone conversation when you asked me if you'd been right in certain suppositions. It never occurred to her that these could concern anyone but her own guilty self. I had a stroke of luck there, too, because you rang off very abruptly, and just afterwards I heard a second click, so I knew somebody had been listening in and it wasn't hard to guess who. When Ellen telephoned me the next morning I was ready to go into action.'

At this point I nearly fell out of bed, in my astonishment. 'Ellen telephoned you?' I said, gaping at him.

'She did, indeed and thereby saved your life. She'd got hold of that card I gave you at the beginning of our acquaintance, and as soon as you and then Matilda had left the house she rang up and told me that you were in danger.'

'What on earth gave her that idea, I wonder? I certainly had no idea that Matilda had rigged the car, so that I'd crash and kill myself.'

'I think Ellen acts mainly on intuition. I've gathered, subsequently, that there was something about the bossy way Matilda was handing out her instructions at the breakfast-table that morning that set up the danger signals. Anyway, it wasn't Matilda who rigged the car. It was Douglas Cornford, and he'd done it on her orders the night before.'

'They were in that together, too, were they?'

'Most certainly, although, as usual, he did the dirty work and she set the scene. It was he, not Matilda, who followed you down the hill, probably just out of range of your driving mirror, while she stayed parked at the top.'

'He had to make sure that I crashed according to plan, I take it?'

'Worse than that. They weren't relying on the crash alone. He had two assignments. One was to finish you off if necessary, and the other to wreck the car so thoroughly that the cause of the accident could never be traced.'

'What a sweet idea.'

'Sweet and extremely neat, because if anyone had come along it would have appeared perfectly natural for him to be there. Any right-minded person would have assumed that he was trying to drag you clear.'

'It didn't quite work out, all the same.'

'Thanks to those two quick thinkers, Ellen and myself, the first people to arrive on the scene after he got there was a car-load of quick-thinking policemen, and they weren't looking for innocent bystanders, either. They knew pretty well whom and what to expect and they caught him in the act, as it were. Only time for one blow to be struck, and that not fatal by the look of you.'

'Yes, I do begin to see, now, why everyone has been telling me how lucky I am. It was a bit of a mystery before. Oh well, it's a mouldy story, Robin, but I'm glad you've told it. I shall try to forget it now, and it's so much easier to forget things when you know what they are, don't you agree?'

'With every word and you look half asleep and half-way to forgetfulness already.'

'Oh, I am, very sleepy. All the same,' I added, rousing myself once more. 'You should have listened to me in the first place. I always said you would find it was the husband in the end.'

'So you did, my love and never more right.'

'I might have said: *"Cherchez la femme"* while I was about it,' I mumbled, with a final yawn. 'These old saws generally turn out to be the best.'

(ii)

'And now, I suppose, you will get married and have lots of little swains of your own and you won't love me best, any more,' Ellen said dolefully.

'Oh, pish and tush! I haven't, by any means, made up my mind to marry him, you know. It might well be beyond me, trying to keep pace with all those high moral standards. I intend to give serious thought to the matter, while I am in Spain. Come to think of it,' I went on, 'How would you feel about coming to Spain, with me? You can swim there, all through October, so they tell me, perhaps even into November.'

'I'd like it all right, but school starts again in a fortnight, and Daddy's very keen on my not missing any.'

'I have news for you, Ellen. I have already been into conference about this with your father, and he has no objection, providing we take along a nice governess as well. How about it? You could learn some Spanish and read Don Quixote in the original. You might even become a famous Flamenco dancer.'

'Or a lady toreador.'

'Just what I was about to suggest.'

'Okay, then; but Swain's going to be awfully disappointed,' she added, looking distressed again. 'He's jolly wrapped up in you.'

'Oh, I know and I'm jolly wrapped up in him, too, in a sense, but there's more to marriage than just getting wrapped up, specially for an actress. Besides, I am not at all sure that I could stand the stresses and strains of police work, even at second-hand. I am much inclined to devote myself to the sweet, sheltered life of showbiz.'

'Perhaps something will happen to make you change your mind,' Ellen said, cheering up a little.

'It has been known,' I agreed.

THE END

FELICITY SHAW

THE detective novels of Anne Morice seem rather to reflect the actual life and background of the author, whose full married name was Felicity Anne Morice Worthington Shaw. Felicity was born in the county of Kent on February 18, 1916, one of four daughters of Harry Edward Worthington, a well-loved village doctor, and his pretty young wife, Muriel Rose Morice. Seemingly this is an unexceptional provenance for an English mystery writer—yet in fact Felicity's complicated ancestry was like something out of a classic English mystery, with several cases of children born on the wrong side of the blanket to prominent sires and their humbly born paramours. Her mother Muriel Rose was the natural daughter of dressmaker Rebecca Garnett Gould and Charles John Morice, a Harrow graduate and footballer who played in the 1872 England/Scotland match. Doffing his football kit after this triumph, Charles became a stockbroker like his father, his brothers and his nephew Percy John de Paravicini, son of Baron James Prior de Paravicini and Charles' only surviving sister, Valentina Antoinette Sampayo Morice. (Of Scottish mercantile origin, the Morices had extensive Portuguese business connections.) Charles also found time, when not playing the fields of sport or commerce, to father a pair of out-of-wedlock children with a coachman's daughter, Clementina Frances Turvey, whom he would later marry.

Her mother having passed away when she was only four years old, Muriel Rose was raised by her half-sister Kitty, who had wed a commercial traveler, at the village of Birchington-on-Sea, Kent, near the city of Margate. There she met kindly local doctor Harry Worthington when he treated her during a local measles outbreak. The case of measles led to marriage between the physician and his patient, with the couple wedding in 1904, when Harry was thirty-six and Muriel Rose but twenty-two. Together Harry and Muriel Rose had a daughter, Elizabeth, in 1906. However Muriel Rose's three later daughters—Angela, Felicity and Yvonne—were fathered by another man, London playwright Frederick Leonard Lonsdale, the author of such popular stage works (many of them adapted as films) as *On Approval* and *The Last of Mrs. Cheyney* as well as being the most steady of Muriel Rose's many lovers.

Unfortunately for Muriel Rose, Lonsdale's interest in her evaporated as his stage success mounted. The playwright proposed pensioning off his discarded mistress with an annual stipend of one hundred pounds apiece for each of his natural daughters, provided that he and Muriel Rose never met again. The offer was accepted, although Muriel Rose, a woman of golden flights and fancies who romantically went by the name Lucy Glitters (she told her daughters that her father had christened her with this appellation on account of his having won a bet on a horse by that name on the day she was born), never got over the rejection. Meanwhile, "poor Dr. Worthington" as he was now known, had come down with Parkinson's Disease and he was packed off with a nurse to a cottage while "Lucy Glitters," now in straitened financial circumstances by her standards, moved with her daughters to a maisonette above a cake shop in Belgravia, London, in a bid to get the girls established. Felicity's older sister Angela went into acting for a profession, and her mother's theatrical ambition for her daughter is said to have been the inspiration for Noel Coward's amusingly imploring 1935 hit song "Don't Put Your Daughter on the Stage, Mrs. Worthington." Angela's greatest contribution to the cause of thespianism by far came when she married actor and theatrical agent Robin Fox, with whom she produced England's Fox acting dynasty, including her sons Edward and James and grandchildren Laurence, Jack, Emilia and Freddie.

Felicity meanwhile went to work in the office of the GPO Film Unit, a subdivision of the United Kingdom's General Post

Office established in 1933 to produce documentary films. Her daughter Mary Premila Boseman has written that it was at the GPO Film Unit that the "pretty and fashionably slim" Felicity met documentarian Alexander Shaw—"good looking, strong featured, dark haired and with strange brown eyes between yellow and green"—and told herself "that's the man I'm going to marry," which she did. During the Thirties and Forties Alex produced and/or directed over a score of prestige documentaries, including *Tank Patrol*, *Our Country* (introduced by actor Burgess Meredith) and *Penicillin*. After World War Two Alex worked with the United Nations agencies UNESCO and UNRWA and he and Felicity and their three children resided in developing nations all around the world. Felicity's daughter Mary recalls that Felicity "set up house in most of these places adapting to each circumstance. Furniture and curtains and so on were made of local materials. . . . The only possession that followed us everywhere from England was the box of Christmas decorations, practically heirlooms, fragile and attractive and unbroken throughout. In Wad Medani in the Sudan they hung on a thorn bush and looked charming."

It was during these years that Felicity began writing fiction, eventually publishing two fine mainstream novels, *The Happy Exiles* (1956) and *Sun-Trap* (1958). The former novel, a lightly satirical comedy of manners about British and American expatriates in an unnamed British colony during the dying days of the Empire, received particularly good reviews and was published in both the United Kingdom and the United States, but after a nasty bout with malaria and the death, back in England, of her mother Lucy Glitters, Felicity put writing aside for more than a decade, until under her pseudonym Anne Morice, drawn from her two middle names, she successfully launched her Tessa Crichton mystery series in 1970. "From the royalties of these books," notes Mary Premila Boseman, "she was able to buy a house in Hambleden, near Henley-on-Thames; this was the first of our houses that wasn't rented."

Felicity spent a great deal more time in the home country during the last two decades of her life, gardening and cooking for friends (though she herself when alone subsisted on a diet of black coffee and watercress) and industriously spinning her tales of genteel English murder in locales much like that in which she now resided. Sometimes she joined Alex in his overseas travels to different places, including Washington, D.C., which she wrote about with characteristic wryness in her 1977 detective novel *Murder with Mimicry* ("a nice lively book saturated with show business," pronounced the *New York Times Book Review*). Felicity Shaw lived a full life of richly varied experiences, which are rewardingly reflected in her books, the last of which was published posthumously in 1990, a year after her death at the age of seventy-three on May 18th, 1989.

Curtis Evans